Also by Karen Casey Fitzjerrell

THE DIVIDING SEASON
Winner of the EPIC Award for Historical Fiction

Praise for *The Dividing Season*:

"...a rare and beautiful book for which other words only begin to describe: exquisitely lyrical, rich in history and emotion, poignant, and intelligently written."
Arletta Dawdy, author of *Huachuca Woman*

"...the author word-paints masterful images - painstaking research is very apparent..."   **Susan Clayton Luton**

"...characters are richly drawn and the plot takes just enough unexpected turns to keep interest without stretching the story's credibility."   **LaDene Morton**, author of *What Lies West*

"...the author manages the reins of both action and introspection skillfully..."   **Judith Austin Mills**, author of *How Far Tomorrow*

"Fitzjerrell...writes with compassion, heart and quiet humor. I loved the book."   **Mary E. Trimble**, author of *TUBOB*

Forgiving Effie Beck

Karen Casey Fitzjerrell

For My Buddy in Word crafts! Helen you're such a good pal!

WKMA Publishing

Karen

Inquiries should be addressed to:
WKMA Publishing
infowkma@gmail.com or kcfitzjerrell@gmail.com

First Edition 2013
Library of Congress Control Number
2013939965

Fitzjerrell, Karen Casey
forgiving effie beck / Karen Casey Fitzjerrell
p. cm.
ISBN 978-0-9847768-1-8 Print
ISBN 978-0-9847768-7-0 Ebook

For Cole and Neva

Author's Note

During the editing process of this book it was brought to my attention that I use several unfamiliar words not listed in most of today's dictionaries. Rather than delete perfectly good words used freely during The Depression Era or interrupt the story with explanations, I include definitions here:

Hoopie

It's my opinion that the difficulty in finding a definition or description of a "hoopie" stems from the fact that *hoopie* was a derogatory term used to refer to ne'er-do-wells, dirty people, bums (especially in the North Eastern part of America) and so it's been more or less swept out of use. To the best of my limited knowledge, in Central and South Texas it was never considered a derogatory remark, but rather a simple reference to a motor vehicle.

I found this single description in Urban Dictionary online, where it's listed as number seven.

Hoopie - A homemade vehicle for back road use. They are usually built using an old car or truck frame with the drivetrain parts intact.They are very minimal and are used for off road purposes as they have very few parts that can be damaged by collisions with trees, rocks, and other obstructions.

Rural settings are the only place you will ever see one of these creations because they are strictly illegal for use on any highway. To get an idea of what a hoopie looks like, think of the Beverly Hillbilly's truck (actually an Oldsmobile Touring Car) without any kind of body. It is said that seeing a hoopie can bring good luck.

Black Draught (pronounced *draw*) - A saline aperient used as a purgative in the 19th and 20th centuries. A laxative.

Blue John - Blue John refers to what is left after skimming cream from whole milk. True farmhouse skimmed milk has a blue cast.

Prologue

There I laid. Old, half blind, stretched out in wet grass giggling like a drunk.

I laughed at myself for ending up that way, and for living such a long time without getting any smarter than when I was a child hoeing red dirt and listening to cicadas bleat like sheep in the tree tops.

But then thunder boomed and crackled again and I felt the ground shudder. My laughing stopped. I sucked rain water from grass and spread my arms hoping to take on the strength of the storm. I'd only planned to rest for a while, catch my breath.

Now, when the sun dips and the sky turns pink and orange and the green jay gripes at the owl, I come up from my resting spot near the spring and go to the rock fence. There I listen to the breathing town.

I've resigned myself to this fuzzy existence on the crooked line between them and me. *Them*, of course, being Cooperville citizens. The Breathers, I call them, including the little seed I gave up so long ago. I've been purified by sorrow, you see, and I hunger to move on, but I have an itch that holds me here. An unfinished task.

This is rawboned country with few places for afflicted hearts to hide. During those last hours, I saw how wrong I'd been, how wrong we all had been. You *can* go back and try to make things right. You *can* change your mind and barrel head-on through uncertainties that might hold you back.

The Breathers are like wreckage caught in an eddy at river's edge, swirling in a never-ending circle of self-deceit. They put their backs to the door of blessedness like humped, eyeless creatures and tell themselves there's no hope for escape, no chance of change, no way to put things right. They believe they are comfortably cocooned by their secrets.

I should know. I was one of them. Now, here I sit weeping, watching, listening.   E.B.

Forgiving Effie Beck

PART I

Bony women, blank-faced children, the absence of hope, the thump of despair. Mike Lemay could not clear the images and thoughts from his mind. They called it the Depression. If it didn't kill you, it altered you, carved holes in your self-respect, made you think about death, clean and quick.

Riding between oil barrels in the back of a truck traveling west through a sleepy little valley, Mike thought he heard cicadas above the whine of truck tires. He had hitched rides halfway across the country, walked much of it, counted each inch, foot, mile he put between himself and the greasy stench of human misery. He'd thought a lot about sorrow and hope the whole way, how both drifted on air thick with heat.

He was sorry for leaving his sobbing mother behind even though he had long since reached the age when a man should leave his mother. She was frail and Texas was a long way from North Carolina, and he'd made her worry, would she ever see him again. The only thread of hope he had – that he dared not bank on too much because he couldn't endure another disappointment – was an honest-to-God decent job. This, after a year of cleaning slop from street gutters for a dime a day.

Mike had been hired to work as an interviewer for the Federal Writer's Project, a government program that was part of Roosevelt's New Deal. But anyone with dog sense knew the United States Government, like God, could take away what was given with ease and no warning. So he kept a tight rein on hope.

The oil barrels shifted when the truck rattled over a bridge. Mike pushed one of his tattered suitcases between the barrels and tried to get comfortable. But images of embittered people forced to endure paralyzing indignities, armies of men standing in line for a bit of bread and the odor of unclean bodies stayed with him. He had been one of them, suffered the same humiliation.

He sat up and rubbed his eyes.

The greatest shame was the one he brought on himself. He asked the FWP coordinator who hired him if he could have an assignment somewhere west of the Mississippi and south of the Oklahoma dust storms. Somewhere far from the filth and rot of cities and the drought devastation in the country's mid-section.

He knew it would break his mother's heart and split up the little bit of family he had left. Of course, he had every intention of sending his pay home to her and his younger brother, James, who had a pregnant wife and no sign of work on the horizon.

Mike tried to make them understand that the one thing that had held him together, the bond of family, could no longer do the trick. He was like a sand castle at high tide, getting washed clean away by shifting hard times. After all, he told himself, James had his wife. His mother had James. And now he, Mike Lemay, had a job. Still, the guilt he harbored for leaving his family overshadowed any enthusiasm he had for the opportunity of work.

The truck stopped in a choking cloud of dust and the driver pointed to a road that angled south off the highway. "Hey buddy! I think that's the road that'll take you where you need to go."

Mike threw his suitcases down and jumped off the truck. He tipped his fedora to the driver as he drove away. Across the road a bird chirped incessantly. It was perched high up in a dead tree, nothing but twisted twigs sticking out against a pale sky.

Down the road, the direction the truck driver had pointed, Mike heard an engine hum faint and far away. He moved his cases to the side of the road and walked off into tall weeds to relieve himself. When he came back, a wavy blue speck appeared around a bend where the road disappeared into a thicket of vegetation and massive trees. The bird jumped to a twig higher up in the dead tree and raised its song an octave. Mike put out his thumb and waited until a rusty blue pickup rolled, slow as syrup in snow, to a stop in front of him. A sun-parched man wearing a straw hat leaned his head out of the window.

"Where you headed?"

"Cooperville."

"By dern, you're in luck. I'm headed that way my own self. Hop in. I'm starved for talk."

Mike hefted his cases on top of some wooden crates in the back of the truck and climbed into the cab.

"Name's Clyde Cheevers."

"Mike Lemay."

Clyde Cheevers drove with his head pushed forward like he was hunkering in a wind. His silver hair stuck out stiff as straw from under his hat. His knobby brown hands were nicked and scabbed. He glanced in his rear view mirror. "Them cases look like a pretty good load. You peddling?"

Mike considered Clyde's question. Where he'd come from, a man didn't ask another's business. More often than not, the answers were foul and hateful, fronts used to disguise the useless feeling of being out of work. "No. Does it matter?" Mike said.

"Why no. I was just trying to be pleasant is all."

Mike clinched his jaw muscles. He'd been alone with his cynicism too long maybe, and it showed. "I'm a FWP interviewer."

"Come again? Don't you mean WPA?"

"Federal Writers' Project. It's a national work relief project like the WPA. I'm supposed to stay in this area for a time, get to know the people, then write about their experiences."

Clyde chuckled. "Now that ought to make for interesting reading."

"Life histories, they're calling it. Interviewers all over the country will eventually compile the transcriptions into a series of volumes."

"Been at it long?"

"No. I worked – my whole family worked – in a North Carolina mill after we lost our farm in the Crash."

Mike let his gaze sweep north. The countryside swelled and then dropped away like a gentle green sea and in the west, hills were the color of bruises. His mind rolled back to the day his family packed to leave their farm. His small wiry father, jaws locked, lips pressed in a tight line, boarded up the windows and doors on the farmhouse. Odd that Mike remembered glancing over at his dad and noticing dirt caked under his fingernails.

His dad had always known what to do to take care of the family, had clear views of the rightness of a matter and acted on his judgments with determination, or some said, pigheadedness. "If your heart is aimed to do right, then don't be afraid to be responsible," he would say.

When his dad finished boarding up the farmhouse, he stood for the longest time in the yawning silence, gazing at the front door. James, his brother, waited in the back of a pickup truck heaped with mattresses, boxed dishes, and a few chairs, while his mother sat on the running board with her forehead cupped in her hand. Then his dad raised the hammer high overhead and hurled it against the house with all his red-faced might.

Six months later he was dead. Withered and wilted away, Mike often thought, like an uprooted oak separated from its sustenance.

Nothing was certain after that. Their lives fell apart like a plodding avalanche, if anyone could imagine such a thing.

Clyde Cheever's old pickup labored down the dusty road snail slow. "Did one of them strikes put y'all out of your mill work?" Clyde asked. "By dern, it's a shame what's happening to this country. But, you'll get along fine, son. We're kind'a off from the worst of it way out here. Things is bad, don't get me wrong, but you'll do all right."

Mike gave Clyde a quick side-glance and wondered if the man had any idea how bad he needed to hear those words. "Do you live in Cooperville?"

"Me? Nawh. I live east of here near Pole Cat Creek, town about ten miles east of Cooperville." Clyde geared down to a crawl as he approached a dirt path leading to a dilapidated house set far back from the road.

"Miss Effie Beck's place," Clyde said. He tapped the horn a couple of times before he rolled forward to the mailbox, opened it and grabbed a cloth-wrapped bundle. A small figure appeared shadow-like in the doorway of the leaning house and a thin arm waved at Clyde. He waved back then handed Mike the bundle and said, "Cake." He wrestled with the gear shift. "The old woman runs her place alone. I helped her worm her cattle a while back. This is how she pays me even when I tell her there's no need to. Help yourself."

Mike bit into a piece of the cake that had been sliced into thick slabs. His heart shuddered in his chest and nearly shut off the flow of air to his lungs. It was ginger cake, just like back home. He wanted to cry like a little child. Instead he swallowed hard, thumbed over his shoulder and asked, "What's in your crates back there?"

"Cucumbers. Taking 'em to the pickle factory in Cooperville. I got a place between here and Pole Cat Creek. I farm mostly cotton and cucumber, anything I can sell, which is not much these days."

Mike noticed a bright metal star pinned on Clyde's shirt pocket. "Are you sheriff?"

"No. Fella by the name of Neal Lackland holds that distinction. I'm a Ranger. I take it you heard of the Texas Rangers?" Clyde propped his arm on the window and accelerated enough to stir a breeze in the cab of the pickup. "You picked a good time to visit our county. Folks'll be gettin' ready for the Pickle Festival. Give you a chance to see how we celebrate in these parts."

"Pickle Festival?" Mike couldn't help but chuckle.

Clyde shrugged in agreement to the corny humor of the name. "Thing is," he said, "you might have trouble finding a place to stay. The WPA has a crew out putting in a new bridge across the Medina River, so the boardinghouse is probably full."

"Is there a hotel in town?"

"Burned down 'bout five years ago. Fella that owned it couldn't afford to repair it so he just walked off toward the highway and hadn't nobody seen him since. There's a widow woman, though, rents a room on occasion. Name's Cora Mae Travis. You ask around. Anybody can tell you where she lives."

Mike held the cake up so Clyde could get a piece. "No thanks, but you go on and have another." After eating a second slice, Mike folded the cloth back over the cake and set it on the seat between them.

Clyde turned onto yet another dirt road that sloped to a valley with a pretty clear water stream running through it. "The Medina River," Clyde said. "On up a ways, Cooperville Spring Creek empties into it. We'll be coming into town the back way since I had to stop by Miss Effie's place."

Low rocky cliffs rose first on the right then on the left of the road that followed the river's twisted path through hills. At times, the river valley was wide and flat and then it narrowed with high rock walls on either side. Occasionally, between the hills or around a clump of trees, Mike glimpsed cattle grazing in apple-green pastures. "This country is different from what I expected," he said.

"Cactus, tumbleweeds and cowboys with six-shooters?"

"Something like that."

"Well, you'll see plenty such as that, but there's more too, as you can see."

Clyde inched the truck across a wooden bridge. "Cooperville Spring Creek," he said, then turned left when the road ended at Main

Street. Six blocks later he stopped in front of the boardinghouse on the east side of town. Mike got out and pulled his suitcases off the back of Clyde's truck. A sharp sour odor turned his stomach. He dragged his cases around to Clyde's window. "What's that smell?"

"Why, that's the pickle factory a few blocks that-a-way. You'll get used to it. Now, if you're ever in Pole Cat, be sure to look me up, hear?"

Mike tipped his hat. "Will do. Appreciate the ride."

As Clyde predicted, the boardinghouse was full. But Mike counted it a mixed blessing. He wholeheartedly disagreed with Clyde about getting used to the heavy vinegar odor that stung his nose and eyes. The lady at the boardinghouse gave him directions to Cora Mae Travis's place and wished him luck.

Mike didn't count on Luck, wanted to tell the lady so, but didn't. Anyone could see that these days Luck was as thin as blue-john milk. When he stepped back out into the sunshine, something about the way his shadow fell across the cracked sidewalk made him pause, as if he'd walked through a gauze curtain into a broad open space in another dimension. With a suitcase in each hand, Mike took a few steps and then stalled. He looked up and down the street, hesitant, but for the life of him, he couldn't determine why.

CORA MAE TRAVIS was getting one of her sick headaches. Jodean had been gone too long for nothing more than eggs and Arbuckle coffee. The last time she remembered feeling like this was when Jodean scheduled three shampoo-sets and a permanent wave, all in one day. Sometimes Cora Mae just couldn't understand why Jodean didn't have a little more consideration, especially after all she'd done for her. Jodean owed her, like any woman owed her mother. Maybe in their case, even more.

In the deep shadows of the parlor, Cora Mae stretched out on the sofa. A few minutes later she heard the screen door at the back of the house rattle. "That you, Jodean?"

"Hello? Mrs. Cora Mae Travis?"

Cora Mae sat up enough to peer over the back of the sofa, through the kitchen and screened porch, at the thin figure standing outside in blinding white sunlight. She wondered what business a man had at her back door. It wasn't time for the peddler for another month. And it better not be a beggar or she'd have to send Jodean for the sheriff.

"What you want?" she called out.

"Clyde Cheevers from Pole Cat Creek said you might rent me a room."

"Did he now? How do I know you're not lying to me, trying to get me to unhook the door so you can rob me?"

"I have a government letter, ma'am. Says I work for the FWP. I've been sent here to conduct government business."

Cora Mae pushed off the sofa and moved through the house, across the porch to the screen door. He looked too skinny to count for anything. "I don't have a room as such. What I got is that tank house yonder. It's got a sleeping loft, toilet and shower. I'll rent it to you for two dollars a week. Pay in advance, no drinking, no smoking, no women. I'm God-fearing and 'spect my renters to be."

The man nodded then set one of his cases on its side and withdrew a letter and two one-dollar bills. He held the letter so she could see it through the screen. It was from the government all right, but Cora Mae didn't bother to read the little print.

"If Clyde sent you, I suppose it's all right. My daughter will be back from the store directly. You'll have to ask her about our rules. You can't be bothering me. I'm sickly."

He nodded again and held up the dollar bills for her to see.

"I'll get the key." *Lord,* she was sure to take a sick headache now with all this bother. She found the key under the sink where Jodean kept it, and returned to the porch.

"Me and my daughter run a beauty parlor in one of the front rooms so we got to be real careful who stays here. Mind you act like a gentleman or we'll get the sheriff after you."

She unlatched the screen door and exchanged the key for his two dollars. Then, from behind a veil of kitchen curtain, she watched as he dragged his tired, skinny self and his big suitcases across the yard to the tank house next to the windmill.

The tank house loomed three stories above the backyard with a cypress water tank occupying the top section. For years the middle section was used for storage and the ground floor, about ten feet square, was used as a wash house for laundry. Back when Cora Mae's father had strings of cowhands working his ranch twenty miles west of town, they'd used the wash house to shower and shave for a night on the town. When the Depression hit, Jodean thought it made sense to get rid of the junk that had collected in the tank house over the years and make a sleeping loft out of the middle section. Then they could rent it to the dozens of spiritless drifters migrating west to California and earn a little extra money.

But, Cora Mae thought, there's something different about this skinny big-eyed man. *Lord*, where *is* Jodean.

JODEAN COULDN'T MAKE herself rush on such a pretty day. She bumped into Ada Kasper on the sidewalk in front of the bank and the two of them slipped into the drugstore for a Grapette. Red, Ada's husband, was busy ordering fertilizer a few blocks away at the feed store.

"The kids are okay in the car waiting for Red," Ada explained. "And he can hold the sidewalk down if he finishes before I get there. Can you believe Tubby wants me to organize the Pickle Queen Contest *again*?"

For the last three years Ada had been asked to take charge of the Pickle Queen Festivities, which, as she put it to Jodean, was a hoot since she never took an active part in all that hoity-toity stuff the town gossips love. But ask they did. *They* being Mayor Tubby Whittaker, his wife Frances and Glory Hughes of Glory's Piano Parlor and Charm School.

"They ask because you make them look good." Jodean sipped her Grapette through a paper straw.

"Well, it wears me out. It's more tittle-tattle than celebration. It seems almost..."

"What?"

"Well, I'd feel better if all this pageant and parade stuff was postponed a year or two. It's disrespectful, somehow, to people having a hard time. Red said he saw a foreclosure sign on the Brady place yesterday."

"I heard. Maybe people need things to do besides mope about how bad things are." Jodean checked the big clock behind the soda fountain. "I better get going, Ada. Momma was fit to be tied when I left. I scheduled her too many hair sets and she was pretty tired."

"You're a saint, Jodean Travis."

Jodean ignored Ada's comment. Both women waved to Leroy, the druggist, on their way to the door.

"Doesn't it get to you, at least sometimes?" Ada persisted.

Jodean squinted against the sun's glare when they reached the sidewalk. Ada was the only confidante she'd ever had. Yet by Jodean's choice, they never openly talked about her family or her position in Cooperville social circles.

"Momma always taught me to be mindful of my station in life so I wouldn't get hurt by expecting too much."

"No disrespect to Cora Mae, but I'd never say something like that to my kids."

They'd reached the intersection of Main and West streets where Jodean had to turn south toward home. At the corner, children hung out of every window of the car. One of them honked the horn, startling Jodean and Ada. When they jumped and screeched, a giggling childrens' chorus chimed in perfect harmony, from the oldest ten-year-old contralto to the youngest three-year-old soprano.

"Scared the wits outta me," Ada shouted at them. "Where's Daddy?"

"Right behind two of the prettiest women this side of the Sabine River."

Jodean spun around in time to catch Red Kasper winking at Ada from under his big ten-gallon Montana slope hat. Red and Ada had been sweethearts since grade school and still behaved like teenagers. It amused Jodean that in this country noted for big ranches, big hats, and big britches, a woman as formidable as Ada could be so attracted to a man as small as Red. Ada hooked her arm around Red's neck and he pecked her on the mouth.

"Oooo, Daddy's kissing Momma." More giggles from the car.

Jodean waved good-bye before hurrying off down the street, thinking her own momma would be in fits by the time she got home. She peered across a hay pasture between the dirt ranch road where Ada and Red bounced toward the spring creek bridge and the tank house two blocks away. The sun was about to sink behind a dark cloud bank.

A couple of butterflies circled each other above a tangle of wisteria growing along the rock fence that outlined three sides of the home she shared with Cora Mae on the outskirts of town. The backyard sloped to the woods all the way to the spring and creek for which the town was named.

Jodean picked a few droopy wisteria blossoms for the kitchen table. But, silly as it was, the wisteria made her melancholy. So did Red and Ada and all their kids hanging out of the car windows like a litter of puppies, squirming for a space. A space was all Jodean ever wanted. A place where she would fit into the lives of those around her. She wanted to be a fertile stem, not a fruitless sucker gleaning what little joy she could between trunk and branch.

She pulled open the screen door at the back of the house, surprised that Cora Mae had left it unlocked.

"Lord Almighty, Jodean, is that you?"

"It's me, Momma." She hadn't meant to let the screen door slam. She dropped the wisteria blossoms on the table, put the groceries away, and then swung around to the refrigerator where she always kept a damp cloth cooled for Cora Mae's headaches.

Cora Mae drag-footed her way to the kitchen where she leaned on the door frame eyeing the wisteria. She scratched under her heavy breasts. "Don't tell me you been out picking posies while I'm here alone with this headache."

"Go on back to the sofa, Momma. You'll feel better soon as I get supper ready." Jodean handed the cloth to Cora Mae then jammed the wisteria in an empty pickle jar and filled it with water.

Cora Mae turned to leave but stopped short. "I rented the tank house."

Jodean looked up from the plate of pork chops she'd taken out of the refrigerator. Cora Mae was holding the headache rag over her eyes.

"Is that right? To who?"

"He didn't tell me his name."

"*Momma*. You didn't ask?"

"You didn't tell me to."

It was Cora Mae's game. She was expert at transferring guilt.

Jodean glanced at the tank house through the window above the sink. "Did you settle anything about meals?" Cora Mae hadn't heard the question. She was already back on the sofa.

Jodean kicked off her shoes, scooped a dollop of lard from a crock and tapped the spoon hard a few times against the side of a big iron skillet.

She heard Cora Mae tuning the old Brunswick radio in the parlor. A snatch of song here, a dog bark from some serial program there. A preacher screaming, "Jeee-suhs." And in between, an empty echoing sheesh, like the sound of someone moving through darkness. Cora Mae found the program she was looking for, a soap opera about a singing cowboy. But after a while, all Jodean heard was the yowl of vibrating air between herself and the rest of the world. She turned the flame under the skillet up high and dusted the pork chops with flour.

Cora Mae ate from a tray in the parlor while Jodean sipped cool tea at the kitchen window where she watched the sky turn to blood. She put a pork chop on a plate along with some green beans and a thick slice of bread. She filled a quart jar with tea and then, with the plate in one hand and the jar in the other, hipped the screen door and crossed the yard to the tank house.

Jodean tapped the door with a bare foot. "Hello..." She waited, tapped again.

The door opened slowly a few inches. A sleep-crumpled man eased his face into the opening. His eyes were a strange blue, like dingy denim and, to her, stuck out too much from his bony face. It was the same with his ears.

"I'm Jodean Travis. I thought you might be hungry."

He looked at the food as if she held the crown jewels of England. Nodding like a mute, he reached through his sleep haze to take the plate and jar.

"I'll be back in a little while with an oil lamp. Around here, every time it rains the electric goes off." She backed away a few steps. "Momma says she didn't catch your name."

"Mike Lemay." His voice was thick with sleep.

"Well, Mike, I'll bring some linens too. I expect Momma forgot."

"Don't want to be a bother." He looked at the food. "We didn't settle anything about meals."

"This is on me. After today, if you decide to eat here, meals are twenty-five cents. I keep a tablet on the back porch for a tally so we can total it up every week."

He nodded.

"Better eat before it gets cold." Jodean backed away and turned to leave.

MIKE WATCHED THE woman walk away. A mass of short brown-black curls blossomed from a bobby pin on the right side of her head. And she was barefoot. At the moment, Mike didn't care if she was naked. He was that hungry.

He carried the food to a tattered, overstuffed chair, the only real piece of furniture in the tank house. Next to the chair a low table had been fashioned from an overturned foot tub, and a single bare light bulb hung from a wire in the ceiling. He'd been too exhausted earlier to notice much about the tank house except where the loft was.

Not long after he finished eating, the screen door at the back of the big house popped shut. Mike glanced out of the window and watched Jodean Travis cross the yard with an armload of sheets and towels and an oil lamp. He held the door open for her.

"Will I need this?" he asked taking the oil lamp.

"I saw the sun settin' behind a bank of clouds. Means it'll rain for three days."

"I see." What else could he say? "I appreciate the dinner. I was pretty hungry."

"Do you know how long you'll be in Cooperville?"

"As long as three months, depending on the project's funding."

"Project?"

Mike explained the Federal Writers' Project and that he had received instructions from a San Antonio office after asking for an assignment in the Southwest. He didn't mention that he had wanted to get as far away from the misery and filth of big cities as he could.

"Where're you from, Mike?"

"North Carolina."

"I thought you talked kind of funny."

The irony was her own accent. Like Clyde Cheevers, she added a "w" or "h" to most of the words rolling from far back in her throat. She said *tawked* instead of talked, *prawh-ject* instead of project. The dialect was different, too, and maybe that was a thing he might to try to capture when he started his interviews and transcriptions.

"Will that be okay with you?" he asked.

She shrugged and laughed. "Mike, you can talk any way you want, so long as you don't use foul language."

"No. I meant okay to stay three months. If not, I can—"

"Oh goodness, yes. But...well, I need to check with Momma to be sure, but I don't know why it wouldn't be." She gathered his dishes and let her gaze drop to the floor before turning to leave.

Mike watched Jodean Travis's small frame move toward the house a second time that day. When she started up the porch steps, he noticed she had put shoes on her tiny feet.

Around three in the morning, the sky crackled with yellow lightning. Mike woke from a dead sleep and wondered how safe he was under the tall water tank. He decided the thing had stood, obviously, for a long time in that same spot without any apparent catastrophe. Besides, if lightning struck and he boiled, he'd be happy to go.

He climbed down from the loft to close the windows. Thunder drummed from far away then clapped overhead, rattling the pipes in the tank house. He struggled with a stuck window, pounded the frame with the heel of his hand. Rain sheeted on a high wind and, in a white flash of lightning, he glimpsed trees thrashing wildly across the way. He managed to close the windows, then fished in the dark for the pull string on the hanging light bulb, found it and gave it a yank. The light didn't come on. Jodean Travis had been right about the electricity as well as the rain.

The sky stayed black and ominous for three days. Late in the afternoon of the third day, Mike had read as much of the FWP guidebook and back issues of newspapers as his brain could stand. He washed and shaved then hunkered against the rain to walk the short distance to town. He found the barber shop a couple of blocks up Main Street. Tom Coker, his supervisor in San Antonio, had written him that barbershops were a good place to find out what people had on their minds.

"Isn't this weather something?" The barber said when Mike burst through the door on a gust of rainy wind. "Be with you shortly," he added without breaking the rhythm of his snapping scissors.

Mike took off his fedora and gave it a shake.

The barber, who didn't have a hair on his head, wore thick, heavy looking glasses. A pudgy red-faced man in the chair stared at Mike's reflection in the mirror.

When the barber swung the chair around, the man said, "You must be the fellow wanting to hang around and see what our town is like."

Mike puzzled a second or two. How could the man know his business?

"I'm Mayor Tubby Whittaker, but we don't hold much on titles around these parts. Call me Tubby. This here's Emmet Anders, the best barber in town."

When Emmet nodded at Mike, his glasses slipped down his nose. He used his right thumb, which was still hooked through his scissors, to shove them back into place.

"...And the worst barber in town." Tubby's eyes disappeared into deep crevices when he chuckled. "You see, he's the *only* barber so he gets both titles." Both men laughed as if the joke was new.

"My name's Mike Lemay."

"I know," Mayor Tubby said. "Clyde Cheevers stopped by my office a few days ago. Told me about giving you a ride to town. I read a while back in the newspaper about the job you're doing. Should be real interesting to see what folks think is important enough for you to write down."

"I'd planned to contact you and the sheriff to explain my job, in case my presence looked suspicious."

"Good idea. If you have time, I'll introduce you to the sheriff when you're done here."

All three men turned to the window when a car, honking wildly, roared up Main Street and skidded to a stop in front of the barbershop. A small man hopped out and made a dash for the sidewalk awning. Another man, tall and broad-shouldered who'd been passing by the barber shop, stepped forward and the two hitched their chins at each other. Mike followed Emmet and Tubby outside. He assumed the second man, wearing a three-inch star on his chest, different from Clyde Cheevers', was the sheriff.

"I'm telling you *something's* happened to her," the small man told the sheriff. He plucked his hat off and rubbed his sweaty forehead on his sleeve. He was bald except for a fringe of pale red hair growing around the bottom half of his head.

"Hold on now, Red." The sheriff held up his hands as if to stop traffic. "She's probably just out checking on her cows. You know how silly she is about her livestock."

"Neal," the man addressed as Red jabbed his first finger at the sheriff's chest. "I was out checking on my cattle night before last and I saw her lantern light out in her pasture that backs up to my place. I drove over to see what was going on and found Miss Effie hunched over one of her old cows out in that sonofabitchin' storm. That old cow was trying to birth."

Red shook his head. "Hell, it looked damned near as old as Miss Effie. The calf was dead before I pulled it. It upset Miss Effie real bad on account of the old cow being so pitiful. Anyway, I went back the next day, yesterday, still pouring rain, and there was no sign of Miss Effie. The feed bucket she keeps by the back door was gone so I figured she's out feeding the old cow. But the oil lamp in the kitchen was lit. I thought it was strange." Red dropped his gaze and let air rush from his throat. "I should've gone looking for her then."

"Sheriff's right," Mayor Tubby said. His jowls jiggled as he spoke. "That old woman has always done the strangest—"

"She'd never leave her oil lamp burning, Tubby. And today, just now, I went to check on her again and there's not a sign of her anywhere. Not a drop of oil left in the lamp either."

The sheriff shifted his weight. "Well, if it'll make you feel any better, Red, I'll ride out and have a look-see."

"Goddamn it to hell! Ain't a matter of making me feel better. Miss Effie Beck is missing, disappeared in that goddamn storm and I figure it's your goddamn job to find her."

Mike could tell by the hunch of Red's shoulders that he was a tired man stretched to his limits. His boots and pants were caked with mud all the way up to his badly bowed knees. A silence stretched. Red's words had hit nerves.

Mayor Tubby cleared his throat then introduced Mike to Red Kasper and Sheriff Neal Lackland, adding, "Why don't we all ride out and look around the Beck place. Mike, you might just as well come along and get started knowing what goes on in Cooperville."

All four men climbed into Red Kasper's car and splashed down the road in steady, unrelenting rain. When they crossed a bridge over a low stream, Mike realized they were on the same road Clyde Cheevers had taken to drive into town four days earlier. Then he remembered Miss Effie was the thin shadow of a woman in the doorway of the leaning house, who had baked the ginger cake that had made him want to weep for home.

JODEAN CLIPPED A towel around Frances Whittaker's neck and adjusted the hot water knob to the shampoo bowl. The beauty parlor had been a bedroom at the front of the Travis house until Jodean's father ripped out a closet wall and hooked a shampoo bowl to the bathroom plumbing. Frances, Mayor Tubby Whittaker's wife, had had a standing appointment since the beauty parlor opened.

Frances wiggled herself into a comfortable position before tilting her head back. "I saw your favorite blonde head a while ago," she said.

"Now who would that be?" Jodean didn't mind humoring Frances' need for gossip but wished every now and then that she'd come up with a subject other than Sheriff Neal Lackland's wife.

"Faye Lackland. She's on the queen's pageant committee again this year, you know. Oh say, what's that man like, the one renting your tank house?"

"Seems nice enough." Jodean knew her own history rated second only to Faye's comings and goings when it came to town gossip. Most likely, Frances and her canasta ladies had wagered on how long it would take Mike to uncover the facts of her past.

"Tubby said maybe I should ask him to help with the queen judging since he isn't from these parts and wouldn't be partial."

Jodean heard Cora Mae padding down the hallway toward the beauty parlor.

"Did I hear y'all say Faye Lackland's name?" Cora Mae held out her hand to study her fingernails. "Jodean, I told Faye you'd set her hair today. Should be in any minute now."

Frances moved to the swivel chair and hitched her dress up far enough for Jodean to see her rolled down stockings below her fleshy knees. *Hams*, Jodean thought. Smokehouse hams.

"Cora Mae, you ever tell Jodean about Faye and that WPA fellow working on the new bridge?"

"Can't remember if I did. I wonder if Neal knows about her sneaky behavior?"

Jodean yanked the comb through a tangle in Frances' hair and wondered if it would do any good to tell Frances to mind her own business. Sheriff Neal Lackland and his wife Faye were favored beauty shop fodder when no disastrous droughts or sinister sicknesses threatened Cooperville. Even the Great Crash hadn't offered as much entertainment as the twice elected, wealthy - by Cooperville standards - Sheriff Lackland and his family. Jodean suspected that was because the Lacklands were easier to snap at and chew on, something the town could watch up close, envy or loathe. It's hard to gnaw on something controlled in Washington, D.C. thousands of miles away. Why, Jodean thought, nobody even knows what a Depression looks like, unless it resembled Mike Lemay or the poor, blank-eyed men working on the river bridge.

Frances continued her nonstop diatribe. "I think Faye hopes Neal will catch her. It'd be like spitting in his face for the way he embarrassed her at church that time, coming in late smelling like a whorehouse drunk. Jodean honey, you're digging in my head with those bobby pins."

"Sorry."

"Cora Mae is sure lucky to have you," Frances added as she watched Jodean in the mirror.

"Yeah, don't I know it," Cora Mae mumbled absent-mindedly while stroking violet nail polish on her fingernails. "I keep telling her someday I'm going to give this business to her. I just hope I can keep my health a little longer."

Every time Cora Mae made those comments, which was often, Jodean felt blamed in a childish sort of way, but she was never sure what she felt blamed for.

"Anyway, Jodean," Frances continued, "a few weeks ago Tubby worked late down at City Hall, till after dark. He walked home like always and when he came around the corner of East Street down by the schoolhouse, he heard a squeaking noise and looked over, and there in the dark was Faye Lackland in one of the schoolyard swings. Tubby could just barely make her out but said he was sure it was her because of that blonde hair kind'a glowing in the starlight, you know? He said about the time he thought to call out a howdy, she hurried off around the corner of the school building like she didn't want him to see her. Then Tubby says when he came to our street and was about to go in the house, there's this man a coming up the other end of the street but he couldn't make out who it was. So Tubby waits a minute, till the man passes through the light coming from our kitchen window, the one facing the corner, you know, and it was that Otis fellow, one of the WPA bridge workers, heading for the schoolyard. Now, you tell me, Cora Mae Travis, if they weren't up to something evil?"

"Faye hasn't got enough to keep her busy now that her kids are, what? Ten and twelve years old," Cora Mae said.

"Tubby says Faye sent her kids off to Dallas to spend the summer with her sister."

Jodean adjusted the hair dryer speed to a roar and waved Smokehouse Hams over. Once Frances' head was capped inside the machine, she wouldn't be able to hear a word being said. To Jodean having that kind of power – the power to stop beauty shop gossip campaigns – was exhilarating.

It was Jodean's gift to Cooperville. Mayor Tubby Whittaker could poke his nose anywhere he wanted. His wife, Frances Whittaker, appointed Pickle Queen committees. Cora Mae maintained proprietorship of the beauty shop from the sofa. Ada and Red loved and made babies. Sheriff Neal Lackland strutted around with a big star on his chest and claimed the prettiest woman in the county as his wife.

Cooperville survived droughts and hard times, erected monuments to Civil War heroes and organized parades to honor a Pickle Queen. But *only* she, Jodean Travis, could stop conversation in the beauty shop simply by using the high fan speed on the hair dryer.

Jodean lowered the hair dryer hood over Frances' head and handed her a LIFE magazine.

A few minutes later, Faye Lackland came through the door. "Hi there, Jodean, I know this is last minute..."

"She doesn't mind," Cora Mae said.

Jodean wrapped a towel around Faye's neck and moved the lever to make the shampoo chair recline. Faye's thick, dark eyelashes made a fan-shaped shadow on her creamy cheeks. Even her ankles were pretty, the way she crossed them on the footstool – and she smelled like peaches. Who could blame a man for tripping in Faye Lackland's wake, sheriff's wife or no?

Jodean checked the water temperature before wetting Faye's silky hair and working shampoo into a lather that covered her whole head.

"How's Neal doing these days?" Cora Mae asked. Jodean shot her a look. Cora Mae shot one back.

"Busy," Faye said. "I take it you hear all the gossip before anyone else so I don't have to tell you no one has found Effie Beck. Neal thinks she's probably lost in a pasture somewhere, still trying to find her way home. We were wondering how old she is."

"Not as old as she looks," Jodean said. "She's had a very hard life." She wrapped Faye's head in a clean towel. They moved to the swivel chair next to Cora Mae while Frances squirmed under the roaring dryer and peeked over her magazine.

"When I came through town just now," Faye said, "there was a crowd of men in front of City Hall getting ready to go out to her place for a search. Jodean, you look a million miles away."

"I was just thinking about Miss Effie out on that ranch by herself all these years. Most people alone that much tend to get testy, but she's always pleasant when I see her in town."

"Looks like a rag lady, if you ask me," Cora Mae said. "And did you ever get close enough to smell her? Lord."

That evening Jodean walked east, on Oak Street toward City Park. Pecan trees formed a dark umbrella overhead, and ahead on the left she heard a little girl banging away at her lessons in Glory's Piano Parlor. Glory, Ada and Faye had been best friends all through their school days, like sisters only without all the fussing. And they always included her, though she never expected it. Jodean often sensed other parents' discomfort with her presence, especially if they had sons. They acted like she was a disease. *Be nice and wave at the plague from across the street but don't invite it in.*

Glory had been the envy of the entire sixth grade class that long-ago Christmas when her parents bought a piano. Jodean paused to listen. Apparently Glory was playing now. The sweet melody resonated like bells in the evening air, expertly paced, a little melancholy, similar to Glory herself, whose high-waisted torso and wire glasses made her appear much older than the rest of them. She'd been the first to marry in spite of her blandness, but widowed young and left childless. A history, Jodean sometimes thought, as pitiful as her own.

Jodean moved on down the sidewalk. At the corner of Oak and Cotton, Fred and Bessy Alvin waved from their porch swing.

Time slowed in the lavender haze settling over the Medina River valley. Jodean loved watching it happen. But on this particular evening, Frances' tale about Faye at the schoolyard troubled her. For a long time now, it seemed that Faye was destined for calamity of some kind and Jodean had this nagging, knowing feeling that it wouldn't be of Faye's own doing.

At City Park she circled the gazebo then sat on the steps for a time to watch two boys tossing a baseball back and forth. Their high-pitched laughter punctuated each pitch and missed catch. Beyond them, the Lackland mansion, as everyone called it behind Sheriff Neal's back, loomed in the shadows of live oak trees. Faye had graduated from high school a year ahead of Jodean, Glory and Ada, and won the title of Pickle Queen the following spring.

The year Faye's first baby was born, Jodean managed to get a job in the pickle factory. Until Jodean's daddy brought up the idea of a beauty shop, she thought she'd spend the rest of her life working up to her elbows in pickling lime, going about her days with a pinched mouth and burning eyes because of the vinegar steam rising from the huge copper vats. Back then, no matter how much she bathed, or how much rose water she splashed on herself, she still smelled like pickles. Jodean's mouth drew up now in the remembering.

The boys moved away down East Street with lowered heads. The tallest had his arm hooked on the shoulder of the other, who kept pounding his fist in his mitt. They looked like great philosophers or leaders of nations, with knees too big and knotty for their thin legs.

Jodean crossed the park and decided to go home by way of Main Street. She took her time enjoying the quiet of early evening, studied new spring dresses in the department store window, and was about to cross the street when three cars bounced across spring creek bridge and stopped in front of City Hall. Tubby rolled out of the car nearest her.

"Evening, Mayor," she said.

He touched his hat. "Jodean." His big red face looked tired. Red, Neal, and Mike got out of the second car. Four men climbed out of the third car, and all of them looked as tired as Mayor Tubby.

"Miss Effie?" Jodean was half afraid to ask.

"Not a sign of her," Tubby said.

At least, Jodean thought, there was hope the woman was still alive. A memory popped into her mind, like a light suddenly flashing on in a darkened room. A few years earlier she'd been in a terrible rush to get to the drugstore for some Black Draught for Cora Mae and then get back to the beauty parlor in time for her next appointment. When she yanked the drugstore door open, Miss Effie, who had been about to walk out, was nearly sucked off balance by the sudden force of air.

She appeared thin and wispy, with a faded rough-woven scarf tied around her head. She wore thick wool socks that stretched up to her knees, even though it was the middle of summer. Her face, with its expressions hidden in a thousand deep lines, made Jodean freeze in her tracks. The woman looked into Jodean's eyes and the deep lines moved, cupped around her mouth to form a smile. Jodean stepped back then, and held the door open for her. When Miss Effie walked by, Jodean, who considered herself small compared to most women, could look down on the old woman's humped back and smell the dusty scent of her moving like brown smoke through the door.

Jodean had collected herself then and turned to see Leroy, the druggist, a clerk, and a few customers staring. Effie Beck could do that. Stupefy people just by passing by. Red said once that Effie Beck had the tight-fisted determination of a wild hog when it came to protecting her home or herd. Grown men counted themselves lucky to have had only their ears singed while arguing cattle prices with her. One rancher claimed she poked him in the ribs with an old Colt and declared she'd as soon barbecue him as sell him a heifer.

"It's just her way," Red tried to explain to anyone who would listen. "She figures that only disreputable vermin with a mind for ill-will could be frightened by the likes of her. To her way of thinking, honest men are hard to scare."

Through it all, Effie Beck bore herself forward, day after day, regal as royalty, serene and poised, wearing raggedy clothes old as Jerusalem.

But here, now, in the middle of Main Street, Sheriff Neal Lackland, with men gathered around him, tried to figure out what to do next regarding her disappearance.

"This is the way I see it," Neal said. "Tomorrow, Sunday after church, we will gather at Miss Effie's place prepared to do a complete sweep of her whole ranch. I'll have the preacher mention it in his announcements after the sermon. I need y'all to call on your neighbors, friends, anybody willing to help. I figure it'll take most of the day and then some." He turned to Jodean. "Maybe you and your momma could tell some of the ladies to set a table for coffee and such for the searchers."

Jodean nodded. Someone behind her asked Sheriff Neal what he thought could've happened to Miss Effie.

"I still say she wandered off to find that cow Red told us about and maybe fell and got hurt...or worse."

"What about robbery, Sheriff?" another asked. "There's been some pretty shady characters thumbing their way through our county. And just look at all them strangers on the bridge crew. Why, Miss

Beck might have come up on somebody poking around her house looking for money."

"Didn't see a single sign of anything to suggest such a thing. Just so everybody knows," Neal paused and gave Red a side glance Jodean couldn't read. "I plan to call on the Rangers – have Clyde Cheevers come out and investigate the house with me."

The men stirred. Some rubbed day old whiskers, others spit in the street. Jodean imagined a grim current ran through them, though she wouldn't consider any of them mean-spirited. Men liked this kind of trouble. It gave them an occasion they could rise to. Looking for a lost woman was a more hopeful thing to be doing than trying to get a good price for rotting cotton or watching hollow-eyed kids with no future loll on porch steps.

Tubby's son-in-law leaned loose limbed against one of the cars and crossed his ankles. He dug a bag of tobacco out of his shirt pocket and rolled a cigarette.

Red pushed his hat to the back of his head and propped his foot on the bumper of his car. He looked heart-heavy and beat down. Jodean knew Red loved Miss Effie like a mother and father all rolled into one. And it was probably a given that Miss Effie returned the admiration. But who could ever guess, really, what went on in the woman's head behind her closed-off face.

Emmet, the barber, and Mike had their heads bent low listening to something the school principal was saying. One man tipped his chin at Sheriff Neal, some shook hands, slapped backs, and Jodean thought she understood. This milling, this huffing and prancing filled their own sense of purpose. True, they worried about Miss Effie's well-being, for her presence among them served as a reminder that they couldn't give up as long as *she* kept going. And no one ever expected Effie Beck to up and quit anything.

"One o'clock Sunday then," Sheriff Neal called out to everyone. "Appreciate your help."

In a matter of minutes they'd all gone, disappeared down side streets and down Main toward the highway, leaving behind a somber spirit that filled the now dark street like water fills a jar.

"Jodean?"

She turned and was barely able to see Mike's outline against the evening's glow.

"Mike, I thought you'd gone home ahead of me."

"Think I could get a sandwich this late?"

"How about bacon and tomato?"

"My favorite."

At the house Jodean fried bacon and sliced tomatoes while Mike washed up at the pump outside the tank house. She carried his food to the dimly lit back porch and then took her time pouring him a big glass of milk so she could study him a little, the way he ate, neat and polite, but eager. He had a gentle look about his eyes, like she could see all the way down into his heart and it was probably gentle too.

There had been few suitors to come to her door because of her "station in life" as Cora Mae liked to put it. Jodean would bet it was Cora Mae's hammering hints about the futility of her as a love interest that discouraged them.

Station in life. Like a sign above bruised bananas at C.J.'s Grocery. *Damaged Produce – Half Price,* or seconds at the Five and Dime – *Marked Down For Quick Sale.*

Jodean grew weary of always wishing she had somebody to love. It was all she ever thought about these days. That, and being loved back. Somebody to reach for every now and then. Someone to touch her on the shoulder or arm to make sure she was real and not some dream, as if her being alive made a difference.

Last night she had squinted at her reflection in the dresser mirror and wondered what a man would see in her. Something shriveled? Wasted? All scabbed over with loneliness? She made herself sick pining the way she did for something she'd likely never have.

Mike's Adam's apple bobbed when he tilted the glass to gulp the last of the milk. She moved to pour him more.

"I've had plenty."

Jodean's tongue stuck to the roof of her mouth. She could only nod and watch him cross the porch and then the yard to disappear into the dark tank house.

"MOMMA, TOOTIE SUE'S got snot running down her lip again."

Ada heard Pete calling out from under the porch where he and the rest of her kids were playing in the cool, dry dirt.

She rinsed the last of the supper dishes and dried her hands. Tootie Sue, almost three years old, was the spitting image of Red and, Ada sighed, hopelessly prone to having a runny nose. Ada glimpsed Pete through the screen door. He petted Bullet, the lanky mongrel dog Red found by the side of the road a few years back. The dog had been shot in the hip and was near death from infection and starvation, but Red nursed him back to health as only he could. That's Red's way, Ada reminded herself. The kind of man who can't walk away from pain or hurt.

As Ada stepped out onto the porch, Pete called out to Bullet and threw a stick. Bullet took off after it, favoring his bad hip with a comical hop about every third stride.

In Pete, Ada recognized the long bones and dark hair of her family. He was so quiet at times she worried he'd shut himself off from the rest of the world and lived in a dreamed-up foreign place inside his head. When Tootie Sue was born, Pete assumed the role of her guardian, exercising the patience of an old man with her while, the others, Jean and Ted, tumbled and writhed from one carefree impulse to another.

"Come here, Sue honey," Ada called.

Tootie Sue squirmed out from under the porch steps and drew her arm across her face. The dirty drip smudged her cheek. Ada swiped at it with a cloth and then brushed strawberry hair from her eyes. It was getting late – that time of day when breezes die down and sounds carried long distances. Ada sat on the steps hoping Red would be home soon saying he'd found Miss Effie.

Pete sat beside her. His overalls were three inches too short and nearly worn through at the knee. Ada thought maybe she shouldn't have had so many kids, wondered if she would have been more careful had she known beforehand about the hard times they all faced.

No matter now. Had them she did and loved each one like her very own arms or legs. Her children rounded out her life with Red here on this little ranch.

Tootie Sue leaned against Ada. "You and Pete want to help me feed the chickens?" Sue sniffed and took Ada's hand.

"When's Daddy coming home?" Pete padded along at Ada's side.

"When he gets here."

"Do you think he'll find Miss Effie?"

"Don't I hope so, Pete honey. Don't I hope."

Ada handed Pete a bucket of crushed corn. He, in turn, held it for Sue as she picked her way among the scrambling chickens tossing tiny handfuls as fast as she could to keep the chickens from rushing at her.

Red was a good daddy and even better husband. Ada knew how much Effie Beck's disappearance haunted him, how much he loved the old woman. In fact, in another life, if he'd been thirty years older and Miss Effie twenty years younger, they probably would have been sweethearts.

But jealousy never entered Ada's mind. Red admired the elder cattlewoman, worked by her side with respect for what she had endured. He was a man's man who nursed a mongrel dog back to health so it could spend its days lounging on a shady porch. Because of his citizenship in the world, Red took it upon himself to be a daddy to it. Ada had never seen him back away from heat when he knew he was right. At the same time, Red figured it was his lot to live by the sweat of his brow and so he did, without complaint.

Lately Miss Effie showed signs of being addled, as attached to her small herd of cattle as Ada was to her kids. Red got real tickled once telling about himself and some cowhands on horseback rounding up cattle for auction and looking over the fence into Miss Effie's west pasture. She wobbled to a hump of land with nothing but a handful of rocks in her old blue bucket. She shook the bucket to rattle the rocks, and waited. After a while here came her cows ambling out of the thickets. They walked right up to her.

"It's a sight," Red said in telling it, "to see Miss Effie, such a tiny tea cup of a thing, with all those big cows hugging around her. Why, they'd follow her into a bonfire. Only Miss Effie could get by rounding up her herd with a bucket of rocks."

Now that Ada thought about it, it seemed Miss Effie's cows were as emboldened by her presence as Red.

Tootie Sue's sudden squeal pierced Ada's thoughts. Pete yelled, "Daddy's home!"

The family's battered green Buick jounced between two gigantic cottonwoods on either side of the ranch gate. Ada could see the familiar outline of Red's big hat through the dusty windshield. His chin was dipped slightly, left elbow propped on the open window and Ada fell in love all over again, the way she did every time he came home after a long day away.

He stopped on the shady side of the barn and as soon as he opened the car door, Tootie Sue jumped into his arms, giggling and screeching, proud that she'd been the first one to reach her daddy.

"There's my Tootie Sue!" Red yelled as he scooped her into his arms. When Pete caught up to them, Red ruffled his dark hair then held him close for a quick hug. Bullet barked non-stop. Jean and Ted joined in the scramble for a squeeze from their daddy.

Red glanced at Ada over the heads of the children. He shook his head side to side. He, the sheriff and the others hadn't found Effie Beck.

RED FIGURED THIS was all a man needed to help him get beyond the heavy feeling of failure. These kids grabbing for a hug, little Tootie Sue wetting his face with a snotty kiss, Jean begging for a toe ride, Ted and Pete running around him on stick horses yelling like a bunch of Indians. These were the things that held him up.

"You kids are going to kill your daddy," Ada said. "Get on in the house. Pete, you start bathwater for the girls."

Red dropped to the porch steps and stuck out a leg so Ada could pull his boot off. "Ada, I swear to God, I just can't get it in my head where Miss Effie got off to." He held out his other leg and told Ada about the search plans for the next day. Ada tugged off the second boot then gave him a hand up.

That night, late, after everyone fell into a rhythm of shallow breathing and deep sleep, Red rolled out of bed and made his way to the kitchen. For once he remembered to step over the creaky floorboard in front of the bathroom. Ada had chewed his tail off at least a hundred times for forgetting and waking Pete, who slept like a coyote with one ear pricked for trouble.

He poured himself a glass of buttermilk and sat at the kitchen table. He shivered, though the night was warm and sultry. Bullet moved outside the front screen door. The heavy wood doors at the front and back of the house were never closed unless it was to keep out winter's cold. From where Red sat, he could look to his right, out the back door to see the barn and pastures. Or turn and look left through the house and front door to see the gate at the road leading to town. Except now, on this godforsaken moonless night, with Miss Effie lost out in the world and him not able to see his hand in front of his goddamned face.

He'd rehashed everything that happened the night of the storm more times than he could count, trying to remember if Miss Effie said or did anything that would give a clue as to what she'd planned to do after he left her. He should have sat with her a while after walking her back to the house, made sure she wasn't too upset over that old cow.

That goddamned worthless Sheriff Neal, Red thought, shaking his head in the dark, was about as useful as a wart on a hog's tit. How a man as lazy and self-serving as Neal Lackland could get elected sheriff was a thing beyond Red's imagining. Maybe that showed how stupid the whole town was to believe slack-jawed Neal was worth a shit for sheriff just because his daddy had owned half the county at one time or another.

Hell, any blindfolded idiot could see Neal didn't do anything day in and day out but sit on a stool at City Hall like it was his throne, drinking coffee, chatting with the lady clerks.

"Red?" Ada stood in the doorway behind him. "Honey, come back to bed. You can't find Miss Effie like this."

"She's out there, Ada. With her blue bucket. I know because it's not at her back door where she keeps it—"

"Red."

"I bet her old black coat is missing from the house. I want to remember to look for it tomorrow. She would have put it on to go out again even though it wasn't cold."

Ada moved to his chair, rubbed his shoulders, then rested her chin on his head.

MIKE WATCHED JODEAN and Cora Mae walk around the house and cross the street headed for church. He rubbed his chin, smiled to himself. Cora Mae reminded him of a rodeo clown. Her turquoise dress blazed with bright pink flowers splashed with orange splotches here and there. Jodean, on the other hand, wore a plain dark blue dress with a white collar and white gloves. As they moved along the street, it struck him how different they were in other ways. Cora Mae, though stoop-shouldered, was inches taller than Jodean. Her walk was heavy with long, plow-pulling strides, while the diminutive Jodean clipped along as if walking in a shallow stream.

He should have planned to go to church, too. Eventually he'd have to meet the preacher and find out what kind of religious doctrine the town practiced. The information might add more insight to the town's attitudes when he got around to writing summaries about Cooperville.

He'd had enough damning and helling from a self-righteous preacher back in North Carolina to last a lifetime or two. Religion required too many shoulds and should nots. It made people shameful instead of hopeful. Hocus-pocus, voodoo, witches' spells. Christianity, Judaism, Hinduism. All the same to him. Religion promised a puffy white cloud world but delivered accusation and guilt. Preachers probably found it easier to cajole people into doing right out of fear instead of teaching the benefits of genuine love and caring. The whole system set up a breeding ground for resentment any way he looked at it.

Shoot, the only thing he got out of hymn singing was his own voice echoing back from a shifting void. Any faith he ever had seeped away over time until none remained. It mortified him to think it, and he'd not dare say it out loud, but Mike believed that when a man loses everything, he doesn't need faith anymore.

To him, it was that simple.

When Cora Mae and Jodean disappeared around a corner, he noticed a slip of paper on the back screen door. He crossed the yard for a closer look. It was a note to him from Jodean, held in place by two bobby pins stuck through the screen mesh said: *Mike, Help yourself to coffee on the stove and biscuits in the oven. Tubby and Frances are giving us a ride out to the Beck place at noon if you care to join us. Jodean.*

He took advantage of Jodean's offer of coffee and biscuits, and after washing his dishes he walked along the rock fence behind the tank house. There he spied a weathered building too small for a barn and too large for a tool shed. Massive trees arched above its mossy roof, and when he leaned over stacks of clay flowerpots to look through a time-hazed window, he saw an old Ford Model A truck covered with a film of dust. The hood was raised and a wrench lay on the fender.

Memories rushed at Mike, images of his father calling out, "Hand me that wrench, will ya, Mike."

Mike tugged on the double doors but weeds grew so thick against the bottom edge he couldn't budge either of them. He dug the toe of his shoe into a patch of nutgrass, surprised at his disappointment when he still couldn't free the doors.

He walked on until the path sloped to a rocky creek, Cooperville Spring Creek, if he had his bearings right. He followed it downstream, occasionally climbing through tangled honeysuckle and tree roots, until he came to a pool where sunlight danced on crystal water and a huge carp lazed in deep shadows.

Mike threw a stick into the pool, wondered about the fact that the whole town gave the impression of being out of plumb because of the disappearance of one old woman. Except for Red, no one claimed to know her well even though she'd lived her whole life a few miles from town.

Cooperville seemed to him a world unto itself, not so much isolated as self-sufficient. As a small boy, he had gone along with his dad once to a clock shop to have a pocket watch repaired. When they stepped through the door the whole place vibrated with ticking and chiming. Behind the counter a thin-faced man leaned over an ornate mantle clock that had been turned so Mike could see inside it, into its heart full of gears and wheels. Each cog fit perfectly into its own mortise. All of it ticking endless little hitches of time.

That's how Mike saw Cooperville, a big clock with everyone fitting into the heart of it. And it was his job to listen to the ticking and record what he heard, to watch the gears and document what he saw.

The FWP guidebook instructed interviewers to pass the time of day with people, let them warm up to you. Find out how different individuals made sense of their lives. Mike considered the possibility of making sense of what anybody lived. To him, life was a joke that everyone laughs at when secretly they don't have a clue what's supposed to be funny.

A tangle of vine and trees across the creek swayed and churned. Odd, because there hadn't been a breeze. He thought he heard breathing, or sighing, and strained to see into the forest, searched for a form, animal or human. The hair on his arms stood on end. He backed up the slope. Ridiculous as it was, he felt watched.

He crossed a wide meadow to return to the house, walked by a small grove of apple trees on his right and then, closer to the house, Jodean's tidy vegetable garden. Rows of Kentucky Wonder beans, Big Boy tomatoes, Northrup collard greens, Honeynut Gold squash, all flourished in bright sunshine. He watched her pull weeds barefooted late one hot afternoon. She hummed softly to herself and when she stood, sunlight shone through the thin fabric of her dress outlining her straight, strong legs.

Back at the tank house Mike jotted a page of notes about the observations he'd made about the town so far. Then he washed, shaved, and walked around to the front of the house to wait for Jodean and Cora Mae on the porch steps. They were already coming back down the street. Jodean glanced up from the ground, smiled and waved. "Been waiting long?"

"We don't have time to stand here chatting." Cora Mae said before he had time to answer. "We need to change clothes and heat the butter beans and rolls before Tubby comes back and blasts his horn."

Jodean hesitated, then followed Cora Mae into the house.

Mayor Tubby and his wife, Frances drove up to the curb just as the women came out again, each with a dish wrapped in heavy towels. Cora Mae shoved hers at Mike and said to Jodean, "Looks like you got the crust too short again."

Whatever Cora Mae was talking about made Jodean flush. The three of them scooted into the back seat of Tubby's car, carefully holding pots and dishes upright. Frances said howdy-do without turning around.

Tubby accelerated away from the curb and said, "Mike, I don't know if you're aware of it but Emmet Anders, remember him, the barber, is acting Police Chief. I had to appoint somebody to fill Chief Goodall's place when he took a sudden fever and died. Emmet don't like it much but the job hardly calls for him to do anything."

"Lord knows," Frances said over her shoulder toward the backseat, "if Faye didn't make it to church, she probably won't be around to help with the food either."

Mike had trouble tracking Frances sometimes. She seemed off subject, more often than not. As if she heard in one language and replied in another.

Cora Mae rolled her eyes, grunted and nodded in agreement with Frances.

At Miss Effie's ranch a group of men had gathered near the barn. Frances took it upon herself, *as the mayor's wife*, Mike heard her say, to organize the food.

Tubby introduced Mike to June Rawlings, the preacher's wife, and to Glory Hughes, the town's only piano teacher, adding the word *widowed* when they were out of ear shot of Glory. Then he commandeered a couple of high school boys to bring sawhorses out from the barn.

"Unhinge Miss Effie's front and back doors," Frances barked additional orders at the boys. "Put them across the sawhorses for tables."

"Somehow that don't seem right," Tubby said.

"I don't think Effie Beck will complain so long as you find her alive."

By the time they had the doors positioned on sawhorses, the road in front of the Beck place looked like a rodeo grounds parking lot. Half the trucks had trailers hitched on back that were loaded with saddled horses ready for the search.

Mike guessed that at least twenty-five men were milling around waiting for Clyde Cheevers to arrive. Sheriff Neal had insisted to Tubby that the search not begin until Clyde arrived to add to the legitimacy to the proceedings. Glory and Jodean circled the makeshift tables, slapping dish towels above the food to keep flies away.

Finally Frances marched over to Neal, who leaned against the barn as if he hadn't a worry in the world. She asked why he didn't tell everybody to go ahead and eat while they were waiting for Clyde.

Sheriff Neal took the hay straw he had been chewing out of his mouth. "Y'all heard the lady." The crowd followed him to the food tables.

Mike counted three kinds of potato salad and one dish of baked sweet potatoes drowning in thick syrup. There was smoked pork, pork roast and ham. Roast beef and beef brisket as well as sliced beef with homemade noodles. That was Frances' contribution, he'd heard her say.

Fried chicken, deviled eggs, roasting ears, turnip greens. Collards and butter beans. Corn bread, sliced white bread, wheat and poppy seed rolls. Someone set a big yellow can of Steen's 100% Pure Cane Syrup near the bread in case anyone wanted to sop bread in it.

He stepped back for a minute to take stock of the tightening in his throat. Troubling thoughts threatened to ruin the warmth of human kindness he'd begun to feel. When he glanced up, he noticed Jodean staring at him from across the table.

A gust of wind churned the treetops and behind the sound of it a cow bawled a long drawn out lament. Jodean kept staring, innocent and questioning.

Mike wondered if she and these good people were exempt from condemnation for not knowing about the hunger and hardship suffered back East. The daily indignities that battered people there?

Shouldn't *he* be condemned for knowing and running away? For in truth, that's what he had done...left his mother and brother to run away to this place of abundance. Sure, county crops withered daily from lack of rain. Banks foreclosed on ranchers then locked their doors and left people without cash. But most of Cooperville was getting by. They raised cattle, goats, pigs and planted small gardens to keep from starving. And it had rained.

How could he ever explain to someone like Jodean how guilt evaporates a man's reasoning. Only a few months ago, he'd helped his brother and mother dig in garbage bins for half-rotted potatoes. And now here he was standing before a feast fit for kings. Mike didn't know which was worse. The guilt or the shame for leaving home.

Tubby announced that everyone should bow their heads so Brother Rawlings could say a blessing over the food. Mike swallowed hard, couldn't hear a word of prayer for the riddling thoughts that drummed in his head.

Most everyone had served themselves by the time Clyde
Cheever's truck crawled to a stop outside the gate. Five men jumped
from the truck bed. Mike recognized the look of them, didn't have to
hear Clyde explain to Sheriff Neal.

"Train rolled into town and these drifters hopped off just as I was
leaving. They're pretty hungry and need work. I figured they could
help with the search in exchange for grub."

Neal nodded and Clyde turned to the bedraggled group, "Come
and get it boys." One man, who looked about sixty years old, hadn't
a tooth in his mouth. Another had yellow oozing sores on his neck
and arms. Mike quickly looked away but not before he glimpsed
Jodean hand the sick man a plate. She told him she was mighty glad
they came to help out. The last man to take a plate stood apart from
the rest. He had a thin brown mustache and high cheek bones. When
he thanked Jodean, his voice had a polished airy sound to it. Mike
pictured him a banker or lawyer who'd obviously fallen far.

Red walked up beside Mike and said, "Might have known ol'
Clyde was driving. The man don't know halt from hurry-up."

Mike watched Sheriff Neal tap Jodean on the shoulder and
motion her aside. She listened then lowered her eyes and shook her
head. She listened some more and shook her head again, only this
time she glanced over at him and Red.

After that, Neal moved to a spot in front of the tables and took
off his hat. "Y'all go on eating while I explain the procedure. Now
Red and Clyde here will head the search of Miss Beck's ranch lands.
On the side of the barn yonder, Red has posted a general layout of
the place showing where the tanks and dry creek beds are so you can
get your bearings. When you're through eating, meet with him over
there. He's gonna divide y'all into groups and assign each an area to
cover, either on foot or horseback, depending on the territory."

Sheriff Neal pinched the crease in the crown of his hat. "As most
of you know, that land 'cross the road belongs to Miss Beck, too, but
she didn't run cattle on it so no reason to suspect she would have
gone there. Concentrate your search over here, on this side. Police
Chief Emmet Anders, Mayor Tubby Whittaker, Mike and myself will

search the grounds around the house and check everything inside. The ladies have informed me they will have plenty of coffee and dessert throughout the afternoon if anyone is inclined to take a break." He put his hat back on and glanced at Red. "Anything else?"

Red stepped forward and faced the crowd. "I think Miss Effie probably had her blue bucket with her when she went out the night of the storm. Keep your eyes peeled for it." He looked at Neal. "And I suspect she had on her black coat. You ought to look for it in the house. If it's not there, you can bet she was wearing it."

"Anybody got questions?" Neal asked. He hooked a thumb in a belt loop. "I've called on Ranger Clyde Cheevers here to help look for evidence of wrongdoing." He shifted his weight. "I reckon we better get started."

As the men stirred, Tubby called out, "Say, Red? How 'bout I have Neal fire his gun when he's ready to call off the search?"

Red, who was on his way to the barn, waved a thumbs-up without breaking stride.

Mike trailed Tubby, Emmet and Neal to the back of the house. A rickety fence surrounded the yard where a windmill whirred in a high breeze above the henhouse. A sagging clothesline stretched from the corner of the house to the barn. A few gray rags hung from it.

Emmet walked to the henhouse, to a pail hanging on a hook and threw a handful of corn on the ground. "Who's tending these hens?" he asked.

"Red and his kids," Tubby answered. To Mike he added, "Though everybody in town at one time or another pitches in to help out the old girl when she needs it. But Red, living so close, does the most."

Inside the back door, Tubby kicked at a pair of old boots. "Her Daddy's," he said. "Been dead thirty years. Tells you how old they are."

The boots sat side by side with their insteps together. Mike lifted one. It was huge and had been patched a hundred times. The other boot had a strip of ducking cloth wrapped around the widest part of the toe and had been tied off in a tight knot on top.

"No cane." Tubby said.

"What?"

"Miss Effie had to have a cane to walk. About eight years ago she stepped on a nail or something, took up a running infection that turned green on her. Doc whacked off half her foot, said she was lucky it didn't get to her *whole* leg. Anyway, she had to have a cane to walk very far after that. Red said she usually keeps it here at the back door. Watch for it and that black coat he mentioned."

When Mike stepped into the shadowy house, he thought it strange that veils of dust and cobwebs covered everything. Hard to believe that it had only been a matter of days since Effie Beck was there, living, doing whatever she did with her time. Except for the sharp, sweet odor of rotting food, the house could have been deserted for years. As if someone in a past decade had stood up from the kitchen table, walked out the door to watch a sunset and never came back.

In spite of the dust and cobwebs, everything was tidy, in place. The wide drainboard on either side of the sink had big jars of flour, lard, and sugar neatly placed according to size. Cups hung from hooks under the cabinets. A filthy, faded green calico cloth strung on a wire curtained the shelves under the drain board. The floor in front of the sink had been patched with squares of tin.

"Good gosh." Tubby blew dust from jars of rotting, unnamable food.

A platter on the table was covered with a layer of green mold. Mike leaned closer. Under the green mold was ginger cake, sure as hell. Sitting to the right of the platter was the empty oil lamp Red mentioned. "Miss Beck must have bad eyesight," Mike said.

"What makes you say that?" Sheriff Neal asked, coming in from the front door.

"Everything appears neat, in place – but dusty and dirty. Anyone who takes the time to be this neat," Mike indicated the kitchen, "would be bothered by the dust and grime. Maybe she doesn't see it."

"He has a point," Emmet said. "That could explain how she got lost...if that's what happened." He opened a closet between the bedroom and parlor and jumped back against the doorjamb when a mouse scurried out and vanished in a hole in the opposite corner. He glanced in the closet and then shut the door.

Mike wandered into the bedroom. A tattered quilt covered the bed. Under the quilt edge, Mike glimpsed the white enameled rim of a chamber pot. A trunk adorned with doilies and a stack of dog-eared Progressive Farmer magazines sat under the window. The walls were bare except for a wedding portrait hanging from a faded satin rope above the bed.

"That would be her parents," Tubby said when he saw Mike staring. "Breezy claims Miss Effie's daddy was the meanest sonofabitch in the county."

"Breezy?"

"Black fellow lives way back down the dry creek bed. His daddy was a tenant of Mr. Beck's in the old days. When old man Beck died, Miss Effie let Breezy and his boys work for ownership of about ten acres." Tubby traced his finger in the dust on the chest of drawers. He sneezed and the whole house shook.

Mike glanced at his own distorted reflection in the splotched mirror above the chest of drawers. He glanced away and tried to imagine what Effie Beck thought of herself. He had always believed such thoughts were more telling of what a person was really like than all the deeds they had done.

"Look at that ceiling, will you?" Tubby said. "If it sags any more, it'll be on our heads."

So that was it, Mike thought, joining the others in the parlor. Three rooms. A kitchen, bedroom and sparsely furnished parlor with a day bed butted against one wall. Newspapers stuffed into a broken window pane and floorboards near the front door were rotted so bad he could see the ground under the house.

They stepped out onto the sagging front porch.

"Well, no cane, no coat, no bucket," Emmet said, then glanced at Mike. "I agree with you about the bad eyesight theory. I see no reason to believe foul play was involved in Miss Beck's disappearance. She probably put on her coat, grabbed her cane and bucket and went out on her own. I bet Red and Clyde find her."

"Dead or alive?" Tubby asked, ducking under the porch overhang. He frowned like a pudgy child and hoisted his belt up and over his belly.

Emmet shrugged.

JODEAN WONDERED, NOT just today but often, if men would roll over and die of starvation if women decided to give up cooking. She always came to the same conclusion – that women would shrivel up from lack of purpose and die right along with them. "Has anybody seen Faye?" she asked.

After washing dishes in tubs hauled from town, the ladies lazed on quilts spread in the cool shade. Frances swatted at a fly with her paper fan. "She ought to be here any minute. Said she'd bring coffee for when the men take a break. By the way, did Glory tell y'all what happened Friday when she was doing her volunteer work down at the library?" When no one answered, Frances turned to Glory. "You tell it. You're the one that was there."

"There's not much to tell. Faye came in real late that afternoon, almost closing time, and checked out some children's books. About third grade level, I would guess they were. She was all breathless, you know, like she'd been running or something." Glory squirmed, looked uncomfortable. She sometimes had trouble dodging involvement in Frances and Cora Mae's gossip.

"Third grade? Her kids are too old for that," Cora Mae said. "Makes you wonder, don't it?"

Jodean moved away from the shade and strolled toward the barn, where most of the corral rails were toppled and scattered on the ground. Beyond the corral, across a little valley and on the next rise, she could see horsemen waving signals to each other as they crisscrossed the ranch.

A sickening dread crept up Jodean's spine and shrunk her scalp. If they did find Effie Beck, she'd be near death or dead, out in the open country all this time, feeble and frail like she was. Up to this point, everything – the announcement about the search, the food planning, seeing everyone pull together – had a carnival feel to it. But now, watching men work in earnest, Jodean's view of what it meant to have a town mindful of your comings and goings somersaulted.

She'd often wished she could live in a city where her difference would blend in, even if it meant being overlooked most of the time. At night, she schemed, built imaginary situations in her mind of how a hair dryer in the beauty shop would overheat and catch fire, burn everything to the ground. Or a spring rain wouldn't let up until the Medina River backed into Spring Creek and Spring Creek backed up until, lo and behold, the beauty shop got washed clean away.

But now, times like this, Jodean knew she loved her home. Cooperville wasn't going to overlook Effie Beck even if most folks thought her a little strange. Jodean just hoped the woman was alive and somehow knew about all this caring and was strengthened by it.

Ada drove through the gate and stopped next to the corral. She turned to the back seat. "I'm going to swat ev'ry one of you if you don't hush!" Her face was pepper red.

Jodean opened the door for Pete, who was hugging a cake platter heaped with globs of cake and icing, some of it mashed against his overalls. Cherries had been placed at exact intervals around the outside edges of the disaster.

"What happened?" Jodean asked Pete.

"Momma sat it down on the porch to run back in the house for her car keys and Tootie Sue accidentally stepped on it."

"I scraped off the dirty part and added the cherries," Ada said as she circled the car and reached for the platter.

Jodean explained to Ada that Red and the men were still out, so there was no news.

Ada put her cake on the table and joined the others in the shade. "It's a bad sign they haven't found her yet."

Frances said, "I keep telling Tubby there's something sinister about Effie Beck vanishing like she did."

"Of course," Cora Mae jumped in. "I think it has to do with one of those WPA fellows. None of this kind of trouble ever happened until they came hanging around. I always heard Effie Beck kept money hid in that shack of hers."

"Me, too." Frances dabbed her throat with a lace handkerchief. "Only I heard the habit went back to her daddy, that he'd collected a bunch of gold bars for fighting for the Confederacy and he hid them in that well yonder."

Ada and Jodean looked at each other.

Little Tootie Sue ambled up with her thumb in her mouth and slouched against Ada.

Frances kept going. "And remember now Effie Beck didn't – *doesn't* have any family? Tubby said so. He checked into it at the courthouse to be sure in case they need to notify next of kin, you know?"

"Then Cooperville has to be her kin," Ada said.

"You ladies are looking mighty down in the mouth." Clyde Cheevers had come from the barn and stood for a beat to catch his breath. "Better turn to and make some coffee. There's a bunch of men a coming." He wheeled around when he heard a car.

"Why, look who we got here," Cora Mae said. Everyone turned to watch Faye Lackland get out of her car.

"Afternoon, Clyde," Faye said joining them. "Suppose I could get one of you to help me unload the coffee? I borrowed one of those big urns from the church and filled it to the brim and now I can hardly lift it."

"We were about to give up on you, Faye. You didn't have to bother yourself, you know." Cora Mae smoothed her apron over her big thighs without looking Faye in the eye.

"Didn't Neal tell you I was bringing coffee around four o'clock?" She looked at the delicate gold watch on her wrist. "It's only three-thirty now."

Cora Mae waved her hand in the air to dismiss the subject and began folding cloths the ladies had spread over the desserts. Tubby and the others, having finished their search of the house, came out of the front door and a group of men, including Otis Bartel, drifted across a pasture and gathered around the barn. Faye approached Otis, said something, then the two of them, with heads tilted toward each other, walked to Faye's car. Jodean watched Faye hand Otis some papers or envelopes maybe. Otis slipped whatever it was inside his shirt then lifted the heavy coffee urn out of Faye's car.

After helping the other women dish out dessert to the men, Jodean asked the mustached stranger Clyde had brought along from Pole Cat Creek if he'd like more coffee.

"Much obliged," he said.

"Where're you from?" Jodean asked.

"Arkansas. Decided to swing south on my way to California. I got a buddy there in the movie business who's looking for a partner."

"Movies? Oh my." He had dreamy dark eyes. Kind of like Errol Flynn.

"My name is Jodean Travis."

He tipped his hat, "John Rice."

Someone jabbed Jodean in the ribs. She twirled around and came face to face with Cora Mae. "I'm going back to town with June Rawlings," she said, giving John Rice a look. "My back is killing me and I figure there's enough help now that Faye and Ada are here."

Jodean watched Cora Mae climb into June's car before turning back to handsome John Rice but he'd already joined a group of men moving back across the pasture. Suddenly she didn't know what to do with her hands. She looked at the ground, folded her arms then let them flop against her sides. Ada was chatting with Glory and Faye on the front porch so she walked that way. When Faye scooted over to make room, Jodean noticed a deep blue bubble-like bruise on Faye's mouth. It looked like she'd tried to cover it with lipstick.

"This is just all so sad," Glory said. "Makes me ashamed of myself."

"How you figure that?" Ada asked.

"Well, we all have each other. I don't ever remember anybody calling Effie Beck *friend*. She knew everybody and everybody knew her but all she did was mess with her cattle."

"I think that's the way she wanted it," Ada said. "I admire her in spite of the way she lives."

MIKE TAPPED THE last hinge pin to Effie Beck's front door into place. At dusk, with no sign of the woman anywhere, Sheriff Neal Lackland fired his gun to call in the last of the searchers. About a dozen or so men were hanging around a campfire between the house and barn. Jodean and Ada were the only ladies still around. They looked as tired and worn out as the searchers, but it was Red Kasper, squatting on his heels staring into the fire, who made Mike take notice. He could almost hear the conversation Red was having with himself and feel the dark regret in the man's weary eyes.

Mayor Tubby Whittaker asked no one in particular, "Do y'all suppose she could've fallen in the tank and drowned?" He had explained to Mike earlier that ranchers made tanks by bulldozing dirt across a low spot or valley so it would hold rain runoff. A pond, on the other hand, is formed by the natural lay of the land.

"I guess we could dynamite the dam and drain it," Neal said.

"Not necessary," Ranger Clyde Cheevers offered. "As long as it's been, a body would have come to the surface because of the gases that get to working in a body. I've seen it happen. Same goes for the well. I already looked."

Red stood, stomped blood back into his legs.

"Got any ideas, Red?" Tubby asked.

Red looked away from the fire, into the dark sky. "It was a mighty hard rain that night. If Miss Effie stumbled into a creek, she might a got swept away. According to the trash line in the trees the water was about ten feet deep in some places."

"Oh my God," Ada said. "Miss Effie could've been swept clear down to the Medina River – who knows how far. We may never find her."

OVER SACKS OF flour at the dry goods store, Effie Beck's situation was subject to detailed examination by local ladies. Around the courthouse square old-timer cattleman friends of Effie's spit and speculated about what possible fate could have befallen her. For a while the weekly newspaper, *Cooperville Gazette*, devoted whole columns on the subject, including opinions from the man on the street. Some said they believed she had fallen in her well while trying to retrieve some of her daddy's Confederate gold bars, in spite of what Texas Ranger Clyde Cheevers had to say about bodily gases. Others claimed she'd been seen roaming the hills near Bandera, a town twenty miles away, reportedly still wagging her blue bucket.

Mayor Tubby wrote letters to all the major newspapers in the state asking them to run a story about Effie in the hope that some long lost relative would come forward to claim the job of fretting about the dilemma. To Mike, it looked as if something at the core of Cooperville evaporated into a heavy hovering cloud. No one could think of anything other than "poor, poor Miss Effie." But he had another opinion, too. That all the guessing and cogitating entertained the town in general. A carnival frenzy took place on the sidewalks as people waited to see what would happen next, whether or not anyone would come forward to claim the purported Beck Confederate gold, or to see Effie's decaying, maggoty body hauled into town to be gaped over.

A self-proclaimed fortune teller read about Miss Beck's mysterious vanishing in a San Antonio newspaper and wrote Tubby a letter stating that, without a doubt, she had been kidnapped by "wet-back Mexicans" and was being held for ransom. The fortune teller said she'd read it in her tarot cards and that if Tubby could raise about fifty dollars, maybe she could meditate on the matter some more and find out who should pay the ransom, how much it was supposed to be, and who to send the money to.

"Some crack pot," Tubby boomed as he tossed the letter at Sheriff Neal.

Mike had joined them on Wednesday afternoon in front of the courthouse where he hoped to kill a little time before his first scheduled interview with Fred and Bessy Alvin, a middle-aged couple who lived down the street from the beauty shop.

"What the hell you want me to do with this?" Neal asked, handing the letter back to Tubby.

Mike had observed Sheriff Neal Lackland for some time now, and pretty much figured out why Tubby and Red had such a hard time with him. Neal watched the world go by from some lofty state of mind, didn't give a damn what happened outside the boundaries of his own skull. He reminded Mike of a caged monkey in that respect, peering out at you with wise yellow eyes when you know good and well that monkeys are dumb as donkey dung. Most people assumed the sheriff was an indifferent jackass, but Mike wasn't so sure about the apathetic part. The hard thing to understand was how in the devil Neal kept getting re-elected. Emmet had mentioned to Mike that the sheriff was in his third term.

Neal dug around in his pants pocket and took out an ivory-handled pocket knife. With more concentration than was required, he opened a small blade and started scraping his fingernails.

"It's been weeks now since Effie Beck disappeared," Tubby said, folding the fortune teller's letter back into the envelope. "I feel like we oughta be doing more."

"You're not paid to lose sleep over it," Neal said.

"We've known her all our lives. It doesn't seem right not to take care of her affairs. She was family to this town, part of our history."

"Every family has a crazy relative, Tubby. Get it right in your head." Neal closed his pocket knife, threw his shoulders back and sauntered off loose-jointed, unaffected, and Mike would bet, proud of it. Even in shadow Sheriff Neal Lackland could be identified by his walk, if nothing else.

The interview with the Alvins could not have gone worse. All their answers were a benign *yes* or *no*. Mike wondered if they were that dull, or was he the world's worst interviewer? Most likely, the latter.

On his way back down the street, Mike caught sight of the sheriff's wife, Faye Lackland, going into the beauty shop. She had the kind of face that made a man want to pound his chest. The day of the search, he'd noticed her moving among the others in a slow easy way, like she was rubbing against the heat of the afternoon. Hard to imagine, but he didn't think Faye knew she stirred air the way she did. A woman like her was a waste on a man like Neal who would never break out of his self-involved state of mind long enough to appreciate what he had.

From the tank house window that same afternoon, Mike spied John Rice, one of the men Clyde brought along to help with the search, coming down the sidewalk from town. He climbed Jodean's front steps, two at a time and tapped on the door. When Jodean came out of the house, she motioned to the porch swing and they both sat. Until long after the marbled pink clouds of late day gave way to a black sky, Mike heard the porch swing chain pop and crunch, Jodean's soft talk, John's manly laugh.

Mike found Jodean as big a mystery as Effie Beck. Her busyness was her hiding place. Her hands moved non-stop. Wipe the table, dust a windowsill, fold a dish towel, straighten this or that – methodical movement that Mike couldn't help but feel was a substitute for something. Jodean wasn't a contributing, working part of Cooperville's clock. He couldn't see that there was a mortise for her cog.

The next morning Mike took his tablet and pencil down to Cooperville Spring Creek, to the same deep pool he'd found the day of the search. He laid back on the grassy slope and tried to formulate new tactics for his interviews. For one thing, he planned to leave his notebook at the tank house. Fred and Bessy Alvin hadn't been able to take their eyes off his note writing when he tried to get them to talk about their experiences. He might even skip questions altogether and simply open up topics and then give people full rein on the direction of conversation. Whatever anyone chose to talk about was, in one way or another, the thing to best define them or their lives.

He felt like a fraud. He had no real qualifications when he applied for this job. He'd written a few op-ed pieces for the local newspapers back home, that's all. But for as long as he could remember he'd found comfort in putting words on paper. He could choose any order for his thoughts and then change his mind and rearrange ideas. The amazing thing was that by the time he finished working on a piece, he had a clearer understanding of whatever it was he wrote about.

He ran his fingers through his hair, tried to recall when he started giving this interviewing job so much energy. All he wanted to do was earn enough to get by and have a little extra to send his mother. He remembered Clyde Cheevers' kind words – that he would be okay in Cooperville. It was a place his dignity could heal, where he could take the time to re-define his scarred life, find another direction.

The faint smell of frying bacon wafted in the dewy air. From the deep woods on the opposite bank came a soft breezy soughing sound, so breathy it could have been a woman. Something inside his ribs shifted like he'd rounded a sharp curve on a bumpy road and now faced a long smooth stretch.

He stood, studied the trees and thickets growing along the far bank and strained to see beyond them, past the blend of leaf and bark as he had the first day he was there. An enticing force tugged at him, his mind. He shuttered as if he'd scratched a blackboard.

Back at the tank house he wrote his mother and brother a letter telling them all about Effie Beck and enclosed two dollars with promises of more at the end of the month.

"YOU MARK MY word, Jodean Travis. That slick hobo only wants one thing and that is to get under your skirt." Cora Mae sat at the kitchen table while Jodean fried bacon. She gulped the last of her coffee and held the cup out for a refill. "Just what do you think everybody up and down the street is saying about you out on the porch half the night with a stranger? You gonna get a reputation – then where will we be? I got a business to think of."

Jodean filled her cup.

Cora Mae knew Jodean hadn't done anything immoral and, by damn, she was going to make sure she never did. Jodean needed to be protected, reminded constantly of how things were. Cora Mae leaned an elbow on the table and blew air out of her mouth.

"He seems very nice," Jodean said. She used a fork to remove bacon from the iron skillet. "He didn't try to kiss me or anything."

"That don't mean he won't. Times like this I wish to hell your daddy hadn't got his brains kicked out and left me alone to take care of everything."

Jodean set a plate of bacon and eggs in front of Cora Mae. "I don't think Daddy planned on it happening so you can't blame him."

"Well, just remember all you and me got is ourselves and we take care of our own. I never kept the facts from you because I always say a person is better off knowing the truth of a situation. And that includes the truth about men. There's not but one thing that interests them and it's—"

"I told Ada and Faye I'd meet them at the school auditorium later this morning to plan decorations for the queen contest."

"What am I supposed to do if somebody comes in wanting you to do a shampoo?"

"Tell them I'll be back around three."

Cora Mae slumped. If it wasn't men poking around – first that Mike fellow and now John Rice saying he was on his way to Hollywood – it was the damned town taking Jodean away from home. Cora Mae always hoped that if Jodean ever married, which didn't seem likely, she and her husband would move into the rooms at the back of the house so Jodean could keep up the beauty shop. But now with so many strangers passing through town, it was harder than ever to keep Jodean reined in close to home.

Cora Mae finished eating, grabbed her coffee cup and went back to the parlor where she tuned the radio to the Lum and Abner Show. *All the way from Pine Ridge, Arkansas*, was the line she liked to repeat to beauty shop customers.

WHILE CLEARING THE table, Jodean glimpsed Mike's silhouette moving around in the tank house. At the Beck place the day of the search he'd stood on the fringe of activity with his hands in his back pockets. He looked so different, standing there in the middle of a bunch of men in boots and Stetsons, some wearing chaps, most with sun-hardened skin. Mike could have been from another planet for all the softened look of him.

Jodean turned the flame under the skillet to high and broke two eggs into hot bacon drippings then thick-sliced two pieces of white bread and placed them on a tray under the broiler. When Mike came out of the tank house with his head lowered to position his fedora, Jodean called out through the kitchen window, "Two eggs, bacon, hot toast and coffee."

He looked up, grinned. "Sounds good to me." He walked toward the house.

She brought the plate of food to the back porch and set it on a small table next to a potted ivy. "I saw you out walking yesterday," she said pouring coffee. "Did you find the swimming hole?"

"And a big carp," he nodded.

"My daddy used to try anything he could think of to catch one of the big critters." She pinched a dead leaf off the ivy.

"Why? I understand they're not very good to eat."

"Just to say he did it, I guess. That's the way he was."

"I take it he—"

"Died about five years ago." She picked up the ivy and wiped the table underneath it. "He was whipping a horse. It reared up, tried to break away. One hoof came down on Daddy's chest and the other right on top of his head." She moved the ivy a few inches to the right and then sat across from Mike and picked at invisible lint on her dress. She hadn't meant to talk so personal.

"Sorry," Mike mumbled with a mouthful of toast. He took a gulp of coffee to wash it down. "You have horses?"

"Not any more. It happened out at the old place. Back then all the land on the other side of the creek belonged to my folks. And before that, the land all the way to the river belonged to Momma's daddy. Everybody down the family line has been selling off pieces of it for one reason or another. This house and a few acres is all that's left."

"You were born here then?"

Jodean had a sudden catch in her throat. No one in all her days had asked such a question. There had never been anybody who would, that didn't know not to. She slapped her hands on her thighs then stood and grabbed Mike's cup. "My manners! Let me get you some more coffee."

"No, I've had plenty," he said handing her his plate. "But..."

Jodean paused at the kitchen door.

Mike's face worked as he tried to find words. "Well, maybe I ask too many questions."

She curled a shoulder, smiled. "I guess I don't have to answer, now do I?"

"It's about that Ford in the shed back there behind the tank house. Has it been driven lately?"

"Not since Daddy died."

"Mind if I take a look at it? If I could get it running, maybe—"

"Won't do any good. Daddy never taught me to drive. Said women had no mind for it."

"Ada and Faye drive."

"Well, I guess that's them."

"Tell you what, if you'll let me try to get it running, I'll teach you to drive. Then maybe we could work out something so I can use it for my interviews. I'll need transportation out to some of the farms and ranches around here."

"Jo-deeean," Cora Mae called from the parlor. "Who are you talking to? If it's me, I can't hear you. You better come in here if you want me to hear you. *Hear?*"

She put Mike's dishes in the sink and turned back to Mike waiting at the door for her answer.

He was different from that first day when she'd brought his supper to the tank house. That lonesome, hungry look was almost gone. "Sure, Mike. What harm can come of it? Now, I have a question for you."

"That's fair."

"The day everybody met at Miss Effie's place for the search…at the food table when we were waiting for Brother Rawlings to say the blessing…what were you thinking?"

"How lopsided life is. After the Crash I went to New York to see if I could find work. I saw women and little kids digging through garbage bins behind fancy hotels looking for something to eat. They looked like bones with rags hanging on them. Then evenings I watched gallons – I'm talking *gallons*, Jodean – gallons of milk from a pasteurizing plant being poured in the gutters because no one could afford to buy it and it had soured." Mike paused to hitch a breath of air. "The thing that sent me packing back south again was one day a woman in the tenement house where I lived was discovered dead with her dead baby at her breast. They'd died because the woman couldn't afford to buy what was being poured in the streets for stray dogs and cats."

Mike's voice had gone all watery. She wanted to comfort him but didn't know how. He glanced at her sideways and continued. "That day at Miss Effie's ranch, it was hard to look at a table full of food and people standing around it who don't know…haven't got a clue…" Mike shook his head, let his voice trail.

"…How lopsided life can be." Jodean finished the sentence for him.

Later that morning Jodean walked to the schoolhouse to meet with Ada and Faye about the queen contest. As she reached for the door she noticed Ada's car parked on the side street near the playground where Pete helped Sue into a swing and Jean and Ted argued over the seesaw. Jean grabbed a fistful of Ted's hair and threw him to the ground. Jodean let the door slam at her back so she wouldn't hear Ted's toe-curling howl.

Inside, the smell of waxy crayons and Big Chief paper flooded Jodean. A million childhood events rushed her mind. The auditorium, which had appeared cathedral-like when she was a child, struck her as seedy and tight feeling in spite of the ceiling-to-floor windows on either side of the rows of seats. Her blood all of a sudden felt thick as syrup, so she slumped in an aisle seat.

Footsteps tapped across the stage floor behind the curtain, then it billowed as someone tried to find the split. Ada found it and stuck her head out. "Thought I heard somebody come in."

"Do you remember our sixth grade play?" Jodean asked.

"October. Before Halloween carnival. I was a pumpkin and you were...?"

"A corn stalk, stage right, back row." Jodean smiled at the memory.

"Did you know Effie Beck was there that night?" Ada walked to the side of the stage and down a few steps to sit with Jodean. "Since I didn't have much of a speaking part, I had plenty of time to look at the audience. She was in the back, over there close to the door, with her hands folded under her chin like she was praying. I could make out the lines in her face from the light in the hallway. Even as a kid I thought it strange."

Jodean thought for a beat. "Now that you mention it, I remember Mrs. Pruitt and Momma clattering on and on about her being there. They thought she was going to try to kidnap one of the first grade kids since she never had any kids of her own. Poor woman."

"Poor Red. I've been tempted to give him a dose of Black Draught and put him to bed. He's got himself worked into a stupor about the situation."

"What situation is that?" Faye asked, coming down the aisle from the back of the auditorium. She was wearing a cranberry red skirt with a snowy white blouse and tiny pearl earrings. A basket of books hung from one arm, and she clutched a bulky paper bag to her hip with the other.

"Red, over Miss Effie." Ada answered. "He's sick with worry."

"Red always had such a soft heart," Faye said, setting the basket of books down in the seat next to Jodean. When it nearly tipped on its side, Jodean lunged to catch it and noticed the books were children's readers.

"Y'all come up on the stage," Faye said. "What do you think about hanging streamers from the back curtain? And I'm open to suggestions about garland."

An hour later the three of them walked out of the schoolhouse, having settled on most of the decorations for the Pickle Queen Contest. Each of the three planned to make ten feet of garland. "Use shrubs, wisteria vine, grape vine, pine, cedar, anything you can find for the garland." Faye moved down the schoolhouse steps, then turned back. "I'm sure it'll all work out just fine."

Jodean watched Faye walk across the playground. At the swing set where Tootie Sue played in sand, Faye stopped, leaned over and said something to her. Then waved to Jean and the boys on the merry-go-round. She passed by the gazebo at City Park and would be in her front yard before Ada and Jodean finished their good-byes. Ada saw Jodean staring and followed her gaze. "Don't envy her, Jodean. She has her share of heartache."

"I don't." Jodean knew, of course, that Ada was talking about Faye's marriage to Neal. Ada had a few dates with Neal in high school before she and Red got serious. During one of their girl-talk sessions, Ada whispered that Neal was about as interesting as a brown beetle. By the end of their third date, he hadn't said much more than "Hidy," "Would you like a soda," or "Want to ride out to the river?"

On their last date, Ada said yes to the river ride hoping he'd loosen up a little. Until that point, she thought maybe he was a little shy – brooding and handsome – that type. But he'd parked on the bluff overlooking the river and started talking about how many deer he'd killed since he was nine years old. He explained why, according to his sheriff father, no one could catch a certain gang of bank robbers terrorizing citizens across the state, and that he hoped to be deputized before long so he could help gun them down if they ever came to Cooperville.

"You kids get in the car now," Ada called out. She mopped a twist of brown hair out of her eyes with a sigh. "Why do I have a feeling this is going to be a long, troubling summer? I dread it so. Why is that, do you suppose?"

Jodean angled her head a little to study the look on Ada's face. It wasn't like her to be morose.

"Why don't you and Red bring the kids over Saturday afternoon. We'll walk down to Spring Creek for a picnic, let the kids swim."

Ada nodded. "Good idea."

THE NOON WHISTLE at the pickle factory blasted away when Mike came out of the post office. He walked up Main Street, passed City Hall and then crossed Cotton Street and headed for City Café, where he hoped to absorb a little conversation. He'd written Tom Coker in San Antonio about how difficult it had been to get people to talk freely about the real substance of their lives when they knew he was about to write it all down. Tom wrote back that Mike could use any method he wished to get the life histories and to take his time doing it.

Mike slid into a side booth and ordered pork roast with mashed potatoes and sliced tomatoes. While waiting for his food, a construction crew from the WPA bridge came clomping through the double doors. Their heavy work boots scrapped on the floor and they laughed and joked among themselves. Dust filled the creases of skin on their sun-fried necks and clung to their hair. Deep Vs of sweat marked the fronts and backs of their shirts like working-man armor. One of them, the man who'd helped Faye Lackland with the coffee urn at Miss Effie's ranch, was the last one to come through the door. He sat at the end of the long counter, away from the others. When he took off his hat, his thin hair clung to his greasy head. Small greenish eyes scanned the café in quick, cautious glances like a nervous animal.

Eventually, all the workmen settled around tables or on counter stools and dropped their voices to hushed mumbles. About that same time, Red appeared in the doorway. He tipped his hat and said something to a wall-eyed waitress who giggled like a billy goat. Mike waved him over since all the tables were taken.

"Damn. Cooperville is getting to be a mite crowded," Red said.

The waitress brought Mike his food and a cup of coffee for Red.

"Now, Doris, how do you know I want coffee?" Red's eyes twinkled with merriment.

"Honey, I ain't never known you to order anything else. Why should today be any different?"

"Well now, maybe I just haven't been hungry any time before." Red dipped three spoons of sugar into his coffee cup.

"Pork roast is the special today," Doris sighed.

"No thanks, just coffee."

"Red Kasper! You're impossible!" Doris turned on her heel chuckling, and threaded her way among the tables, filling coffee cups as she went.

"Anything new on Effie Beck?" Mike asked, reluctant to bring up the subject, but wanting to know.

Red shook his head. "Not a thing."

"I find it hard to believe she had no family or kin anywhere. Did she ever travel, maybe to visit somebody who could help Tubby settle her affairs?"

"I never knew Miss Effie to go any farther than town."

"What about her folks?"

"Her mother died when Miss Effie was a child. Her daddy hit the bottle pretty bad. We used to hear him yelling from clear out on the road when he was on a binge."

Red glanced around the café, nodded here and there to some of the locals. He pulled a slow breath of air into his lungs then started talking again before looking back at Mike. "One daybreak, long time ago, my daddy woke me in a big hurry. Said to get my pants and boots on. Old man Beck's place was on fire. We didn't even take time to saddle our horses, hopped on 'em bareback. When we got there, Miss Effie was dipping buckets of water from the trough while Mr. Beck tried to get the spooked animals out of the burning barn. We managed to help him save the animals except for a few chickens, but the barn was pretty much destroyed. Mr. Beck stood in the yard looking at the smoky ashes while Miss Effie pumped water for me and Daddy."

Red picked up his spoon, stirred his coffee then tapped it three times on the side of the cup. He looked Mike in the eye. "Beck's white hair was standing straight out from his head every which a way with the sun about treetop high behind him. He was a scary sight for a little kid like I was back then. A damned big man, too. Well over six feet tall and lean, even as old as he was – coming up on eighty, I'd guess. Miss Effie, a little older than my own mother at the time."

"What started the fire?"

"I'm getting to that. Miss Effie kept pumping water quiet as a mouse. She almost looked like she was shrinking, you know what I mean?" Red took a sip of coffee.

Mike pushed his empty plate aside.

"Beck walked to the trough where she was pumping water then turned to my daddy and says, 'I done told her every day of her life to hang the lantern high on the hook, never sit it on the ground where it can get knocked over.' Then he bent down to look Miss Effie in the face on account of she's so small, and yells, 'Ain't that right?' Before she could answer, he reared back and clubbed her upside the head with his big fist. I tell you Mike, both her feet left the ground before she flopped onto her back like a dead fish."

Red motioned to Doris with his coffee cup. She worked her way over and filled it.

When she left, he began again. "My daddy stood there, did nothing, and that – to this day – is hard for me to stomach. If I'd a been grown, I'd a killed old man Beck with my bare hands. He wasn't much better than a mad dog as far as I could tell."

Red squared himself in his seat. "My daddy grabbed my collar and we left in as big a hurry as we went. Two days later, half the town showed up to help Beck build a new barn." Red dropped his eyes and traced the pattern of scratches on the table top with his finger.

"I take it that sort of thing happened a lot. Him hitting her." Mike said.

Red shrugged. "The unspoken rule was – *is* – that neighbors always help out but never interfere. But here's the thing, Mike. It looked to me like Miss Effie needed help saving herself more than that worthless piece of shit old man needed help building another barn."

Red fished around in his pocket and threw a few coins on the table before standing to leave. "You getting by okay, Mike?"

Mike followed him outside. "Sure. Slow getting started with the interviews but there's no hurry. Hope you don't mind me asking about Miss Effie."

Red shook his head. "Nawh."

"For me, a stranger in town, well, I wish I could have interviewed Effie Beck before she disappeared."

"I just had a thought," Red said. "Old Breezy the Negro lives behind her place. I bet he could answer more of your questions than me. Especially going back before my time."

MIKE USED JODEAN'S garden hoe to clear thick weeds growing along the bottom edge of the car shed doors. Inside, the dead stillness stirred and the putrid smell of rats closed off his nostrils. On a low, homemade table strewn with tools, he found a screwdriver to pry open the windows. When he turned back to the table a small bird flew into his face, chirping wildly. Mike reared back and raised his arm against the attack, but it was only a tiny house wren that, in a brown fluttering flash, flew through a hole in the corner where the walls met the roofline.

He circled the Model A pickup. One tire was flat. He'd roll it around the corner to Hank's filling station and get it fixed for little or nothing. A new battery and spark plugs would be the biggest expense, but the rest would be a simple matter of cleaning and oiling. He squatted low under the rear and found a massive dirt dauber nest in the exhaust pipe. By using a hammer and the longest screwdriver he could find, his was able to dislodge the nest and scrape the pipe clean.

When he grabbed the driver's side door handle, the door popped out and dropped to an odd angle. Inside, he found the key rusted in the ignition and hoped he'd have as easy a time working it loose as he had the dauber nest. Using an oil can with a pencil thin spout, he squirted oil on the key, then tapped it a few times with the hammer. It wouldn't budge. He coated it with oil a second time and left it to soak while he crawled underneath to examine the gas tank.

At some point during the day Mike lost track of himself in the physical labor required to make a useless thing worthwhile again. The metallic odor of motor oil, the chink and clang of tools gave him a boost, a new focus. That night he crawled into bed exhausted. His sleep was deep and healing.

Days after that, his signal for time to wrap up his tasks was the smell of Jodean's cooking as it wafted from the open windows of the house. Fried chicken, salmon patties or meatloaf. Sometimes sweet potato pie or chocolate cake, hot rolls or cornbread. And always on the same hazy blue air of late day he heard the muffled sound of Cora Mae's radio music interspersed with her braying. Mike marveled that Jodean was so pleasant, in complete contrast, after sharing a lifetime with the woman.

"Seems like you're going to an awful lot of trouble in there," Jodean said one day from where she stood at the shed's door. Mike looked out from under the hood. She had a glass of tea in each hand.

"It'll be worth it if I can get it running."

She moved closer, handed him a glass. "I forgot what a mess this old shed is. Don't see how you can manage with all this junk in your way." She kicked at a box of old magazines rotting on the dirt floor.

"Uh, well, I—" Mike chuckled, embarrassing himself.

"What's funny?"

"I was going to say I hadn't noticed, but you'd think I was pretty sloppy if that was the case."

They both smiled. She opened the cab door opposite him, brushed away a cobweb then climbed in. "My daddy sure thought he was the cat's meow the first time he drove this truck up the drive. I'll bring you some old rags. Maybe I could help clean the inside."

Mike gulped tea.

"Do you think it'll take much longer to get it running?"

"It would run now if it had a new battery, but I don't get paid for another week."

"I expect to share the cost and I bet Red or John Rice would be glad to help with the work."

"Did John get hired on with the bridge crew?"

"Yeah, but he says it's temporary. His business partner in California claims there's more money to be made there than in all of Texas. He just needs to earn enough to get to California then it'll be smooth sailing from then on."

"Jodean, a lot of people are selling hope at a high price."

"Oh, I know. I told John that same thing. But he says he has complete faith in his friend. The one in California, I mean."

Mike decided it would be useless to tell her he thought John was the one selling hope.

She sipped her tea and looked around inside the cab. "Sure is a mess."

That evening, when Mike went up the back steps to get the supper tray Jodean left for him, he overheard voices inside the house. It was dark out, no light in the kitchen. But the parlor and dining room lights were shining bright as day.

Through the thin curtain on the door window, Mike saw John Rice sitting at the head of the dining room table with Cora Mae on his right and Jodean on his left. Jodean stood, went to the sideboard and returned to the table with a bowl of food. She was wearing shoes and the same dress she had worn to church the day of Effie Beck's search. Cora Mae's lips were pressed in a grim line until John Rice leaned toward her and said something that made her smile. When John turned back to Jodean, Cora Mae's eyelids pinched around anger-flecked eyes.

JODEAN RACED AROUND the kitchen while throwing cookies and sandwiches in a picnic basket right up to the time John tapped at the front door. She'd had the day's appointments all taken care of with enough time left to tidy herself a little. Then, at the last minute, Cora Mae decided she wanted her hair set and that threw Jodean late with everything.

As she and John walked out the back door, picnic basket in hand, Red and Ada turned into the drive with all their kids in tow. Red seemed a little stiff when he shook hands with John. Red was cowboy, pure and simple. The best there was. And, John, all citified polished talk. The four of them, John, herself, Red and Ada, loaded down with picnic baskets and old quilts, fell in line behind the children scurrying down the path toward Spring Creek. When they got close to the shed where Mike was working on the Model A truck, Red called out in surprise.

"Gall dern, old buddy. You should a hollered. I could give you a hand with this."

"So far, two hands have been enough, but I may call on you in a few days to give me a push."

"Count on me to help."

Jodean noticed Mike had built a few shelves and swept the cobwebs out of the corners. "We're going down to the creek for a picnic. Want to come along?" When Mike hesitated, Red palmed his back and reminded him that he needed to take time to eat anyway.

"When you put it like that..." Mike said. "But go on ahead. I'll put my tools away, wash up and join you in a while."

It was the kind of rare day Jodean lived for. She felt no separateness from the people around her. Like smooth water, the day was, and they were little paper boats floating wherever life took them, so full of merriment there was no room for complaint or worry.

The children shouted and chased each other through tall reedy grass while the sun blazed overhead unnoticed. Red, never one to show modesty, stripped down to his underwear and dived with great fanfare into the carp's pool. One by one his children climbed rocks and jumped to his waiting arms. Only Tootie Sue hung back, afraid to jump.

"Come on Tootie Sue," Red called up to her. Sue stood as if made of stone with a finger in her nose. Pete knelt next to her to try to talk her into jumping but she twisted away from him.

John reclined on a quilt while Jodean and Ada peeled hard-boiled eggs and talked about the Pickle Festival. Mike came down the slope a little later, greeted them and then moved to the pool to watch Red and his antics. He took off his shoes and socks, rolled his pant legs to his knees and sat with his feet dangling in cool water.

"By golly, that looks like a good idea. Think I'll give it a try," Ada said. She sat next to Mike, dangled her feet in the water and clicked her tongue. "Sometimes," she said, tipping her chin toward Red and the children, "it's hard to tell which one is the daddy." Red struck a comical pose and squirted water out of his mouth.

"I can see why," Mike said.

"Jodean and I were just wondering if Frances ever asked you about judging the queen contest."

"Yes, as a matter of fact. I ran into her at the post office a few days ago." Mike looked from Ada to Jodean. "I was surprised since I'm so new in town."

"It gets mighty hard to find three judges that aren't involved in small-town social politics," Ada said.

"Who are the other two?"

"Paddy Blue and me," Jodean answered for Ada.

"Have I met Paddy Blue?"

"Doubt it. You'd remember," Ada said.

When Mike looked puzzled she added, "You'll understand when you meet him."

"But why you, Jodean? I would have thought social politics were written at the beauty parl—"

A piercing, toe-curling scream split the air above the pool, and for one red flash, Jodean was relieved that Mike had been interrupted. It was little Tootie Sue who screamed. She was on the bank downstream a little past Mike and Ada, batting at her ears and clothes. Red lunged from the far side of the pool and struggled against the weight of water to get to her. At the same time, Mike sprang into action and was at Sue's side in a heartbeat. He grabbed her like a heap of rags then jumped feet first into the deepest part of the pool. Ada, Jodean, and John stood petrified at the water's edge, staring down at the dappled surface, breaths held, puzzling over Mike's bizarre act.

"Sonofabitch!" Red yelled as he continued to fight water to get across the pool. "Su-u-ue!" He looked to Ada as if she might understand better than he what had just happened. But Ada had gone bug-eyed and gape-mouthed.

Sounds magnified. Birds twittered in the distance. Water dripped from Pete's elbows and made plinking noises in the pool. And above those sounds came the distinct hair-raising buzz of wasps.

"Tootie Su-u-ue!" Pete yelled.

Sue burst from the surface of the water like an urchin fountain ornament held aloft in Mike's long-fingered hands. After a beat, Mike's head splashed above water, too. He gasped for air, yelled *wasps* to Red who took the drenched, screaming child in his arms. Jodean realized then that Tootie Sue had stepped on an underground wasp nest and only Mike had been close enough to see she was being attacked.

Red carried Tootie Sue, blue lipped and trembling, to one of the quilts where Ada stripped off her clothes. Red ran his callused hands all along her little arms and legs to dislodge any remaining wasps. He reassured her again and again that he wouldn't let the bees come back.

Ada squeezed water from Tootie Sue's clothes while Mike dived to the bottom of the pool, to where Jodean imagined icy water bubbled from a cavernous dark place deep in the earth. He came up with a handful of cold mud to pack on Sue's stings. Jodean marveled at his unwavering purposefulness. She wouldn't have thought he'd be like that – so deliberate.

In the end, Sue had three stings and one of those, the one on her elbow, had left only a little red bump. Everyone agreed, Tootie Sue was lucky Mike acted so quick.

After the excitement died down, Jodean noticed Pete bird-dogging Mike like a newfound hero. He asked Mike what it was like to write for newspapers and was he ever afraid he'd make people mad by what he wrote. Mike explained to Pete from behind a thicket of brush, where he'd gone to wring out his clothes, that the U.S. government was founded on freedom of speech. "The way I see it," Jodean overheard Mike say, "is that if I write the truth, and not use the truth for the sole purpose of hurting somebody, then I'm practicing free speech the way it was meant to be."

"But don't some people say things or write things just to get what they want?" Pete asked.

"Yes. It's the reader's responsibility to decide what he believes is truth." Mike stepped out in the open to button his shirt and saw Jodean listening. She turned away, embarrassed to have been caught eavesdropping.

She and Ada handed out sandwiches to the shivering swimmers and John. Mike sat in the sun to eat so his clothes would dry faster. Red, slouched on the ground beside him, fiddled with his sandwich until he dropped half of it. "Mike, I'm mighty thankful to you for grabbing Tootie Sue the way you did."

Mike mumbled, "You're welcome," and changed the subject. "Is it true you were a big-hit rodeo clown at one time?"

"Sonofabitch. Who told you about that?"

"It's my job to ask questions, remember?"

"Hell, hanging around that beauty shop you ought to be able to find out anything."

"Why'd you quit?" Mike asked, not willing to be detoured.

"'Cause I was a busted piece of horseshit, that's why."

"Hush that talk in front of the kids," Ada said.

Jodean had heard Ada ask Red a hundred times to watch his mouth around the children. In truth, his salty language was so much a part of Red, like his bowed legs or bald head, that most folks had long since taken it in stride. Red liked to poke fun, and in a way his foul language was just one more way of teasing. As if he liked to see people blush for his own entertainment.

"I won $750 bronc riding in 1927 and decided to quit while I was ahead and could still walk. Hell, time was, I had to be wired back together, so busted up I wasn't worth a damn for nothing. I bought out my brother's share of our folks' place, where me and Ada are now. Good thing I did too, before the Crash."

John Rice had eaten his sandwich and stretched out on a quilt with his hands behind his head. Sue clung to Ada and the rest of the children grew drowsy from a day of swimming, food and warm sunshine. In spite of Tootie Sue's scare, the day ended as bright as it had begun, with all of them packing back to the house with red noses and full stomachs while evening hugged Earth in an indigo cloak and fireflies blinked on and off in the tall grass.

WHEN MIKE DROVE up to Breezy Parker's yard gate, the pickup misfired, shuttered and died. An elderly black man sat hunched in a ladder-back chair on the front porch watching six or eight little brown children jump rope under a cottonwood tree. The children took one look at Mike and scurried around the corner of the house, flapping their arms like a covey of quail. Breezy, at least Mike assumed that's who he was, pushed up from his chair but his body remained bent at the waist.

"Hello, Mr. Parker?" Mike called when he stepped out of the truck. Breezy strained to raise his arm then shook a few fingers in an attempt to wave. He had skin like an iron skillet, crusted with age, and cloudy, wet eyes. A silver crow teetering on a leafless twig, Mike thought. "Mind if I come in your yard?"

"No, no. Come right on."

"My name is Mike Lemay. Red Kasper said I should call on you."

"That right now?"

"I'm traveling around this area talking to people for a government report and I'd like to ask you about Effie Beck."

A woman appeared in the doorway behind Breezy. She wiped her hands on a towel. Mike nodded, touched his hat brim, and explained his job with the FWP and his disappointment in not having had a chance to interview Effie Beck.

"Lordy mercy. Miss Effie. Now there's a story," the woman said.

Breezy ticked his head back toward the door. "Trudy here is my daughter-in-law."

Mike tipped his hat a second time in acknowledgement of the introduction. "What do you mean, 'there's a story'?" Mike asked.

"Breezy and all his boys think she just about Holy, but I say she was a practicing voodoo woman mahself. She done the strangest things."

"Like what?"

"Well sir, for one thing, she wandered that road yonder from here to town and back in the middle of the night more times than I can count. I tried to get Jericho, that's mah husband, to follow her. See what it was she was a-doin' roaming 'round like that."

"She just lonely is what I say," Breezy said. "Night time can be bad when you ain't got nobody."

A little girl toddled up to Trudy and started a noisy fuss. Trudy lifted the child to her hip then asked if either of them wanted a dipper of water. They both declined and she moved back into the shadows of the house.

Breezy eased himself back to his chair. "Me and Miss Effie go way back, that we do. But mind you now, she not old as me. I reckon we's the last of the old folks." Breezy dropped his eyes and shook his head. "Mmh-mmh-mmph. I reckon she on the other side by now."

"People in town don't know what to make of it."

"She dead. Tell 'em Breezy Parker said so. I knowed her better than anybody 'cept maybe Red, and he don't go far back as me."

"I asked Red if Miss Effie ever had visitors or traveled anywhere. He thought you might know."

"Well now, let me see. Seem like I recall a time she was sick, some bad disease Mr. Beck said it was. See, me and mah chil'ren was picking cotton for him at the time and we missed Miss Effie bringing us cool water, you see?"

"Disease?"

"That what he said. Some sickness. Only thing I noticed was her eyes was red and swole a lot."

Breezy Parker had the profile of a hound. The skin under his eyes hung nearly to his cheek bones, and his hands, like twists of black rope, were tipped with jag-edged fingernails. Mike followed Breezy's gaze across the yard to a cotton field. He sensed nothing would be volunteered from the cast iron patriarch. If Mike wanted to know particulars, he'd have to ask.

Mike leaned against a porch post. "Did she travel then? To see a doctor?"

"Some hospital, I heard it was, in New Mexico or somewheres way off like that."

Two little boys peeked around the corner of the house at Mike then jerked back with their hands over their mouths to hide giggles. Breezy heard them and called out, "Here now. That ain't no way to do."

"How long was she gone?"

"Long time. 'Bout a year, maybe longer. Fact was, couldn't nobody guess why she come back."

"Red said he saw Mr. Beck hit Miss Effie once."

"He done whipped us all, Mr. Lemay." Breezy stomped his foot when he said the word *whipped* as if adding an exclamation point.

Mike let a minute or two pass while they watched a Negro man come into view on the other side of the road. He moved along in the wavy heat of midday behind a plow-pulling mule, and his gruff geeing and hawing rose above the crackling noise of cicadas. Not a whisper of air stirred. Mike mopped his wet face with his handkerchief.

"That there's mah boy, Jericho," Breezy said after a while. He nodded toward the man calling out "haw-haw" so deep in his throat it sounded like a growl. Jericho did a double-take when he saw the truck parked in front of the house. Mike waved and Breezy nodded. Jericho reined the mule's lead, looped the lines on the plow handle and crossed the road.

Breezy spoke first, "Red done told this here Mr. Lemay I could tell him a thing or two 'bout the bad times and Miss Effie."

Jericho wiped his hands on his dusty clothes. "Lord, I reckon Pa can tell you anythin' you want to know 'bout either one." Jericho's wide smile showed large teeth. He scooped off his straw hat and rubbed sweat from his forehead. His hair was almost as gray as Breezy's. Trudy moved through the door and handed Jericho a jar of water.

"Hard times ain't nothin' new to us colored folks," Breezy said. "We's born to it. I feel sorry for the white man doncha know. Low as he is, the black man is lower."

"Pa." Jericho looked embarrassed. He turned to Mike. "Anybody find Miss Effie?"

"I'm afraid not," Mike said.

"Mmh-mmh-mmph." Jericho shook his head in the same manner Breezy had. "That Miss Effie, she's sompin. Did Pa tell 'bout that time she lit out after us boys?"

Breezy swatted air. "I'll swan! I forgot 'bout that. You tell it."

Jericho motioned Mike to the porch steps. They both sat.

"It wasn't too long, you see, after Miss Effie's daddy died and she worked out a way for my Pa to buy this here cotton patch from her. To have for his very own. Little bit at a time for next to nothin', too.

"So...I'm not one bit proud of what I'm about to tell you." Jericho glanced at Breezy. "I's still green wood, know what I mean? Young and full of mahself. Just gettin' some whiskers, so was my brothers. Six of us in all but I'm the only one stayed here with Pa. Anyways, back then we had a hard time of it. We 'bout killed off the rabbit population tryin' to keep ourselves fed, and one bad winter got followed by a real dry spring. We's gettin' mighty hungry, Mr. Lemay. So one night, moon high and shinin', me and my brothers crossed that field there." Jericho pointed to the rows he'd been plowing.

"We crawled under Miss Effie's bob-wire, hiked – oh, I guess it's two miles to her place through there, and stole two of her chickens.

Back then she had this old dog and he went to howlin' and then here come Miss Effie with a shotgun. Ooow-wee." Jericho paused to chuckle. "Course, it weren't funny then. She could a killed us. We lit out for home and her right on our tails the whole way. She weren't no young thing at the time as I recall, but she stayed right on our tails. One of my brothers a screamin' it was a ghost after us, her white nightgown blowin' out behind her the way it was. Hair a flyin' down her back. Looked like cobweb, yessiree."

"Mmh-mmph." Breezy stomped his foot and shook his head as if listening caused him pain.

Jericho continued. "Miss Effie fired that big old gun of hers and scared us so bad we froze right where we was. When she caught up to us, she whacked me a good one with the stock of her gun like she was swingin' a ax. Thought she'd kill me for sure."

"What about your brothers?" Mike asked. "Did she hit them?"

"No. Jus' me. Guess 'cause I's oldest."

"I heard the shot," Breezy said. "And I come out here to see what was goin' on. Yonder come my boys, they heads down and tails 'tween their legs. This'n here look like he been whupped pretty bad. Yessir."

"And Miss Effie did that?" Mike asked to be sure he understood. Somehow this didn't quite fit what he'd come to believe of the woman.

"Yessir," Breezy said. "She come on mah porch here with a tote sack of chickens in one hand and that old gun in the other. She said if she ever catched mah boys stealin' again, she'd shoot 'em." He paused a minute then leaned forward and pointed a knotty finger at Mike. "Then you know what she said?"

Mike shook his head.

"She said if mah boys want a chicken to eat they'd best come to her door in the daylight and ask for it proper."

Mike found it hard to believe a woman, who had suffered the blows of an unreasonable father, would do the same thing to another human being. She hit a starving boy with the butt of a gun and yet found it in her heart to nurse an old cow through stillbirth in a raging midnight thunderstorm.

"She done a good thing for mah boys, Mr. Lemay." Breezy must have read Mike thoughts. "They learnt it takes a proud man, be he colored or white, to ask outright instead of sneakin' 'round on their bellies like snakes, stealing what ain't theirs...what people would give if you ask."

Mike shifted his gaze from Breezy to Jericho's clear dark eyes. "Miss Effie hit me," he said, "because I insulted her, not because I tried to steal her chickens, don-cha see?"

Mike nodded, but he didn't understand any of it.

Jericho lifted the jar of water Trudy had brought him and gulped until his head tilted far back. A clear drop of water trailed down his black, dusty throat and disappeared under the faded fabric of his blue work shirt. He handed the jar back to Trudy, then stood and said he needed to get back to his plowing.

Mike sat with Trudy and Breezy a while longer. An odd comfort settled on him as he watched heat slur up from the dusty cotton field while Jericho hollered gee-gee to his mule and little black-eyed children giggled because a white man was sitting on their grandfather's porch.

After a time he fired up the little pickup and made a wide circle on the washboard road. He waved to Breezy, then to Jericho out in the field, and headed back to town.

It stumped him. Neither Breezy nor Jericho seemed bitter. Questions boxed back and forth in his head. Effie Beck had a right to defend what was hers. But to hit a starving boy the way she did? And, years before that, had the town been right to help her father rebuild the burned down barn when *her* situation was so desperate? How on earth could a small old woman, who had lived such a harsh life, be so crusty and mean?

The road made a right angle turn where cows grazed along the fence line. That particular corner of pasture was low and caught more rain water than the rest of the field, so grass there was deep green and thick. Mike slowed to a stop, felt the brakes grab. Cows rolled their big ebony eyes his way, angled their ears toward him, too, as if waiting for him to speak wisdoms.

The riddle of Effie Beck's life and the mystery of her disappearance had him hooked. She had a hard life, left town because of some illness, then returned after being away for a year or more. Why? What would've brought her back? Did she risk injury at the hands of her father to inherit his ranch? Had Beck hidden Confederate gold in his well as town gossips claimed? Why did Effie Beck roam Spring Creek Road at night?

Mike was glad to let the puzzle occupy his mind. It distracted him from the flashback images in his head and that old city feeling of something eating at him from the inside out.

He'd have another talk with Red to see if he could shed a little light on Miss Effie's night roaming. And he'd ask Jodean why she was considered impartial enough to judge the Pickle Queen Contest when she grew up right here in Cooperville, and even had a beauty shop in town.

Mike clutched and slipped the truck into gear. In town he passed the turnoff for West Street and the tank house and headed straight for the benches outside the boardinghouse. People there were always aching for conversation. It was their favorite pastime. And tomorrow he planned to be at the pickle factory in time for the noon whistle.

CORA MAE CLIMBED the courthouse steps, glanced over her shoulder, then swung the tall wooden door open. Once she was inside, she unclasped her purse, withdrew an envelope, and proceeded down the hall to the deed office.

"Hidy, Cora Mae." The young woman behind the counter was too cheerful if you asked Cora Mae.

"Hi." Cora tilted her chin and touched her hair. "I stopped by to see if any of you ladies here want to enter the baking contest at the Pickle Festival this year."

"I thought Frances was handling that duty?"

"Well, she is – was. She just gets so busy…thought I'd help her out a little." Cora Mae side-glanced into the hallway, then added,

"Might save Frances a little time this way." She took a sheet of paper out of the envelope. When she heard footsteps in the hall she jerked around. "Oh! Sheriff Neal." He stopped and leaned into the doorway.

"Hello, Cora Mae. You doing all right?"

"Mighty fine, thank you. As a matter of fact, I hoped I'd catch you. Been too long since you and me had a chat." Cora turned back to the woman behind the counter. "Y'all pass this sign-up sheet around among yourselves while I visit with the sheriff. Take your time."

"What's on your mind, Cora Mae?" Sheriff Neal asked as he tapped shut his glass-fronted office door. She glanced around, gave her dress a tug. Neal adjusted the window blinds to a full open position and stood for a beat looking down on the courthouse lawn.

"Why nothing in particular, Neal. Like I said, it's just been too long since you and me talked. I mean a *good* chat, you know? How are those kids of yours? In Dallas I heard."

"That's right." He motioned to a chair.

"Faye must be sick with loneliness for them."

"She manages to keep busy."

"Don't you worry about Faye home all by herself? I mean with that bridge crew working right there, not a mile from your house? All those strangers messing around all the time must make your job extra hard."

"I can handle it."

"Don't I just know that. Why, your daddy would be so proud of how you've carried on in his footsteps, in that big house, and keeping the law here in this county."

Neal leaned back in his chair and folded his arms across his chest.

Cora licked her lips. "You know, that reminds me. Did you ever stop to think that one of that WPA crew could have done something to Effie Beck?"

Neal pulled his pocket knife out and studied his fingernails.

Cora Mae dabbed her upper lip with a lace-edged handkerchief. "I certainly get worried for my Jodean. That new fellow, John Rice, is hanging around our house, Neal. All his big talk about Hollywood makes me nervous. You know how Jodean is. The girl gets impressed so easy."

"Jodean is no girl, Cora Mae."

"You know what I'm talking about – *innocent*. And, you know I hear most everything in my beauty shop. Well, Neal, I-I—"

Neal sat forward, leaned his elbows on his desk. "Why don't you just get to the point?"

"You better keep your eye on that pretty wife of yours."

"I said, what's your point, Cora Mae?"

"That Otis fellow from the bridge crew has been seen sneaking around the playground across from your house after dark. And that slick Hollywood yokel, John Rice, is hanging around my front porch till all hours and Effie Beck is dead. I don't care if you haven't found the body. You know it's true."

"Look, Cora—"

"—And I want to get rid of Mike Lemay. I tried to tell Jodean it's indecent for two women to keep a man boarder. It's damn strange Effie Beck disappeared the same day he showed up at my back door."

"I'm a step ahead of you. I questioned Jodean the day of the search. She said Mike didn't leave your place any time during the three days it rained. He had no way of getting out to the Beck place anyway unless he walked, and that would've taken the better part of a day. Jodean would've known if he was gone that long."

Neal leaned back into his chair. "Besides that, Clyde Cheevers and Tubby Whittaker checked with authorities in San Antonio and he's okay. But, hell, it's a free country. If you want him gone, tell him to leave. As far as the other two, Otis and John Rice, are concerned? I have no reason to suspect them of anything illegal."

"You might have a reason you don't know about yet."

"What the hell does that mean?"

"Let's just say I'm still gathering talk from the beauty shop." Cora returned her handkerchief to her purse and stood. "In the meantime, you better keep a close eye on that pretty wife of yours like I do my daughter."

NEAL TOOK OFF a little early that day. The sky had turned mean with thunderheads sliding in from the southwest. When he turned onto the long, half-circle drive in front of the house, a squirrel scurried out of his way. The double front doors of the house – hand-carved mahogany depicting a mounted cowboy roping a longhorn steer – were never locked. Neal entered the large foyer and hung his hat on the horns of a mounted ten-point deer head.

He went through another double doorway into the dark-paneled den and poured whiskey from a decanter. When he turned to the window, he saw Faye in the backyard on her knees in a bed of tall yellow flowers. Clouds boiled overhead and wind whipped her blonde hair across her forehead and neck. Neal sat in his leather chair and watched. His jaw muscles jerked. He sipped the pale brown whiskey, licked his lips and felt his insides heat.

MIKE TAPPED THE the carburetor with the handle of his screwdriver and yelled at Red who was inside the truck. "Try it again."

Red turned the key and stomped the starter button on the floorboard. It fired, coughed a few times, then died.

"Try the choke."

Red adjusted the choke, mashed the starter. The Ford fired again and this time kept running. Mike stuck his head out from under the hood and gave Red a thumbs up. Red got out of the cab and both men stood listening to the engine purr.

Neal Lackland turned in the driveway behind Mike and Red. He stepped out of his car, asked, "What's going on?"

"This thing's a bitch to get started," Red said. "I wouldn't be surprised if old man Travis hadn't tried to run it on kerosene."

Mike nodded in agreement.

Neal leaned his weight to one hip. "Tubby and Clyde got it in their heads that Effie Beck's well ought to be checked out for those gold bars town gossips insist is down there. My guess is that Frances is behind it. Tubby says it's cause kids might try to have a look-see and get drowned if we don't prove once and for all there's nothing down there."

"Tubby knows kids is gonna be kids one way or another," Red said. "And town gossips will always find something to gnaw on."

"Just the same, I'm going to see if Paddy Blue will agree to go down the well since he's the smallest man in town. If not, Red, you might have to be the one."

"Not a chance in hell that's going to happen. I hate tight places, always have. You better work on Paddy to do the deed."

"On my way to talk to him now. If he agrees, I'll pick up Tubby then head out. I'd appreciate it if the two of you'd meet us out there."

"Give us time to wash up," Mike said. "I've been wanting to meet Paddy anyway."

Red left immediately to swing by his place to tell Ada what was going on and to load the block and tackle he used for loading hay in his barn loft. He'd explained to Mike that the little pulley on Miss Effie's well wouldn't hold a man's weight.

Mike washed his hands at the outdoor pump, glanced up and noticed Jodean hanging out her wash. Bed sheets and towels whipped in a strong breeze, all but hiding her.

"Hello," Mike called out. When she waved, he walked over.

"I saw Red helping you with that old truck."

"Yeah, well…there's still work to do yet. Right now I'm on my way to the Beck place to help Red and some others check out the well. Seems Tubby is anxious to quiet the Confederate gold gossip."

Jodean chuckled and bent down to get a piece of laundry from her basket. When she straightened, her face went blank for a second and she held a hand to her stomach, just below her waist.

"Jodean, you okay?" She looked fragile, as if the slightest touch would knock her off her feet.

"Of course," she smiled but the look in her eyes tensed.

"Would you like to ride along? Maybe visit with Ada while we…"

"John is coming by this afternoon, but thanks just the same."

She held onto the clothesline. There in blaring sunshine like that, Mike noticed anew her pale skin, small features, and big dark curls. Her bare feet. If things were different, if he wasn't just pausing here in Cooperville for a few months, could he be serious competition for Rice? Would Jodean even be interested?

When Mike rolled up to the Beck house, Red was in the process of getting his equipment in order above the well while Tubby chatted with a man no bigger than Jodean.

"Hi ya, Mike," Tubby called out. "Meet Paddy Blue, Cooperville's undertaker."

Paddy Blue's appearance shocked Mike. People can't help what they look like beyond keeping themselves clean and groomed and Paddy Blue was groomed, to be sure. But his odd shaped face, with one eye lower than the other and a mouth sloped to one side, could make a man pause. Mike held out his hand for a shake. When Paddy hesitated, Mike realized that the man's right shoulder and arm drooped. Paddy, nonetheless, grasped Mike's hand with his dropped right hand and gave it a limp bob, saying, "Howdy do," in a raspy voice. His teeth were piled one on top of the other so bad he couldn't close his mouth all the way.

Red called out that he was ready. While Paddy stripped down to his underwear Neal and Tubby gave him a few instructions. If Paddy was nervous about being lowered down the well he didn't show any sign of it. Red secured a strap similar to a saddle cinch around Paddy's middle then tied a rope onto a D-ring at the back of the strap. He yanked on the rope a few times to test it. Mike, Tubby, and Neal lowered Paddy down while Red watched and gave hand signals to the others.

Paddy worked his way down the narrow walls of the well. Above ground, they heard him heave and huff for a lung of air before he went under water to feel around the bottom. Seconds later he splashed above water and gasped. He held up a muddy rectangular chunk about six by four inches.

"Pull him out." Red gave the hoisting men a hand signal. Paddy's head peeked above the edge of the well. He handed Red the object. It turned out to be an old brick that apparently had been dropped down the well at some point in the last fifty years.

Red looked back at Paddy. "You all right? Rest a bit before you try again." Three times Paddy kicked against the sides of the well to work his way to the bottom. Each time he came up gasping and empty handed.

Their efforts were for nothing.

"Well now," Tubby rubbed his chin. "Guess the next step is to get the *Cooperville Gazette* to report this event and maybe keep some poor local idiot from trying the same thing and getting drowned."

"While you're at it, have them run another missing report," Neal said. "Going to be lots of folks coming to town for the festival who might see the paper and have something come to mind about Becks' affairs."

"Good idea," Tubby said. "And we can put posters in store windows. Red, you happen to know if Ada has a photograph of Effie?"

When Red answered no, Tubby turned to Mike, "Why don't you come inside and help me look for one while Paddy catches his breath. It might help if the papers run a picture of her along with the other information."

Mike followed Tubby inside where he kicked at the old boots next to the back door as he'd done the day of the search. Only this time a mouse popped out of one of them. "Damn!" Tubby jumped sideways and knocked over a tub of rags.

Inside the house Tubby rummaged in the closet while Mike headed for the dresser in the bedroom. Ada had been in the house to clean. The ginger cake was gone. In reality though, the place needed the same kind of overhaul he'd given the pickup.

"How about this old trunk?" Tubby said as he got down on one knee, his big jowls jiggling with the weighty effort. He cleared the farmers' magazines and doilies from the top and pried it open. Tubby groaned. The trunk was stuffed full and in no particular order. He grabbed a piece of paper on top of the jumbled mess. "Says here this is a receipt for a hog Mr. Beck purchased in 1918. Now why do you suppose that's on top?" Tubby looked exasperated.

He moved a wadded, stained tablecloth aside and handed Mike a clump of letters tied with string. Mike sat on the edge of the bed to thumb through them, five in all, addressed to *Miss Effie Beck*, all in the same handwriting but mailed from different locations. One was postmarked Santa Fe, New Mexico, two from Fort Worth, one from Dallas and one from Oklahoma City. The post dates ranged from April of 1908 to December of 1909.

Tubby held up a left foot baby shoe of soft white leather browned with age and a crumpled hat. Under that he found the deed to the ranch, an unfinished sewing project and a damp damaged tintype. The person in the tintype was unrecognizable.

"Anything in those letters?" he asked.

Mike opened the one on top. "It's signed Joseph Dunlap. '*My Dear Effie, I arrived here in Santa Fe in a downpour the likes of which I have never seen. Wish I could send some your way for I know your good father would like to have some of it on his cotton fields.*' " Mike looked at Tubby.

"Go on."

"'*I will travel the neighborhoods here for a while then make my way to Oklahoma City where I hope business is good. If it is, I will head back to Texas in October to see you. You are the sweetest woman a man ever held close. My very fondest regards.*' It's signed *Joe.*"

"Well I'll be hornswaggled," Tubby whispered in amazement. "Who would've ever thought Effie Beck had a sweetheart?"

"I could have my supervisor in San Antonio see if he can find out who this man is."

"Or was. If he was old enough to court Effie, he may be dead."

"Worth a try." Mike unfolded the next letter in the stack. It was postmarked Fort Worth and felt thicker than the others. When he slipped the folded paper out of the envelope, a photograph fell in his lap.

Tubby grabbed it. "Hot damn!" He held it so Mike could see too. It was the type of photograph taken at carnivals by amateur photographers back when pictures were still a pretty novel idea. A small, dark-headed woman sat on the lap of a man who looked much older than she. He had a square-shaped head and huge mustache. They were smiling, squinting into the sun.

"Is that Miss Effie?" Mike asked.

"Think so, though a whole lot younger version than I can call to mind. Need to have Breezy take a look at it to make sure. He may be able to tell us about that Joe fellow, too." Tubby shook his head. "That just beats all... Miss Effie Beck had a gentleman caller. Imagine that."

Outside, Red finished loading the block and tackle in the back of his car and coiled a rope while chatting with Neal and Paddy at the well. Mike showed them the photograph. Red was as surprised as Tubby, but Neal just stared for a minute then passed it back. Mike volunteered to show the photo to Breezy since he'd planned to make another trip to talk with the Parker family anyway. If Breezy confirmed that it was Miss Effie in the photograph, then Mike would see to it that all the newspapers in the area ran the photograph along with a column about her mysterious disappearance.

Tubby was glad to let Mike have the responsibility. "To tell you the truth, I got my hands full. The Committee for Advancement of Commerce is all in a squabble about getting a new festival banner. Then, too, I got to supervise a crew putting together the platform for the queen ceremonies. Why don't you take the photograph and the letters, see what you can find out about them."

"Ada invited all of you to supper when we're done here," Red said.

"Count me out," Tubby said. "I got things to do."

Paddy and Neal declined too, but Mike accepted the invitation, glad to have a chance to talk with Red a little more about his rodeoing days and Effie Beck. He followed Red the short distance up the road to his place.

They washed at the water pump just inside the yard gate. Red's children swarmed around them while a gimpy dog barked high pitched and constant. Little Tootie Sue kept a finger hooked through one of Red's belt loops while eyeing Mike suspiciously.

Supper at the Kasper house was an experience Mike would not soon forget. Pots and pans clanged, bubbled and steamed. All the while, Ada stirred, chopped or issued commands to the constant stream of children in and out of her kitchen. She ran an efficient, tightly-organized home but Mike had a feeling she'd toss it all aside in a heartbeat to devote full attention to a child discovering a tobacco worm on a bean vine.

After supper the children drifted to another room where Pete supervised a child's game of dominoes. Red leaned his chair back on two legs and picked at his teeth with a broom straw. Mike showed Ada the photograph he and Tubby found in the trunk.

"I have no idea who that man is," she said after studying it for a few minutes. He handed her the letter he'd read out loud to Tubby and she read it for Red. When she finished, they sat for a time staring at the picture and Joe Dunlap's faded handwriting.

Mike said, "Breezy's daughter-in-law told me they'd seen Effie walking the road to town at night. They never figured out why. Did either of you ever see her out at night like that?"

"A couple of times," Red said. "She's just out checking her fences or late getting back from town." Mike looked puzzled so Red explained, "She always walked the distance to town and back for her supplies. She quit riding a horse years ago – bad hips – and never owned an automobile."

"What about the time we saw her walking along Spring Creek?" Ada asked Red. Mike held his plate out to her so she could scoop him a big slice of apple pie. "Before Ted was born. Remember? Jean had a fever and we were taking her to see Doc in town, about midnight."

"Oh, yeah. We saw Miss Effie near Spring Creek behind Jodean's house. The headlights beamed right on her so I stopped and got out, you know, thinking something was wrong, late like that." Red chuckled. "She bit my head off. Told me to mind my own *goddamn sonofabitching* business."

"The older she got, the crankier," Ada said. "Only person in the county that could out cuss Red."

Red chuckled again. "I won't argue with that. But all the same, Miss Effie was good at heart. In the last few years though, I didn't see her out like that much."

"That trouble with her foot," Ada said.

Red said, "Tubby told you, didn't he, about Miss Effie having some of her foot lopped off?"

Mike nodded.

"After that she'd get in the car when I offered her a ride, but she always wanted to pay me. It'd make her mad if I didn't take the money, usually a nickel, so I did." Red dropped his chair forward to all four legs. "You know, I never heard Miss Effie complain or ask for a thing. I don't know if she had any regrets or longings. I guess that picture and those letters prove that we sold her short. She had a life and feelings none of us knew about."

Ada started clearing dishes. "You never sold Effie Beck short on anything Red Kasper."

The children came bounding back into the kitchen wanting to ride Gyp, an old nag of a horse that, according to Ada, Red couldn't bear the thought of shooting.

Red groaned but winked at Mike and let his children pull him out the door. Mike carried a stack of plates to the sink.

"You don't have to do that," Ada said, a little surprised when he started washing dishes.

"Nice bunch of kids you and Red have."

Ada looked out the window. She was a sturdy woman with sun-browned skin. A scrubbed-face beauty unlike city women. "I named them all one syllable names so they'd be easy to call up. When I was expecting each one, I'd go to the back door and call out a name. You know, drag it out the way mothers do, to see how it'd sound. The only one I messed up on was Sue. Sounds like I'm calling hogs. Su-ue, Su-ue!" She shook her head with a smile.

"Is that why Red calls her Tootie Sue?" Mike handed her a rinsed plate to dry.

"Not really. She's just our Tootie Sue."

"Have you lived in Cooperville all your life?"

"Yes, 'bout all of us have, except the bridge crew."

"So you've known Jodean all that time?"

Ada paused for a beat. "Yes."

"The day of the picnic, Jodean didn't get a chance to explain why she's a judge for the queen contest along with me and Paddy. You'd said the position required impartiality..." Mike had trouble forming his next question.

Ada stared at him.

"How does Jodean fit that role? I mean with Paddy Blue and me, it's obvious. But if she's lived here all her life...?"

Ada sparked. "It's the role Cooperville placed on Jodean a long time ago, Mike. And if you're as kind as I think you are, you'll not ask any more questions about it."

"Sorry, I—"

"No need to be. It's puzzling for me, too."

Red's infectious laughter filtered through the open window. Mike dried his hands while Ada put the last of the dishes away. The two drifted to the porch and there, in the drawn-out shadows of dusk, they watched Red lead Gyp around the yard with kids stacked on her back like books standing on their ends. Alice In Wonderland, Huckleberry Finn, Nancy Drew, Hardy Boys.

DURING THE DRIVE back to town, Mike let his bitterness slip away, but then his old cynicism kept it from leaving him altogether. Things that occurred during the day stayed with him into the night to be hashed over and over. Effie Beck staring at him from a photograph. Red's giggling kids on Gyp's back, a smile from Jodean.

Tootie Sue felt like a pouch of bones in his arms the day of the picnic, wet and cold, screaming "Daddy, Daddy" at the top of her lungs. And tonight, Ada's strange response when he tried to find out why Jodean seemed removed from the town's hierarchy. He felt like a cockroach for asking about it, but her reply confirmed that the situation was, in fact, not as it appeared as far as Jodean and Cooperville were concerned.

Mike couldn't wait to write his brother James and his mother and tell them he was to judge a queen contest. They'd get a laugh out of that. But like sails gone slack in the doldrums, his spirits plunged when he thought about them. He was far away from all he and his family had suffered, and harbored bright eye-stinging shame about leaving North Carolina. Even when he reminded himself he'd done it for work.

James had a baby on the way and had to shoulder the responsibility of caring for their mother alone. Mike wondered if that was the thing inside him – guilt – trying to reverse itself? The gloom of wasted ambition had left him smoldering and bitter. But here in Texas there were huge spaces between clumps of grief and ruin. He'd like to think that in those spaces he could recover the parts of himself that he'd lost along the way.

Around nine-thirty he swung into the drive beside the beauty shop and glimpsed John Rice and Jodean in the front porch swing. Jodean jerked around and froze for an instant in the headlights, like a rabbit caught in cross hairs. His spirits slipped another notch.

Mike drove past the house and into the shed then made his way to the tank house. It had been a tiring day. His bones ached. He dropped in his chair and took Effie Beck's picture out of his shirt pocket.

Every now and then he could hear Jodean and John talking in hushed tones through the open window of the tank house. He tried to make out their words then shook himself mentally. It wasn't so much that he was nosy, just that hearing them, knowing they were there, tugged at him. Rice was a dead-end street where Jodean was concerned. The man had priorities that didn't include her, which wasn't bad. Every man had a right to set his own priorities. But Jodean was being fooled and John Rice knew it.

Mike had already washed for bed and turned off the light when he noticed the tone of their voices changed. Jodean's rose a half octave while John's took on a pleading aspect. Mike peered into the dark night, though he couldn't have said what he thought he'd see since the tank house sat at the back and a little to the side of the house. The porch swing chains crunched and someone *shooshed*. Mike saw a shadowy figure hurry down the drive from the front of the house. It was Jodean's thin-boned frame barely lit in star glow. John Rice rushed up behind her, grabbed her arm and whipped her around to face him. Mike's insides coiled. He shoved through the screen door and waited at the corner of the house. They hadn't seen him.

John let go of Jodean's arm and jerked away. "You're nothing but a tease! And not a very good one at that." He wheeled off in a huff, looked back once.

She touched her face then looked right and left before bumping into Mike with a gasp. He couldn't see her face in the dark, but he could hear her breath coming and going in short hitches.

"You okay?" he asked. Her head moved up and down before she rushed by him and headed for the back door.

BREEZY PARKER STOOD in the doorway to watch as that new white man parked his truck in front of the house. He couldn't figure what Mike Lemay's business was this time. A right nice fella, and from a farming family, too. That's what Breezy told Trudy after Mike's first visit. When Trudy asked how he knew that, Breezy said he just *knowd*.

Jericho, who stood behind Breezy, called out a howdy.

"You find Effie Beck?" Breezy asked.

"Afraid not," Mike answered. "I told the mayor I'd write another story to run in the newspapers though. We found a picture to go with it but thought you might take a look at it first and tell us for sure it's her. It was taken a long time ago."

Breezy took the picture Mike handed him. "I be a suck-egg mule. That her all right." He handed the picture to Jericho. "And that be the medicine show man she's with." Breezy moved to his porch chair and backed up until his legs touched the seat then let himself drop down. "Mmh-mmph. Don't nobody know what these old bones feel like."

Mike followed him. "Medicine show man?"

"I remember him," Jericho said. "He'd come 'round now and again peddling stuff outta his wagon. Can't imagine what Miss Effie's doing with him – sitting on his knee like that."

"Could he have been a friend of Mr. Beck's?" Mike asked.

"No suh," Breezy said. "Becks didn't have no friendships or relations neither." He shifted his gaze to the road behind Mike. Paddy Blue came rattling by in his mule-drawn coffin cart. All three men on the porch waved at him.

When Paddy had moved down the road a piece, Mike asked, "What's he doing way out here?"

"Ain't enough people dying off here 'bouts to keep the gravedigger busy. He got to chop wood to earn his keep."

"I thought he was the undertaker."

"That he is. *And* the gravedigger, *and* the one what keeps the graveyard." Breezy knew what the next question was going to be so he figured he'd save Mike his breath. "Don't nobody know what happen to him. He come to town all crippled that-a-way."

"Where did he come from?"

"Baby train," Jericho said, watching Paddy's cart disappear into the thickets. "He come here on one of the baby trains."

"Mmh-mmph." Breezy stomped his foot. "I can hear them little babies crying to this day, I can. You see, way back – long as I know 'bout – folks up north, church people, sent their orphans all over to get adopted. Mostly to farm country so's the babies, and bigger chil'ren some of em, could live on farms and help out and have a good home, you see."

"Only some didn't have it so good," Jericho added.

"That so. But lemme tell you, ain't nothin' sad as them little babies. The preachers, sometimes nun ladies, they'd get off the train and line up the chil'ren and just stand there with the crowd a lookin' 'em over. And the chil'ren just a bawling, scared to death they was."

"And someone adopted Paddy Blue?"

"Brother Jake Blue. He was the white-man preacher back then. He dead now. He felt sorry for the little boy with the twisted face, the last orphan on the train and nobody want him. I was there that time, yessir. Brother Jake give Paddy a big hug and says to him that he was just the little boy he'd asked Jesus to send him." Breezy watched Mike fix his eyes on Paddy's dust cloud.

"I reckon Paddy was lucky," Breezy added, hoping to put a bright light on the telling. "Brother Jake, he all right."

Mike moved down the porch steps after thanking them for taking a look at the picture, but stopped short. "One more thing. Do you remember the medicine show man's name? Was it Joseph Dunlap?"

"I reckon I cain't recall," Breezy said. He raised his arm as high as he could to wave good-bye, but he only managed to shake his fingers a little. Right nice young man that Mike Lemay. *He be back.*

MIKE WATCHED A city crew stretch a banner from the second floor of the bank building across the street to an electric pole in front of City Café, close to where he stood. The banner read, "Pickle Festival – Friday and Saturday." The word festival was missing the *l*, and the *S* in Saturday had peeled off so that part of it flapped in the breeze.

Doris came out of the café to shake crumbs from a table cloth. "That sign is one and the same used for the last fifteen years. That faded, wrinkled old thing seems to fit the times, don't it?"

Paddy Blue rode by in his coffin cart chock-full of wood. He waved at Doris standing now with her arms folded across her bosom.

"Where's he going with all that wood?" Mike asked.

"Boardinghouse. It's one of the few places in town that still uses a wood stove."

Paddy turned onto Front Street where a car full of high school kids came close to running him over. Doris clicked her tongue. "Kids out drumming up mischief for the festival. Every year the town's teenagers feel it's their duty to out prank the sneaky deeds of the year before. I hear Mayor Tubby and town officials promise formal charges and jail sentences for anybody that causes trouble. But no one takes them serious."

"Jail sentences are pretty serious."

"Poor Paddy has suffered more pranks than anyone. One year a bunch of thugs rolled him out of bed during the night, tied his hands and feet and put him in a casket they'd dragged out of the funeral home. Just before the parade next morning, they loaded the casket – with Paddy in it – on the coffin cart, hitched up the mule and set off a string of firecrackers they'd tied to the animal's tail. The mule tore through the parade and nearly broke a kid's leg in the confusion." Doris gave the table cloth another shake. "The *Cooperville Gazette* that week said Paddy Blue had the by-god scared out of him."

"I think I'll try to catch Paddy at the boardinghouse. This might be as good a time as any to interview him."

"Sure thing, Mike. You come back for supper now. We got ham and beans on special today."

Mike caught up to Paddy in the alley behind the boardinghouse. After the two greeted each other, Mike asked, "Mind if I tag along with you a little while this afternoon? I'd like to watch what you do and maybe ask you a few questions."

Paddy wrinkled his good eyebrow.

Mike knew Paddy didn't understand his interest. "Have you heard about what I do? I'm writing reports on people's histories."

Paddy nodded but still looked a little unsure of himself, so Mike offered to help unload the wood in the hope it'd put Paddy at ease. He couldn't help but wonder how Paddy could eat with his teeth all bunched in the front of his mouth the way they were. His hair looked like matted cotton, an awful dirty-water color, neither blond nor gray.

Bill and Bart Steves, the boardinghouse proprietor's boys, came out to help, too. The youngest climbed onto the cart and tossed logs down to them. Paddy worked for the most part with his left hand and arm since his right side – face, arm and leg – sort of sagged. The other boy told Paddy that a tree just off the road near the Bat House blew down in Effie Beck's storm, that it would be good cut wood if he needed it. Paddy gave the kid a nod of thanks.

When they finished unloading, Mike climbed in Paddy's cart and they rumbled out of town. Paddy pivoted his head right and left watching for the downed tree the Steves kid mentioned. About three miles from town, they saw a fancy yellow coupe convertible, like the one the sheriff's wife drove, parked under a big shady oak beside the road.

"Usually town folks stay away from the Bat House," Paddy said, whispery and hoarse through crowded teeth. "They think bats are evil creatures. But I never mind them. The Bat House was built to attract bats that feed on mosquitoes carrying yellow fever. Nothing morbid about that."

Compared to the *Tex-isms* Mike had come to expect from most of the town's population, Paddy's speech sounded polished.

Paddy pointed to the downed tree on his right and turned onto a cattle trail leading into a thicket. He stopped in the deep shade of a huge tree and reached behind the seat for the ax and bow saw. The sun was high and hot. Insects buzzed around their heads, not so much as a stir in the air.

Mike climbed down from the wagon and followed Paddy a few steps into the weeds. Paddy stopped, held up his hand, to signal that he'd heard something. He used the ax handle to move aside yaupon branches and get a better look at a flat open area across the way. A man and woman, their heads barely visible above tall golden grass, were sitting in the shade of the bat house. Mike squeezed his eyes to make out who it was. He and Paddy exchanged looks.

The woman was Faye Lackland, the sheriff's wife, but that wasn't the sheriff with her. Mike recognized the man from the bridge crew, the one who sat alone in City Café.

Faye stood and brushed at her clothes and handed the man a basket. She reached down and picked up a quilt, shook it and then rolled it under her arm. The two tromped through the high weeds to her car and drove off.

MIKE DELIVERED THE story of Effie Beck's disappearance, along with the photograph, to the newspaper front office as soon as he finished writing it. Like Sheriff Neal, he hoped folks coming to town for the Pickle Festival would see it and maybe come forward with information. The girl at the front desk told him to wait while she made sure the editor had room in his layout to run the story. When she came back, a tall, lanky man followed her. She introduced Mike to Rudy Cochran, the *Cooperville Gazette* editor.

"I've been hearing about your work for the Writers' Project," Rudy said. "Interesting, but do you think it'll go all the way to being printed up in books?"

"I'd like to think so. No way to know at this point."

"I looked at your story. It's good. I'll run it in the next copy."

Mike shifted his weight, didn't know what to say.

"Come on back and let me show you my operation here. It'll seem small after some you've seen."

Rudy lead Mike into a room, dark and crowded with two ancient-looking printing presses. Long layout tables with mason jars full of scissors, bladed knives and ink pens lined each end of the tables. Everything, even the walls, had been splattered with ink. An unoccupied desk was heaped with old newspapers. A glass-fronted door opened into Rudy's office where he offered coffee. Mike accepted. Rudy remained eager to talk shop even after Mike assured him he didn't have any real or practical newspaper experience.

"Tell me," Rudy said, "you've seen a lot more of the country than the rest of us, do you think the hardest times are behind us now?"

"It's hard to say. Keep in mind that some regions were just naturally hit harder by the Crash. And the effect will drift around to the rest of us for years to come."

"A couple of ranching families in the county lost everything they had down to the shirts on their backs. I hear some are living under a bridge somewhere in New Mexico. They never made it to California." He offered Mike more coffee. "How long do you think you'll be in town?"

"I'd guess another couple of months." Mike took the chair Rudy pointed at then changed the subject. "You may be able to help me out a little. I just heard something about baby trains. Know anything about them?"

"Not a whole lot. Most people called them Orphan Trains. I remember reading that in the late 1800s a man by the name of Brace organized a way, using the country's rail system, to move orphans from the slum streets of big cities in the Northeast to the farming states. I don't think it's been all that long since the practice stopped. Anyway, thousands of children were adopted that way. Some of the kids had been abandoned, some became orphans when their parents died in epidemics or from plain old poverty."

"I heard Paddy Blue was one of them."

"Now there's a case where the system helped. No doubt some of those adopted ended up little more than indentured slaves. Paddy's life hasn't been a bed of roses, but no doubt, better than if he'd been left on city streets."

"How many were adopted here – in Cooperville?"

"There's no way to know for sure because there were no public records kept for local adoptions. But I'd guess several still live in this county. A stigma exists where the adoptions are concerned, Mike. I've heard the term "bad blood" used referring to the orphans."

Rudy walked around to the front of his desk and leaned against it. "A few folks will tell you orphans are bearers of sin or some silliness, and that nothing short of massive doses of Christian doctrine can change what those children are supposedly predestined to become. Many don't even believe *that* can make the orphans acceptable. No doubt some children were born to prostitutes and illiteracy but..." Rudy shrugged. "I never heard of any in

Cooperville being harmed or mistreated. Ostracized? Yes. But not physically hurt."

"I take it the adoptions are not an open subject?"

Rudy nodded. "And that makes it hard to know much about them."

"Then how can you be so sure that none have been harmed?"

"Good point. It's unfortunate our society holds such bigoted attitudes about adoption."

Mike stood to leave. "Maybe we'll live long enough to see it change. Thanks for the coffee."

Rudy took Mike's empty cup. "Before you go...well, I may be getting my cart before my horse here but when you finish your work for the Writer's Project, stop by to see me. I'd like to hire someone with your skills. Trouble is, I got to gauge how business is, or will be, before I can make that decision."

Mike grinned in spite of himself. Nice to hear the offer even if it didn't pan out. "Sure thing," he said.

From the newspaper office Mike walked to C.J.'s Grocery where he picked up some crackers and cheese. It was Jodean's beauty shop day and he didn't like troubling her to fix his lunch on the days she worked. On his way out of C.J.'s, he held the door for Emmet's wife. She said hello and made a little pleasant talk about having him over for supper sometime. Mike crossed the street, waved at Hank standing in front of his filling station, then stopped by the bakery to buy a discounted day-old donut.

He tried to imagine where he'd fit into Cooperville's comings and goings, into the gears and wheels that ticked little hitches of time. What if Rudy did offer him a job? Would he accept? What about his mother back in North Carolina? The last letter he'd received from his brother hinted that their mother wasn't well. Nothing James could put a finger on, he'd written, just that she didn't act right, forgot things. Mike wrote back asking if he should head home to help out, but hadn't heard anything since.

Thoughts of his mother brought Effie Beck back to mind. Her musty house, that old trunk full of wadded-up secrets stuffed in a dark place so no one would know. And the town's secret children whose wrecked lives it saved, only to hold them at arm's length as if tainted – as if orphans could infect them somehow because of a life they'd been born into.

Mike wanted to understand Effie Beck, find out what happened to her during her long and troubled life. And he wanted to understand this town, how people here could be so prudent in taking care of each other yet hold prejudices against innocent victims of circumstance. He planned to re-read all of square-headed Joseph Dunlap's letters first thing when he got back to the tank house. Then he'd write Tom Coker in San Antonio and ask him to see what he could find out about the man and orphan trains.

A lady climbed the steps in front of the Travis house as Mike walked by. He hadn't seen Jodean since the night John Rice took off and she'd run into the house. No doubt she wanted it that way. She'd be embarrassed by what had happened – or almost happened. He hoped to catch her soon to remind her of his promise to teach her to drive.

Jodean, it seemed, occupied as big a chunk of his brain as Effie Beck, though for different reasons.

BILL AND BART STEVES headed for the old abandoned cotton gin as soon as lunch time boardinghouse dishes were washed and put away. The cotton gin was the tallest structure in the county. Their grandfather had helped build it, but they gave their grandfather no thought whatsoever as they concentrated on the mission at hand.

"Did anybody see you?" Tommy Crane asked when Bill and Bart climbed onto the loading dock. Beads of sweat glistened the fuzz on his top lip.

"Lots of people saw us," Bill said. "But we didn't look like we's doing anything so different. You get the tarpaulin?"

"Yeah. I need some help getting it unloaded and set up. Bart you stand watch."

Tommy, the self-appointed mischief-maker for the Pickle Festival, led Bill to the back of the dark, oily smelling cotton gin.

Their footsteps gritted on the rough cement floor that was caked with years of dirt and rot. At the far end of the huge barn-like building, behind a ten-foot partition, Tommy pointed to the rolled tarp on the back of his hoopie truck. Bill jumped up on the back and grasped one end of the tarp and Tommy the other.

"We have to figure out a way to hang it so Calvin can paint it."

"It's awful dark in here. How about there close to that window? Is he bringing the deck of cards?"

"Yep, and his paint."

"How'd you talk Calvin into going along with the plan?"

"Easy. Offered to let him come with me next time I head to San Antonio. You can come, too, if you want. If we pull this off without getting run out of town, we'll owe it to ourselves."

"What's so interesting about San Antonio that Calvin'd risk his neck for?" Bill dropped his end of the tarp and looked around. "I reckon we can hang it on these bale hooks. That ought'a work."

Tommy grinned, shook his head.

JODEAN WALKED TO the parsonage the day before the Pickle Queen contest to help June Rawlings fold programs. As she was leaving with the programs tied and bundled under her arm, she spied John Rice strolling down the sidewalk with a duffel bag slung over his shoulder.

Her heart thumped and her mouth formed a little *o*.

John kept his eyes narrowed on her until he was close enough for her to see the little patch of dark skin on his cheekbone. She'd teased him about it once when they were sitting in the porch swing, said it was shaped like a pumpkin.

John tipped his hat in greeting and set his bag down.

"Leaving town?" Jodean asked.

"Yep." His eyes were aimed toward the train tracks.

Jodean's throat closed off. She didn't know if she was disappointed or relieved. Either way, her spirits had already started flowing through the soles of her shoes and were spilling across the sidewalk disguised as her shadow. Obviously he hadn't planned to run into her. He was simply going to jump a train away from Cooperville without so much as a blink of concern.

"California is waiting for me."

He reached out to touch her cheek but she moved back a step, hoping Brother Rawlings or June weren't watching from the window. "Good-bye, John Rice."

His grin mocked her, like she was the butt of a joke. His white dress shirt was so bright it made her eyes sting. Like a proud rooster, he picked up his bag, threw his shoulders back and moved down the sidewalk with a deliberate jounce.

Just as well, she thought. *Better now before she'd made too much of a fool of herself.*

Jodean kept telling herself that all the way home. As she approached the house she heard the Gospel Hour on Cora Mae's radio, a choir singing *Give Me That Old Time Religion*. Inside, Cora Mae sprawled on the sofa with her bare feet propped on the coffee table. "Better get on to the cookie baking or you're not going to get it done before supper."

Jodean dropped the programs on the dining room table. Yesterday's newspaper was tented above a bowl of soggy, cold oatmeal. She looked at the back of Cora Mae's head, at the radio blaring away, and then moved to the hall. She looked left into the beauty shop where shades were drawn and the scent of wave solution hung in the air like a permanent fixture. She turned right, walked down the short hall and peered into Cora's bedroom. The bed was unmade and a veil of lose face powder covered everything. Beyond Cora Mae's bedroom a narrow stairway led to her own bedroom upstairs, but she moved straight ahead, past the stairs to a door that took her out to the back porch – the opposite end from the kitchen. She plopped on the bench where Mike sat every now and then when he had time to share small talk with her.

"A penny for your thoughts?"

Jodean jumped. "Mike!" He stood outside in the sun, squinting through the porch screen at her. "I thought you were gone."

"I was earlier," he said. "I saw Sheriff Neal giving Rice the run around..."

Jodean nodded. "He jumped a train."

Mike opened the screen door and stepped into the shade of the porch. After a quick glance into the house, he said, "This might be a good time for you to learn to drive."

She shook her head.

"Sure it is, Jodean. Just think how much easier chores would be if you didn't have to walk everywhere, especially in the boiling heat of summer or freezing rain in winter."

"I've got to bake cookies for tomorrow night—"

"I'll help."

"Then first thing in the morning I have to make garland for the auditorium."

Mike held his first finger to his lips, tiptoed across the porch, and went into the kitchen. Curiosity got the better of Jodean. She followed him. He closed the door to the dining room then grabbed a dish towel and tied it around his middle. He pulled a drawer open, looked in, shut it, opened another and grabbed a big wooden spoon. He turned to Jodean. "You measure and I'll stir."

Jodean stared. Was this the same man who had dragged his bones up to the back door weeks ago, whose smoky sad eyes were sunk so deep in their sockets he could've passed for dead?

"Why are you doing this?" she asked.

Mike shrugged and tapped the spoon in the palm of his hand. He drew a lung of air. "I like your company."

Jodean gave up trying to put herself back together after he said that. If the pieces of her were going to scatter, then so be it. John Rice hadn't surprised her with his abrupt departure as much as Mike Lemay had by saying something so sweet. Maybe she wasn't worth a fig for knowing how a man thinks – like her momma always told her.

While measuring butter and sugar for the cookies, she told Mike all about the queen contest. He stirred, slopped a little on his hand then licked it off with a grin like a little boy caught with his finger in the pie.

"This year there are four contestants," Jodean explained. "Since there're only four positions, queen, first, second, and third runner-up, all we have to do is decide on the order. Paddy never says a word about which girl he thinks should be queen, and I feel awful because I know them all, so I'll just leave the decision to you. It'll be fairer that way."

"Who were the judges last year?"

"Me and Paddy and a WPA supervisor visiting town. I told him the same thing I told you. Just pick one girl who you think looks like a Pickle Queen and put the others in any order you want."

"Why do they even bother? I mean, it seems it'd be just as fair to put the names in a hat and draw."

"It would. But tradition makes people feel secure."

Jodean showed Mike how to roll the cookie dough into balls then roll the balls in sugar while she flattened them with the bottom of a spoon. In no time they had baked four dozen cookies and washed the last of the dishes. Mike untied his dish towel apron. "I don't know any more about garland than I do making cookies, but you can show me. Want to get started first thing in the morning?"

Jodean nodded. "If you're sure…" Her ears grew hot. She had to bite the inside of her mouth to keep from grinning like a goo-goo-eyed school girl.

The next morning Jodean and Mike walked past the tank house and stopped at the car shed to get the wheelbarrow and pruning shears. From there they worked their way down the rock fence along the road. Jodean cut lengths of wisteria vine, boughs of cedar, and thin branches of yaupon. "We'll take these back to the porch and wire them into ten foot lengths. The hardest part is keeping the leaves from wilting too much."

Mike didn't say much all morning but watched her every move. To break the long silence, she said, "Ada told me you and Red and some others went back out to Miss Effie's place."

"We lowered Paddy Blue down the well to confirm there were no gold bars."

She clipped a small cedar limb and handed it to him. "It's just so awful, Mike. I know she's probably dead. But how? Where? I can't help but think she suffered."

"Red and Breezy said they'd seen her walking this road late at night. Did you ever see her?"

"Oh, yeah. She roamed a lot." Jodean handed him another cedar bough. "There was so much space between Miss Effie and the rest of us, you know what I mean? But at the same time she was close at hand. Even when I was little I could feel it."

She grabbed a yaupon branch overhead and pulled it down to clip but it caught in her hair. The more she struggled to free herself the more tangled she became.

"Hold on." Mike reached to help her.

She got tickled, had to shut her eyes to keep from being poked by twigs. When she opened them, Mike stood still as a fence post, staring down into her face. She cut the branch he held and told him they had enough.

They said little on the way back to the house. More and more Jodean felt comfortable with Mike and their quiet spells, as if she'd known him longer and better than she actually had.

MIKE STUDIED THE list of contestants Ada handed him and wondered how the hell he could pick one girl out of the four to be queen. Only a handful of early arrivals gathered at the back of the school auditorium. Mike watched Paddy Blue gimp down the aisle and head straight for him. Paddy had on a too-large suit and a stained tie. His hair had a striking resemblance to tangled wire. Mike looked the other way for a minute.

Ada hurried from the back of the auditorium to the stage, trying to get everyone settled. "Mike, you and Paddy need to take your seats and get out of the way. Folks are going to start filing in any minute now." The judges' table sat directly in front of the stage where they'd have a ringside view of everything that went on.

Mike looked at the names again and decided to pick a queen right then and there before he ever saw any of them. He picked

Doreen Crumps. For first runner-up he picked Esther Wiggins, second would be Evonne Noble and third, Dee Dee Bishop. He leaned towards to Paddy and showed him the list. Paddy smiled big enough to show all of his brown teeth.

More families drifted into the auditorium. Mike hadn't seen Jodean since the morning they'd finished making garland. He offered her a ride to the schoolhouse in the truck, but she declined, saying Ada was coming by, that they had lots of details to take care of.

The Alvins came in and took a seat to the left. They reminded Mike of two aged cats. He'd seen them on their porch most evenings, lounging in slanted light, as if sunning themselves. She was wide-faced and slick-haired. He, graying, drooped and thin.

Glory rushed by the Alvins and blabbed something to Frances about a problem with her sheet music. Frances told her to hush before she worked herself into hysterics. Red and Ada's kids ran up and down the aisles screeching at the top of their lungs. Others, who Mike hadn't met, came strolling in from the back, some in faded cotton and overalls, others in polished shoes and white gloves. All of them seemed happy to be where they were. Even Paddy Blue. Mike hoped Cooperville would still be speaking to him after the Pickle Queen winner was announced.

Faye walked across the stage headed straight for the judges' table. Mike rubbed his chin. A man could hear jungle drums just looking at her. She leaned forward with her hands on her knees. "Jodean said to tell y'all she'll be out in a minute. One of the girls is having a case of nerves."

Mike nodded.

A little later Jodean rushed up behind them to take her seat. With the place packed to a standing-room crowd, Glory Hughes banged fanfare music on the piano.

When she finished, Mayor Tubby Whittaker stepped onto the stage. "Okay, folks. Y'all settle down. The ladies running this show asked me to remind everyone about the parade and street dance tomorrow starting at four in the afternoon. And just so's everybody knows, city officials are aware of a broken water line out near the pickle factory. Crews will have it fixed in no time."

As it turned out, Doreen Crumps, the girl Mike picked to be queen, had skin like pea gravel. She lost her place halfway through a dramatic reading and had to start again. C.J's Grocery had sponsored her.

Esther Wiggins was prettier. She twirled a baton, performed a cartwheel and ended her talent portion by executing a cheerleader split. In Mike's younger days, girls like Esther made him want to puke. She bounced too much when she walked, acted like everyone's best friend and confidant, and grinned twenty-four hours a day. Good looks, false sincerity. The girl would go far in a town like Cooperville.

Evonne Noble wore glasses and breathed through her mouth. Jodean whispered that Evonne was expected to be valedictorian of her graduating class. Evonne sang a song Mike had never heard before. Or maybe he had. She was so off key he couldn't be sure.

Dee Dee Bishop, the best looking of the group, gave the impression of being the least interested in what she was doing. She'd been sponsored by Hank's Service Station and played a Sousa march on the piano. Dee Dee took her bow right in front of Paddy Blue, flashing a four-inch cleavage. Paddy squirmed and doodled on his note pad.

When Ada proclaimed that the contest was over and that the judges' decisions would be announced after the parade the next day, everyone cheered and bee-lined it to the cafeteria for refreshments.

RED FOUND SIX empty chairs along the far wall of the cafeteria. He told his kids to sit down and dared them to move or make a sound. He wished to hell Ada had just let them all stay home.

"Pete, go get cookies for your brother and sisters." Pete took off for the refreshment table.

Red watched Sheriff Neal Lackland and wife Faye walk in from the hall. Neal had his hand on Faye's back, but he might as well have had a noose around her neck. Red had seen enough trapped animals to know the look, and Faye had it. Who could guess her hell? Faye introduced Neal to Otis. She was playing with fire. Neal nodded at Otis stony faced, said something, then pulled Faye toward the punch table.

"Wha'cha looking at?" Ada asked Red when she joined him.

"Ah, that jackass sheriff."

"You might find watching Mike more interesting." Ada used her chin to point over Red's shoulder. Across the room, Mike was handing Jodean a glass of punch. "I sure do like that man," Ada said. "I wonder, now that John Rice is out of the picture..."

"Jodean is destined to be an old spinster, so you can stop your wondering."

While they were still watching, Cora Mae walked up to Jodean. Ada moaned. "I'll never understand why Jodean doesn't tell Cora Mae to go to hell and leave town for a clean start somewhere."

"Help Jodean out a little," Red said. "Go on over there and tell Cora Mae you need her to do something. Make it sound special so she'll go along."

Ada kissed his cheek. "You're such an old softy. How 'bout I tell Cora Mae that Rudy from the newspaper is looking for her so he can to take her picture for the spread he's doing on the festival committees? He's gone home already so she'll spend half the night looking for him and the other half regretting she missed him."

"That ought'a do the trick." Red winked.

Ada sauntered off.

Pete navigated his way back through the crowd carefully carrying four cookies on a napkin. He dodged a man who'd stepped back suddenly and the movement made him drop a cookie. He flashed a guilty look at Red who nodded a *that's-okay* look. Pete handed his siblings each a remaining cookie then sat down. Red ruffled his son's hair and told him he thought it would be okay if he got another for himself and to be sure to pick up the one he dropped and put it in the waste bin.

Tootie Sue climbed on Red's lap with her cookie and held it to his mouth. Red pretended to take a bite.

Frances Whittaker rushed by mopping her face with a handkerchief while husband Tubby rolled back and forth over the toes and heels of his new boots. Each time he dropped back on his heels, blubber jiggled head to foot. He was talking to Hank, owner of the service station, and the preacher. All three stuffed their mouths with sweets and washed it down with punch.

Behind them, Evonne Noble sat against the wall with her face buried in her mother's shoulder, bawling her eyes out, most likely because she forgot half the words to the song she sang. Her daddy, on the other side of her, looked at air, like he wished he was in the parking lot getting a snort.

When Ada came back, she handed Red a glass of punch. Red shared it with Tootie Sue, who managed to spit half-chewed cookie each time she gulped. He pushed hair out of her eyes. "Ada, darling, if you ever put our girls through this goddamned queen horseshit I'll put a bounty out on your head."

Ada gave him a wicked grin. "You know how excited I get when you talk like that."

Tootie Sue and Jean fell asleep on the way home. As always, Bullet was waiting for them at the end of the long drive. When he saw the Buick turn in, he stood and gimped the way to the house. "Just like we don't know where the house is without him showing us," Pete said from the back seat.

Red waited for Ada to make the last of her rounds checking on sleeping kids like she did every night before coming to bed. When she sat down heavy on her side of the bed with a tired sigh, Red reached to squeeze her shoulder muscles. "Do I need to talk rough some more or save my breath tonight?"

Ada chuckled, leaned back so her head rested on his stomach.

Red smoothed her hair and touched her mouth with his callused thumb. "You're queen of my world, Ada Ann Kasper."

They fell asleep like that, with Ada's head on his stomach and him holding her face like it was a fine jewel. Sometime in the middle of the night Ada stirred, slipped her nightgown over her head and lay for a time watching Red breathe. She nuzzled his neck and face then slipped her hand down his belly and into his underwear.

Red hiccuped air, rolled his eyes open with a sleepy grin. "My queen."

BILL STEVES HAD never seen anything like it – a whole deck of playing cards with a different naked woman on each card.

Calvin Lewis had been an ace at drawing cartoons and painting pictures since they were all in grade school, so it was only natural that Tommy asked him to paint a likeness of one of the naked women on the big tarp. They decided on the four of hearts, a brunette, laying all stretched out on her back with one arm under her head. Where her legs came together she held a little red heart-shaped pillow with pink fringe on it.

Bill, Bart, and Tommy watched as Calvin transformed the drab green tarp into a fine work of art. Bill figured the lady, once Calvin copied her likeness, was eight feet long from her head to the tip of her red toenails. The red toenails were a special touch they'd all decided on at the last minute.

It had taken Calvin two days to finish. They left the tarp hanging for a third day so the paint would dry. Tommy and Bill returned to the cotton gin the night of the queen contest, rolled the tarp into a tight bundle and hauled it to City Park. They secured it in place while most of the town gathered in the schoolhouse cafeteria for punch and cookies.

PARADE DAY DAWNED bright and clear with bird song everywhere. In the distance, down the sloped land behind the tank house, Cooperville Spring bubbled from a deep underground crevice then gurgled softly over rocks above the carp's pool. Mike could smell spring water all the way up the slope. He rolled to his side in the narrow loft bed, climbed down, pulled on his pants and imagined how Jodean would look this morning coming to the back porch with his toast and eggs. Sometimes she was as pale as gardenia petals, others flushed as a rose.

During the night he decided to let go his hold on bitterness. From now on he wanted to view the future from Cooperville's perspective. That of acceptance. He glanced at the back door to the house and tried to name what he risked by dropping his guard. He came up with nothing.

The shower, which was nothing more than a faucet positioned high in a corner of the small room, was ice cold and smelled like moss. Mike was quick about showering and shaving and afterward moved to the arm chair to watch for Jodean.

He had no idea how long he'd sat there with his mind drifting in and out of a shallow doze when he heard Cora Mae caterwaul from inside the house. Jodean called out a reply and a minute later Cora Mae appeared at the back door wearing a nightgown and a thick black hair net tied around her head. The ends of the hair net trailed down her broad back like a tail. She pinned a note on the screen door.

The note confirmed what Mike had guessed. Jodean would be too busy all day with her beauty shop appointments to mess with breakfast. He wadded the note and struck out for City Café, hoping it wasn't too late for a breakfast order. According to the newspaper and Tubby's announcement, the parade was scheduled to start at four in the afternoon so he had a few hours of free time.

The café was full of people. Even if he hadn't known about the scheduled parade, he'd have guessed something was afoot by the high pitched voices echoing louder than usual under the tall tin ceiling. Eyebrows were raised in anticipation of the day and every face sported a smile. The air felt sharp to the skin, colors were brighter.

The excitement appeared out of proportion to Mike, but maybe the day offered a change of pace, or a demarcation that meant one cycle was ending and another beginning. If Cooperville was like the rest of the country, *any* change could be good.

"What'll it be?" Doris asked.

"Too late for breakfast?"

"Nawh." She withdrew a note pad from her apron pocket. "Where's that side kick of yours?"

"Red? Haven't seen him this morning."

"He told me that one of these days he's going to bring in his young'uns and let me dip 'em some ice cream."

Before Mike could comment, Doris hollered at a group of men coming through the door. "I guess Emmet will have to deputize extra men to watch over Cooperville with the likes of y'all in town."

They laughed and shuffled to a booth across from Mike. Doris knew just about everything there was to know about anyone in town or passing through. More so than the ladies at the beauty shop. Here the men, as well as the ladies, shared their news and gossip.

After breakfast Mike walked north on Cotton Street toward the railroad tracks. With the distinct chug and wheeze of an approaching train in the background, he spied Otis standing on the deserted platform. The marks of comb teeth showed in his thin, plastered down hair. Otis stared up the tracks with so much concentration he didn't notice Mike.

"Morning," Mike said. Otis swung around and nodded.

"Leaving town?" Mike asked.

Otis shook his head. "My wife and kiddies. They are a coming. All the way from Oklahoma."

"I see."

"Haven't seen 'em for pert near three months now." Otis stretched his spine and rubbed his mouth. Mike heard the train whistle, turned to watch it huff through a thicket of trees and roll to a stop. A long quiet tugged on Otis, standing there almost haggard in anticipation. The engine hissed and spewed clouds of steam.

Not wanting to intrude, Mike backed away a few steps before pivoting around to leave. He moved off a few paces and then glanced back. A woman with a baby on her hip stepped off the train and all but flung herself at Otis. Otis buried his face in the hollow between her shoulder and neck. Behind them a conductor helped a little boy off the train and set a heavy looking suitcase on the ground. Neither Otis nor his wife noticed the conductor.

Mike jammed his hands in his pockets and moved on.

No sign of life at the pickle factory so Mike meandered south along the highway until he came to the schoolyard. He cut across the playground to City Park just before the noon whistle blew. A platform had been assembled on the backside of the gazebo. The roof of the gazebo provided the framework for a backdrop that looked like one of the heavy velvet auditorium curtains from the schoolhouse. In fact it was. Mike recognized a tear about six inches from the floor. He'd noticed it the night of the Pickle Queen Contest. The top of the curtain draped from one side of the platform to the other with red, white and blue bunting hiding the top edge.

It appeared to him that anyone not at City Café was at City Park. At the baseball diamond, men were setting up sawhorse tables and big umbrellas. Ladies arrived with all manner of bundles. Mike moved among them unnoticed, hearing bits of conversation here and there. He knew it would all come back to him late at night to repeat in his head. He'd analyze it, find the patterns and rhythms of the local way of speaking. Little pieces of information like "...Bobby Jean'll need this ribbon for her table skirt..." Or "...That was the year it rained the whole time and we had to move everything into the schoolhouse..." And "...We've always done it this a way. Now scooch that table over a foot or two."

They resembled ants scurrying back and forth around the park in confusion and calamity.

Last night at the queen contest Mike overheard that a Mister Asa Adams, who owned the pickle factory, would be in town to crown the queen. Mike asked Rudy Cochran why Mr. Adams wasn't more active in the community. Rudy was under the impression that as long as Mr. Adams' manager kept the factory in the black, he didn't much care one way or another what was done to honor his business. In the end, the town was tickled pink to have factory jobs and Mr. Adams was happy to have nothing more to do with the town than to appear year after year to crown some starry-eyed girl whose future ended at the city limit sign.

The Pickle Festival served as a yardstick by which citizens measured their lives. Mike wondered what they'd do, what they'd talk about when it was over. Return to speculating about Effie Beck? Or would everyone forget her?

He worked himself around the park and ended up walking down Oak Street past Glory's Piano Parlor and the Alvins' house. Tommy Crane roared by in his dad's old hoopie. Mike didn't recognize the kid in the front seat with him, but Bill and Bart Steves from the boardinghouse were riding in the back.

He swung by the tank house to put on a fresh shirt but he still had more than an hour before time for the parade. He stared out at Jodean's garden, drooped and wilted in the hot dry heat. He thought of her bare feet there in the dirt and how her dark hair whipped in the breezes late of an evening when she weeded and watered. He still hadn't asked her about her strange habit of not wearing shoes or why everyone considered her "outsider" enough to judge the queen contest. Truth was, Ada's reaction to questions about Jodean made him think twice about upsetting the thin relationship that had budded between the two of them.

He checked his wallet for cash, three dollars and seventy-five cents. He slipped it into his hip pocket and glanced in the small mirror above the sink one more time. When he pivoted around, his eyes fell to the makeshift tub table where he'd tossed Effie Beck's letters from Joseph Dunlap. He picked them up and moved to the chair, where he held them to his nose. He drew a deep breath and immediately felt stupid, as if he hoped to inhale answers to the endless questions. Why were the old letters tied in a small bundle? And why were they sitting at the top of all the rest of the stuff jam-packed in the trunk?

There had been other letters, but most were concerned with the business of running a ranch, insurance notices, inquiries about the sale of livestock and so on.

When Mike had returned from Red's the night they'd lowered Paddy down the well, he'd read each one, probing every word for hidden meaning but found nothing to explain the relationship. The letter Joseph Dunlap mailed from Santa Fe resembled a tourist's rendition of the sites and a brief history of the place. One of the Fort Worth letters was not much more than a dry list of items he sold to a rancher's wife. The second Fort Worth letter was the one he'd read to Tubby. Dated a month later, the Dallas letter mentioned that he'd been to see a picture show and that he hoped some day to take Effie to see one. Mike gathered that, because Joseph Dunlap wanted Effie to experience something pleasant like movies, it meant he cared for her more than the average customer on his peddling rounds across the state. He signed that letter, '*Love Joe.*'

The last letter, the one from Oklahoma City, was the longest and most telling. In it, Joe Dunlap wrote the usual descriptions of the town and the weather, but added that business had dropped off because of the "god-awful drought."

Mike flipped the envelope over and compared the postmark with the others. All the letters were mailed at about four-week intervals except the last one, the Oklahoma letter. It was dated nine weeks after the Dallas letter. The tone was different in the Oklahoma letter, not as personal or deeply sincere.

The last paragraph read: "This is a nomad's life, not suitable for a family man. I cannot bear to be hemmed. I have heard that business is better in Chicago so I will be on my way there first thing tomorrow morning and leave these great dry plains behind." He signed it *Mr. Joseph Dunlap*, more formal than the others.

Mike slipped the letter back into the envelope. Was it his imagination or was the Oklahoma letter more tattered than the others? Had Effie Beck read and re-read this last letter? Had she written letters to him? Mike leaned his head back on the chair and let his mind drift. When he glanced at the clock, he realized he'd dozed for over an hour. He popped out of the chair, scattering the letters across the floor. When he stooped to pick them up, an odd awareness, maybe from having slept so hard for such a brief time, sent a thread of thought reaching back across time and distance. Effie Beck had a secret other than this relationship with Joe Dunlap, and the letters were a significant clue to what that secret was.

He positioned his fedora at a jaunty angle before rushing out the door. He found a good place to watch the parade on the corner of Main and Cedar Streets facing the courthouse. Crowds packed in the shady spots of sidewalk and little kids yelled at each other back and forth across the street. It was hot as hell, a terrible time of day for a parade. An hour or two later and a breeze would stir out of the south. But, as Mike had observed, events were unalterable from year to year in Cooperville. The mere suggestion of change was frowned upon.

He spied Red and Ada and their kids on the southeast corner of the courthouse. Red threw his head back, laughing with some man in a straw cowboy hat. Ada shaded her eyes with her hand. Reverend Rawlings and wife June, had found a good shady place on the courthouse steps.

It dawned on Mike how alone and removed from life he'd been for months. The thought swept over him so suddenly he shivered, then looked around to make sure no one standing close had seen him. Laughter echoed, little kids screeched and yelled. He was healing. Mike actually felt it happening.

Sheriff Neal walked down Cedar Street, right down the middle of it, scanning the crowds. The shadow of his big hat covered most of his face but Mike could see well the determined set of his jaw. The big star on his chest shone bright against his dazzle-white dress shirt. Tall with huge shoulders and a flat gut, his footsteps fell heavy and sure.

Mike couldn't imagine what the sheriff was doing in the middle of the street like that, eyes glued on the crowds. But no one else seemed to think the sheriff's behavior strange or paid much attention to him. Mike watched until he moved out of sight.

According to the clock on the courthouse tower, the parade wasn't due to begin just yet. So Neal couldn't be a part of the parade, though to be sure that's what it looked like. A self-proclaimed patriarch, initiator of all things, surveying his kingdom and leading the way for all others to follow.

Paddy Blue stepped down off the curb next to Mike and sat. Mike gave him a nod and asked, "Any idea what the sheriff was doing walking down the street like that?"

Paddy shrugged. "He always does it when there is a parade."

A slow thrump-rump, thrump-rump sound - that of a pounding drum gave Mike the first indication the parade was approaching, though from his vantage point, he couldn't see it. A minute or two later a fire truck stacked high with kids rounded the corner. A little boy cranked the siren with such enthusiasm people oohed and covered their ears. A Cavalry Division Band from a nearby army base followed the fire truck. They played a popular marching tune well enough, what he could hear of it over the siren, but their formation was a mess.

Everyone stood with hands or hats over hearts when the American flag fluttered by. Two girls followed the flag with a banner announcing Mr. Asa Adams, Parade Marshal. A big black open-top automobile inched by with Mr. Adams sitting on top of the back seat. He had a shock of red hair and appeared much younger than Mike would have thought. He would bet, too, that Mr. Adams hadn't a clue about Cooperville community concerns. Mike didn't recognize the man driving the car but, Emmet, wearing his police chief hat, was in the front seat, cartoonish and uncomfortable.

Next, a brand-spanking new Buick rolled by carrying a few gray haired men with confused looks on their faces. The sign on the side of the car said *Confederate War Veterans*. Behind the new Buick, a group of Veterans from the Great War marched in loose formation. Then, of all things, a bunch of jack-a-dandy cowboys and cowgirls mounted on prancing horses whooped and waved like they were having the time of their lives. One of the riders yelled at Red. Red waved his hat and whooped right back.

It appeared that every conceivable elected official had a truck, car or float in the parade. Justice of the Peace, County Judge, County Clerk. The Republican Party float was decorated with wilting flowers but the Democratic Party float sported a four-piece band and pretty girls throwing hard candy to the kids. Farmers got in on the fun.

Some drove their cotton combines down the middle of the street, others their hay baling machines. Clowns turned cartwheels and snapped balloons to the spectators lined up along the street.

The high school band marched by and again the crowd roared and clapped. A couple of twirlers pranced and waved, and Mike glimpsed Bill Steves blowing kisses to the drum major. She blushed and grinned, showing all her teeth, but never missed a high prancing step.

C.J.'s Grocery and Glory's Piano Parlor had gone in together on a float. C.J. had stacked boxes of produce and caged chickens at one end of a flatbed truck with his kids dressed like a butcher and housewife. Glory's piano had been secured to the back of the cab and some girl hammered away on the keys while Glory stood at her shoulder waving to the crowds. When the truck turned the corner a little too short, the rear wheel jumped the curb and Glory had to grab onto the girl to keep from falling. The piano let out an ugly *clong* noise and the crowd roared with laugher.

The last float in the parade carried the Pickle Festival Queen contestants. Jodean explained to Mike that the whole purpose of the parade was to lead the queen contestants to City Park for the announcement of the winner and the official crowning ceremony. Behind the queen's float were two open-top cars. Cora Mae Travis and Faye Lackland were riding in one, and two older women Mike didn't recognize rode in the other. Paddy stood, leaned to say, "Past queens."

The crowd filled the street behind the last of the parade and trailed it out to City Park. Mike had hoped he'd see Jodean but so far, no sign of her. Hearing a car approach from behind, Mike and Paddy moved aside.

Tubby drove up next them and rolled his window down. "How 'bout a ride boys?"

Paddy climbed in the back, Mike in the front.

Tubby said, "Frances is with the other ladies at the crowning platform. No need to rush getting there though. They can't get started without the mayor." Tubby chuckled at his own joke. "I told Emmet there wouldn't be any parade trouble from mischief-makers this year. Once you convince kids there'll be consequences to pay they'll cool the merry-making. Yessirree."

"The day isn't over with yet," Paddy said from the back seat.

"No, now, I even put Tommy Crane in charge of the platform assembly so the high school kids would feel a little pride by taking a part in things, you know?" Tubby tooted his horn so the crowd would part and let him pass.

TOMMY CRANE AND Calvin cut through an alley on the way to City Park. Bill and Bart Steves were ahead, waiting for them on the corner.

Tommy clamped a hand on Calvin's shoulder. "I told that skinny Larry Jenks from Pole Cat Creek he could borrow the naked women cards for a week if he'd pull the rope to drop the tarp."

Calvin watched the ground as he walked. "Somebody will figure I was the one to paint that lady. My old man is going to kill me."

"No way. All of us can stand right there in front of the gazebo and can't nobody accuse us of anything. Larry runs like a rabbit. Nobody'll ever know it's him dropping the rope, let alone catch him. They'll be too busy gawking."

"I ain't goin' within a block of that platform. You know everybody's gonna know I painted it." Calvin was on the verge of tears.

"You should have worried about that before now." Tommy wheeled around and took off across the ballpark toward the gazebo.

Bill and Bart Steves looked at one another. Bill said, "He's right, Calvin. If you're with us in front of the platform, it'll sure be hard for anyone to point a finger our way. On the other hand, if you're off hiding, you gonna look guilty right off the bat."

Calvin slumped against a cottonwood tree. "I had other things on my mind when I agreed to paint that…picture."

"I never did figure out why you agreed to do it."

Calvin looked surprised. "Why…didn't Tommy tell you? Didn't I hear him say you were coming to San Antonio with us tonight?"

Bill turned to Bart and told him to go save the three of them a place close to the platform. With Bart out of hearing range, Bill turned back to Calvin. "I never said I'd go. I just asked what was so special about San Antonio and Tommy laughed at me."

"*Whores*. That's what's so special. Tommy claims he knows right where to go to get all of it you want. Cheap."

Bill's mouth dropped. "Oh." He shifted his weight. "Well, like I said, we just as well get a place to stand in front. We're either going to get blamed for this or not."

Calvin pushed away from the tree and walked with his head dropped forward. "Bill?"

"Yeah?"

"If we get through this, are you gonna to go to San Antonio?"

"I ain't sure San Antonio is ready for me, Calvin." Bill chuckled at his own chicken self.

JODEAN HELPED JUNE arrange jars of pickles and baked goods on the same church sponsored table she'd worked at for the last five or so years. She'd managed to see most of the parade as the procession arrived at the park and disbanded around the gazebo.

It hadn't rained since the week Mike arrived and Effie Beck disappeared and the hot, dry air squeezed Jodean, made her lungs feel too small to hold the amount of oxygen she needed to move about. Perspiration rolled down between her breasts, her stomach quivered and she wanted a cool drink of something sweet in the worst way.

When she looked up, Mike was crossing the gap between the crowd and the sweep of booths and tables outlining the park. He carried a Coca-Cola in each hand, stared at the ground as he walked. He stopped at her table and handed her one of the drinks. "I bet we can see the announcement ceremony if we stand on that bench I spotted over there in the shade."

Jodean sipped her drink, let the blessed cool liquid trickle down her parched throat. She followed Mike to the bench he mentioned and took his offered hand so she could step up onto it. He climbed onto the bench beside her.

Tubby moved to the center of the gazebo platform. Asa Adams followed him. Jodean had seen men like Mr. Adams pass through town often on business and couldn't imagine what they thought of a place like Cooperville.

Faye, along with Frances and Ada, followed Mr. Adams, and all four took a position at the far side of the platform. The Pickle Queen contestants stood opposite them. From Jodean's vantage point, it looked as if a wind stirred the curtain behind the platform, but she hadn't felt a breeze.

Tubby drew a deep breath to begin his announcements but Evonne Noble started a noisy sneezing fit. Tubby stared until her daddy stepped forward to hand her a handkerchief.

When Tubby was satisfied he had everyone's full attention, he said, "As mayor of Cooperville, Texas, it is my honor and pleasure to welcome all visitors to our fair little city—"

Evonne sneezed a couple of times more, then snorted into her daddy's handkerchief.

"At this time, I'd like to introduce the Queen Committee…"

Jodean sipped her Coca-Cola and glanced at Mike. He'd rolled his shirt sleeves to above his elbows and caught her looking.

Tubby finished with the announcements and introduced Mr. Adams, who took Tubby's place in the center of the platform.

"Ladies and gentlemen, it is an honor to announce the third runner up in this year's Pickle Queen Court, Miss Dee Dee Bishop." Dee Dee moved to center stage behind Mr. Adams with a forced smile on her face. Everyone applauded.

"Second runner-up, Miss Evonne Noble." Evonne started sniffling. Mr. Adams looked around as if ready to bolt and run. He continued. "First runner-up, Miss Esther Wiggins." Esther bounced across the stage waving and smiling, using her well-rehearsed cheerleader, crowd-pleasing technique.

Mr. Adams shuffled the bits of paper in his hands then smiled at Doreen Crumps. "And, finally, ladies and gentlemen, this year's Pickle Queen, Miss—"

As Jodean watched the proceedings, the curtain moved behind Dee Dee. Mr. Adams noticed the movement too and lost his place reading from his card. Before he could find it again, the red, white and blue bunting fell on top of the girls. They dropped to the floor screeching like mashed cats. Where the bunting had been attached at the top of the old auditorium curtain, a wide dark cloth unfurled and the whole platform swayed ever so slightly.

The crowd let out a collective gasp. Jodean clamped her hand over her mouth but couldn't bring herself to look away from what would, no doubt, go down in the annals of Cooperville history as the most shocking festival prank since its organization in 1899.

There, painted on a banner, for the whole town to view, was a reclining naked woman. Her long dark hair fanned out over a pillow and a huge gold crown topped her head. Bright green jewels in the crown – Jodean assumed they were supposed to be emeralds – were set in place to spell *Pickles*. A small heart-shaped red pillow covered the place where her legs came together and her big red lips stretched into a wicked grin.

Mr. Adams stood with his back to the townspeople and gaped. Esther's dad climbed onto the platform and made a desperate attempt to disentangle the girls from the bunting. All four screamed hysterically, not having any idea what had happened. Tubby shook his head in defeat. Then, red-faced and flustered, he stepped to the center of the platform and held out his arms in an attempt to hush the crowd.

Half the people turned their backs and started to move away, dragging little children by arms or collars. The other half, mostly men, stared or guffawed and slapped each other on the back. When Tubby's efforts to gain control proved futile, he rushed to the banner and attempted to pull it down. Sheriff Neal and Acting Police Chief Emmet joined him, but the thing wouldn't budge.

Jodean couldn't stop laughing in spite of her embarrassment looking at nakedness with Mike right next to her. He yanked off his hat and doubled over with laughing tears in his eyes. Finally he jumped down from the bench and held out a hand so she could do the same.

After that episode, the rest of the festival went by so quick Jodean would wonder later if it really happened. Mike walked her back to the church booth where Ada, scheduled to help with the first shift, and Red were trying to designate a place to meet later. Mike and Red greeted each other like old friends.

"By damn, Mike, I always say, leave it to the kids to liven things up around here."

"Any idea who did it?" Mike asked.

"Oh, yeah. But Emmet and Tubby are never going to be able to prove a thing…" Red let his voice trail when Otis Bartel walked by with a baby in his arms and a willowy woman at his side.

"Hi there," Ada called to them, not leaving the slightest opportunity for uncomfortable quiet.

Otis licked his lips and said, "Like y'all to meet my wife, Eula."

Mike and Red tipped their hats.

"Pleased to meet you," Jodean said. She didn't dare look at Ada who surely was having her same thought – that sooner or later a logical explanation for Faye having been seen with Otis on occasion would surface and crush town gossips once and for all. Namely, Frances and Cora Mae. They'd blabbed about an assumed affair so much the whole town had already tried and convicted the pair behind their backs.

"And this here's our baby girl, Jessie, and little boy, Luke," Eula said.

"Otis," Red said. "I hope you explained to Eula that things such as that fiasco over yonder are rare occurrences here in Cooperville." Everyone grinned at the ground.

"Boys is boys," Otis said.

"Red knows that better than just about anybody, right honey?" Ada said. "Back in his heyday, he masterminded festival shenanigans. Painted a bunch of pigs lime green and set them loose on the auditorium stage in the middle of the queen contest."

Jodean changed the subject. "Eula, me and my momma have a beauty shop right down that street there, on the left. There's a sign in the window. All newcomers get one free shampoo and set. Come by anytime you like."

"In fact," Ada added, "we should time our appointments one after the other. That way we can watch after each other's kids."

"That's mighty nice of both of you," Eula smiled.

"I was just about to take my kids over to ride the merry-go-round," Red said. "Maybe Luke there would like it if y'all come along."

"Think I'll go see what Tubby found out about the little mishap on the platform," Mike said.

"Oh yeah?" Red's eyes twinkled. "You goin' to try to find out who posed for the picture, I bet!"

Everyone laughed and began to drift in different directions. Ada waved good-bye to Eula and then whirled around to Jodean. "This ought to be real interesting!"

"Now stop, Ada. I always said, and you know it too, that there's an explanation. Faye would never run around behind Neal's back."

"I know, I know, but I can just hear Frances—"

"Hear me what?" Frances set her big handbag on the table. "Did y'all see that woman with the man Faye keeps company with?"

Ada and Jodean held their ribs and shivered with laughter. What would Frances have to nag about now that Otis had a wife right here in Cooperville?

"Wish you'd share a little of your fun," Frances said in a huff.

Ada opened her mouth to say something but was seized by another fit of snickering. Jodean tried to concentrate on helping a lady who couldn't decide whether she wanted June Rawlings' coconut white cake or Glory's German chocolate. Frances drifted off and, after the lady made her purchase, Jodean side-glanced Ada. They leaned against each other and pealed with laughter all over again.

June Rawlings and Bessy Alvin appeared two hours later to relieve them. As Jodean and Ada moved around the grounds – Jodean heading for home and Ada looking for Red and the kids – Ada asked, "You're coming to the street dance aren't you?" When Jodean hesitated, Ada stopped and looked her square in the eye and waited.

Jodean sighed. "I need to go home and check on Momma. She left after the parade. One of her headaches."

"So you rush home to wait on her hand and foot?"

Ada had always sparkled with an inborn goodness. Since they were in grade school she'd been the one to take a stand for what she believed, most often making herself unpopular in the process. Ada had an uncanny gift for seeing into things, could detect pretenses, or determine the true nature of a person by the glint in their eyes. Jodean witnessed it often over the years. So the few times Ada spoke up against Cora Mae, Jodean took notice.

But the arguing points in Jodean's head never came to a concluding resolution. She knew Ada thought Cora Mae was bleeding her, using her to feed her own inadequacies, that Cora Mae used the circumstance of their lives together like a hangman's noose. And Jodean could understand why Ada would think that, but she couldn't see a way to change it. The few times Jodean tried to take charge of her life – in little ways, of course – Cora Mae reminded her of how much she owed her, would ask where she thought she'd be without her. Then Jodean would feel ashamed and trapped and wished she'd never mentioned the subject of leaving. Better to find whatever contentment she could in the way things were.

Ada dropped her eyes, "Sorry."

"To tell you the truth *I* haven't felt too good lately. I may just go home and go to bed."

Ada studied her.

"Truly, Ada."

But by the time Jodean walked the three blocks home, she'd made up her mind to go to the street dance after all.

Cora Mae was in the kitchen making a sandwich. "I gave up on you ever coming back to fix something to eat."

Jodean opened the refrigerator and poured herself a glass of milk and walked out of the kitchen.

Cora Mae smirked. "Well, hello to you, too."

Jodean bathed, powdered her face and brushed her hair until her scalp was sore and then climbed the stairs to her room and stretched across the cool sheets. She decided to wear her yellow dotted Swiss dress from Easter two years back – without stockings. They were hot and too hard to come by.

"Where do you think you're going?" Cora yelled louder than the radio noise when Jodean came down the stairs an hour later.

"To the street dance."

"You needn't bother. I heard that drifter you's so sweet on left town."

Jodean let the front door slam at her back, drew herself together and thrust her chin forward. It was twilight already, that dark blue time of day, a sort of benediction for the eyes, affirming the end of light had come.

When she rounded the corner at Cotton and Main, a four-man band, fiddler, guitar, bass and piano, were playing a snappy cowboy song from a little stage built a foot above street level. She stopped where she was and let her eyes and ears take it all in. Little Pete danced with Tootie Sue but Red and Ada were nowhere in sight. Couples whirled around in the middle of the street.

"Jodean?"

She turned. Mike held his hand out to her.

"Care to dance?"

She had to ball her hands into tight fists to keep excitement from spilling out of her palms. Whether it was Mike's sweet eyes – so like deep water, neither blue nor gray but a shimmering shade in between – or the ague causing her to feel that way, she couldn't guess.

MIKE DECIDED JODEAN felt like air in his arms, as if he shouldn't exhale too heavy or she'd blow away. "I've never been to a street dance before."

"They don't have them in North Carolina?"

"Guess folks back home don't know what they're missing."

When she smiled, he filled his lungs and tried to hold his breath until the tune ended. He walked her back to the sidewalk.

"Mike, you've been here for two months now. I'm curious to know what you think of our little town."

"Friendly. But there's a social order here that I haven't quite figured out."

Jodean moved her eyes away from his face. "When you do, will you explain it to me?"

Her voice was flat when she said it. In the next instant, the band struck a loud tune that turned out to be Cotton-Eyed Joe. Mike held out his hand and was relieved when Jodean took it because he hadn't understood the sudden change in her. Back in the middle of the street, they moved in and out of the other dancers like they'd been doing it all their lives. It amazed him how Jodean fit perfectly into the crook of his arm.

When the Alvins bumped into them, Mike had to tighten his hold around her ribs but she didn't seem to mind. Little kids jigged on the outskirts of the dancing throng. Teenagers made a line and locked arms and kicked and scooted in circles, most in big cowboy hats and boots, all yelling like a pack of coyotes. Across the way, Mike glimpsed Red yelling a cattle call.

After that he deposited Jodean, panting and fanning herself, on the courthouse steps and went to get cold drinks. When he came back she was talking with Clyde Cheevers and his wife. Mike hadn't seen Clyde since the day of the search at the Beck place.

"Well, would you look here," Clyde said when Mike returned. "I've been meaning to give you a call. I read the piece in the paper about Effie Beck that you wrote. Have you heard anything?"

Mike handed Jodean a Grapette and shook Clyde's hand. "No. Afraid not."

"The reason I been meaning to talk to you is a neighbor lady of ours, lives the other side of Pole Cat Creek, had her elderly aunt move in with her, you see. And this old aunt saw the picture you put in the newspaper. Said if nobody rushed her about it sooner or later she'd place where she'd seen that woman. Meaning, of course, Effie Beck."

"What about the man in the picture?"

"She didn't mention anything about him — Ho! There's Ed Noble over yonder. If you'll excuse us, we'll go say hello to Ed. Me and Ed been talking back and forth 'bout time sharing a haymaker."

"You'll let somebody know if you hear any more?" Mike called after Clyde.

Clyde waved and nodded. "Sure thing. Oh, and say, Miss Jodean, you keep up whatever you're feeding him. He looks a mite better than the day I give him a hitch to town."

Clyde's remark made Jodean blush. When she recovered, she asked Mike, "It's not just a matter of curiosity is it? About Effie Beck, I mean."

"Did Red or Ada tell you about the letters we found?"

"Ada and I have been so busy getting ready for this brouhaha that we haven't talked about much of anything else."

"Jodean, I have a feeling Effie Beck had a whole other life – one that none of you knew about, a different purpose, different from what everyone thought. The letters don't say much, not in words."

"Who are they from?"

"Man by the name of Joseph Dunlap. Signed some of his letters *Joe*. Breezy remembers he was a peddler some time back. Jericho confirmed it but he was a small boy at the time and couldn't offer much more. I wish you'd read the letters, tell me what you think."

They were quiet for a while after that, sat on the courthouse steps to watch people move around the square. Red and Ada switched partners with Tubby and Frances and later Mike glimpsed Glory Hughes dancing with one of the bridge crew.

"Tell me about Glory," Mike said.

"Her husband was killed in a horrible tractor accident. About six months later she gave birth to a little baby boy and he died, too. The years since have been pretty hard for her."

When Otis asked Ada to dance, Red asked Faye. Faye, who was about three inches taller than Red, appeared completely out of character, less reserved and laughing. In fact it was the first time Mike had seen her laugh. They were doing a kind of jitterbug and Red spun her away from him then twirled her back in. Impossible to imagine Red not having a good time anywhere, at any time. Women and children, even men, were drawn to his big happy grin.

Beyond the dancers, standing in the shadows, Mike glimpsed Neal watching every move Red and Faye made and the look on his face was not what he'd call sweet. Neal never smiled, never participated, set himself apart, above everyone, like some pompous-assed god. Poor Faye.

The last song Mike and Jodean danced to was a slow tune about being somebody's darling. Mike would bet the word *"darling"* originated in the deep south. Georgia, Alabama, maybe even the Carolinas. But Texans turned it into an endearment of unlimited proportions. He wished he could keep dancing in front of the courthouse in Cooperville, Texas for the next month or two, stay lost in the maze of the town's riddles and puzzles. He touched his chin to Jodean's temple and she went soft in his arms.

Around midnight, with the street dance winding down, and a slip of silver moon on the horizon, Mike walked Jodean home. She paused at the front porch steps. For once her hands were still, clasped behind her back. Her chin tilted up to him but in the dim light all he could see was the moon's reflection in her eyes. "Thank you," was all she said.

He leaned forward and quickly kissed her cheek, afraid to touch her any more than that – alone and away from the crowds, he couldn't trust the heat behind his infatuation. She tucked her chin and went into the house.

Mike's insides quivered too much to think about going back to the tank house. He walked along Cooperville Spring road to the spot where Red said he and Ada had seen Effie Beck wandering around in the dark. From there he took the fork in the road that led to the Bat House. In moon glow he crossed a meadow to double back toward town. *Cooperville.* Mike whispered the name and thought of Jodean, her father, the pickle factory. All of it capsulized in his mind, a tiny fairytale kind of place.

He had read that people flocked to this valley as far back as 1800 to escape religious constraints. Later, Civil War criminals arrived hoping to escape prosecution. The Irish came here fleeing the potato famine. And here he was, Mike Lemay, running from – what? Hard times like everyone before him.

Most of the families in the county considered themselves ranchers – livestock men who bred and raised cattle, goats or sheep. Those who could stomach the gamble were farmers. It was easy to tell the two apart.

Ranchers walked upright and tall but had bowed legs, wore boots with two inch heels. They tucked the inside seam of their heavy jeans in their boot tops. Hats were wide brimmed Stetsons, beaver if they were the *haves*, Mexican straw if they were the *have-nots*. Ranchers' fingernails were clean, boots dusty and most grew thick bushy mustaches to protect their lips from sunburn.

A farmer didn't need a mustache because his head was always turned down to the earth, hoe in hand. Mike thought of his father out in the fields long after others called it a day. He was glad in a way that his dad died before the worst of the hard times hit the country.

Farmers in Texas wore Dickie overalls, as had farmers back in North Carolina, and brown brogans packed thick with dirt. They had humped backs to match the ranchers' bowed legs and wore slouch hats pushed low on the head.

Ranchers' tools were rope, thick leather gloves to protect hands from rope burn, chaps to protect legs, jiggling spurs, branding irons. Most had hay meadows wired off from their herds where summer grass was left to grow tall so it could be cut and baled three or four times a season, depending on rainfall. Neighboring ranchers got together to cut the tall bluestem and grama grasses using a bar mower, bull rake, and baler. Necessary ranching supplies were few. Barbed wire, staples for fence posts, various medications for livestock, oats for the horses.

Farmers' tools, on the other hand, as Mike knew so well, were hoe, plow, and cultivator. By the calendar, farmers planted and harvested. What they didn't sell or use was fed to hogs and chickens. Farmers around town grew mostly cotton and corn. The farmer's work animal was the mule; the rancher's a horse. Ranchers and farmers talked about the land as if they knew it intimately all the way down a hundred feet into the soil where they found life-sustaining water.

On the sidewalks in town, farmers and ranchers discussed bottomland, black land, sandy land. Post oak savannahs, river bottoms, rocky hilltops and cedar groves.

Red, a descendant of the Irishmen who immigrated to Texas shores, claimed farming was a "crap shoot." His take on farming was that if the weather held with decent amounts of rain at reasonable intervals, the boll weevils would get your crop. If it turned out to be a dry year, grasshoppers were the scourge. And any year, wet or dry, mites could be the ruin.

"If all that don't blow your goddamned skirt up," Red had said, "the sonofabitching prices could drop out from under a fella just because everybody had a good crop and cotton so plentiful it's not worth a man's pissant sweat!"

Men like Clyde Cheevers and Breezy, though, complained that raising livestock required too much time on horseback. Cattle were stupid, nasty animals that were hard to handle and sometimes dangerous. Ranchers had to battle screwworm, black leg, mastitis, and grass bellies. Ranching required a lot of land to graze enough cattle to make a profit. But a cotton farmer could raise a pretty fair crop with a little acreage and good weather. Ranchers were always off over some hill – at least in their minds. And they ate supper out of a tin can while squatting under a tree – if they were lucky enough to find a tree.

Ranchers hired cowhands to help with branding in the spring and roundup in the fall. Most of the cowboys moved from ranch to ranch to help with seasonal chores much the same way tenant farmers and migrant workers moved back and forth across the state following harvest seasons.

It was a complementary existence. Ranchers bought the farmers' corn and oats for winter stock. *Tick.* Farmers needed winter work and an occasional calf to butcher. *Tock.*

Land, Cooperville's common element, flourished thanks to the respect of the farmer and the rancher. Pity the people in states to the north where the land was literally blowing away. People here were genial robust souls, all of them. He thought the town would sing and play and dance just the same in the worst or best of times.

Mike tried again to imagine where he might fit in. And if, by some chance he managed to find permanent work, would Jodean fit in with him? Would she be willing? In reality that was the meat of what gnawed at him.

The sky twinkled like a dark umbrella held aloft by a sliver of moon. Mike moved in the night more by feel than sight. He heard the muffled music of the four-man band back in town. Until that moment, he'd thought he suffered the loss of dignity alone. Then, like voices whispering from times past, the truth of his self-indulgent self-pity came clear to him and he was repulsed. But just as sharp was the feeling of relief, for a man can change only when he recognizes his truths.

Mike walked across Cooperville Spring Creek bridge back to the tank house where he watched a light in the upstairs window at the back of the house. He was pretty sure it was Jodean's window. A thin black shadow of indistinguishable shape moved, bent over, straightened. A moment later the light went out.

There were lessons to be learned from all his searching and pecking around. But for now, he was content to climb to his loft bed and let his tired mind untangle.

PART II

CORA MAE SHUT her mouth and then tried to lick her lips, but they stuck together. She thought it was morning, but soon realized that light filtering into the room came from the hallway. It was just like Jodean to bang around at night when she, Cora Mae, needed sleep the most. She pulled up onto her elbow and opened her dry mouth to let air rise from her stomach.

She heard Jodean cough a few times and flush the toilet then the light went out.

Cora Mae plopped back onto her pillow. She had a hard time thinking about Jodean being all grown sometimes. The idea had a worrisome edge to it. Of course that was stupid. Jodean was way past childhood, but still... They'd come a long way together with a lot working against them.

She couldn't imagine what would become of Jodean, what her future held. The girl just couldn't make a sensible decision. Jodean needed her momma – always would.

Cora Mae stared at the dark corners of her bedroom. Who could guess how much better off she would have been all these years without the worry of a skinny little child hanging on her? For one thing, she wouldn't have had these health problems. Buddy – God rest her husband's shifty soul – had insisted on a kid and all these years her reputation suffered because Jodean had been in the picture. Probably, Cora Mae thought, she wouldn't have been passed by so many times when everybody was picking committee people and such as that. Just this week the girl went and made a mess of the pie crust and caused her, Cora Mae, not to win the pie contest at the festival for a second year in a row.

Still, Jodean was all she had and she guessed she'd better stop tearing herself apart like this. Eating her heart out was what was happening, making her have gas and sleep with her mouth open and giving her a headache and all.

No. Since the day Buddy died, Cora Mae had pinned all her hopes on Jodean. And God knows how much she loved the girl in spite of everything. Tears welled in Cora Mae's eyes. She did love the girl. She loved Jodean like nobody else could. Like nobody else ever would.

The hall light came on again and Cora Mae heard Jodean open the medicine cabinet above the bathroom sink.

Buddy had been crazy about Jodean. The day he brought her home he couldn't say enough about all that dark curly hair. Sat her on his lap, he did sometimes, and brushed it like it was black silk from China. And he'd laugh at her for kicking off her shoes as soon as he put them on her.

When Cora Mae heard Jodean cough again, she untangled herself from the sheets and moved down the hallway to the bathroom. The door was half shut so she gave it a little shove. Jodean was kneeling in front of the commode. "What's wrong?"

Jodean shook her head, grabbed the sides of the toilet and spewed yellow water.

Cora stepped over her and opened the window to clear the sour smell. "What the hell you been eatin'?"

When Jodean didn't answer, Cora Mae went to the kitchen to get her headache rag and while there fixed a glass of warm salt water. Back in the bathroom she handed the glass to Jodean. "Sip on this. It'll help. Can I get you anything else?"

The girl just looked blank-faced, the most unfeeling child a mother could ever have. "Well, call out if you need me for something, hear?"

RED TOOK ONE look at the brindle cow he'd penned the day before and knew it was time for some serious doctoring. Her swollen bag was as big as a feed sack, her udders red as berries. Her calf, curled into a tight ball in the corner, was in big trouble, too. It hadn't suckled for three days and now lay in a starving stupor.

Pete walked up beside Red with a bucket of milk and a huge baby bottle. "Momma washed out the bottle." He held it up for Red to see.

"This might get a little tricky, Pete. That ol' momma is mad as hell at me for penning her up and she's not likely to thank me, or you, for feeding her baby. I'll have to get the calf out of the pen before you can see to it."

Red eased the gate open. The cow lowered her head, dug a front hoof into the ground and threw dirt over her back.

"Ooo-doggie, now ain't I scared," Red whispered to her. "You better let me get to that young'un of yours or he's gonna starve." The cow laid her ears back and swung her great horns at Red in a gesture of threat.

"You better tie her to a post, Daddy."

"Hell, Pete, I's sweet-talking these beauties since before Jesus was born." Red moved closer to the calf without taking his eyes off the cow. She dug at the ground again and let out a ferocious bellow.

"Now, now, momma." Red cooed to her. He was now between her and the calf. "You know I'm not going to hurt your sweet little baby, now, don't you? Yeah. Sweet little momma, you are." He backed closer to the calf.

The cow blinked her large onyx eyes and side-glanced Pete waiting outside the pen with his bucket of milk. Red stopped moving for a minute, let her take in the situation. "See, we aren't going to rush you," he said to the cow.

Slowly, he reached down and grasped the calf by the ears and tail. When it didn't struggle or whine, Red thought it might already be dead. But then its warmth registered on his hands and he knew that the strange animal sense he'd seen so many times had kicked in. By some trick of nature, a calf can sense a doomed situation, and will go limp as death and take its chances.

Keeping his eyes locked on the cow, Red began to drag the calf down the rails back toward the gate. The cow pawed the ground with each front foot and let out a lung's worth of air through her nostrils, blowing dust everywhere. "Now there's a sweet ol' girl," Red whispered.

Pete had seen his dad work this way enough to know to stay far back from the gate. When Red decided to make his escape it would be quick and dangerous.

"Son, take a look…make sure the gate is unlatched."

"Yes, sir. It is."

Red burst through the gate, dropped the half-conscious calf at Pete's feet and slammed the gate latch so quick it was all a blur. The cow charged then, but more for show than anything else. She could have busted through the flimsy boards and rusty latch with ease. It often seemed to Red that gates and fences had come to be mental barriers as much as physical barriers for his cattle.

And the same probably held true for humans too. Most never test the strength of the things holding them back.

He reached in a back pocket for his handkerchief and wiped his sweaty face. When he turned, Pete was already on his way to the barn, struggling under the weight of the calf in his skinny arms. Red picked up the boy's bucket of milk, the bottle and followed.

Inside the barn, Pete lowered the calf onto clean hay he'd scattered in an empty stall earlier. He held the bottle while Red filled it with milk.

"Now dip your finger in that little bit of milk left in the bucket and rub it on his mouth," Red said. Pete did as he was told and the calf worked its nostrils. "Some more on his nose so he can get a good whiff." The calf twitched its tail and licked.

"Do you think he'll be all right?" Pete asked.

"Hard to say, Son. But one thing for sure, if you get him to suck that bottle, he'll think you're his momma and it'll be up to you to feed him until he can graze on pasture grass and chase heifers."

Pete cradled the calf's head in his lap and worked the huge nipple into its mouth.

Later that same day, Red drove to the feed store in town to buy some Underwood Udder Balm for the cow. As he got out of the car, Faye called his name from across the street. "Is Ada with you today?" she asked when she caught up with him.

"No, I'm making a quick run to the feed store is all."

"Oh, well. I, uh...I have to stop by Neal's office." She glanced at the lunch basket in her hands then at Neal's courthouse window. "But after that I'm going home and...would it be too much trouble for you to stop by? I have some of Ada's tablecloths she loaned me for the queen contest and a platter that belongs to her, too. It'd save me a trip out to your place."

Red told her he'd be glad to, but when he knocked on Faye's front door about an hour later, it was Neal who opened it just enough to stick his head through.

"Faye has some things she wants me to take to Ada." Red said.

Without a word Neal walked off into the dark house. Red heard movement, Neal's lowered voice, then Neal re-appeared with a platter stacked with tablecloths.

"Much obliged." *Asshole sheriff*, Red added to himself. As he drove away from the Lackland mansion, he thought how sad and low-down that whole marriage was.

That night he told Ada what had happened and Ada relayed all the town gossip concerning Faye and Otis.

"You know," Ada said, "if any of it turns out to be true I don't think anyone would blame Faye. Neal is such a cold-blooded man, like he's missing a measure of warmth in his heart."

"Darling, if Neal ever figures out the rest of us are on to his shortcomings, Faye'll be the one to pay."

"What do you mean?"

"A big fish like Neal has to feed off little fish and Faye is the handiest one. It's how he makes himself feel noble. And the need to feel noble is what drives Neal Lackland."

MIKE ROLLED TO a stop in front of Brother Matthew Rawlings' modest home next door to the church. He'd put off interviewing Matthew and June as long as he could and would rather bathe in boiling acid than sit at a preacher's dinner table. For a time he'd considered taking them off his interview list, but Tom Coker insisted he needed to round out the range of occupations of interviewees.

Mike was short on patience when it came to gospel talk and not at all sure how he'd handle it if Brother Rawlings started a spiel. It irritated the hell out of him that preachers thought they had all the answers. One Sunday the topic would be about the sin of judging others and the very next Sunday the same preacher would stand in his pulpit and tell his flock they were all a bunch of sinners doomed to hell for breathing air. If that wasn't judging others, Mike didn't know what was. Preachers were the most judgmental lot under God's blue sky.

The day had already been too long. On the spur of a moment that morning he decided to pull the brakes off the Model A pickup truck to check for wear. They looked safe enough. He figured it was a hundred degrees in the shade when he finished getting everything adjusted and back together. By the time he backed out of the drive, the air inside the tank house smelled like burned toast. It had been days since he'd seen or heard anything of Jodean. He'd thought she might show up if she heard or saw him working on the truck.

Cora Mae kept pinning notes on the screen saying Jodean wouldn't be cooking on this or that particular day. The only sign of life had been the low garble of radio music. And the only thing *that* told him was that Cora Mae was holding vigil with the radio like always.

Matthew Rawlings was waiting for Mike at his front door. Mike turned off the ignition and glanced at the funeral home across the street. And the burned out hotel across a side street from the funeral home. It just didn't feel right to start an interview with preconceived notions about the preacher's attitude. A waste of time for all of them.

June Rawlings served lemonade from a tray and said maybe they could relax and talk a while before rushing to eat. The manse was light and airy with thin curtains tied back exposing the windows. The house smelled of pine oil mingled with the aroma of slow cooked beef and fresh bread. Wood floors were waxed to a high shine, hooked and braided rugs had been placed to catch the heaviest foot traffic. Clearly, June Rawlings spent a lot of time dusting, polishing, and fluffing. Mike imagined her using a level to make sure the pictures – the efforts of an amateur artist no doubt – were in precise alignment. Or was it Brother Rawlings who performed the rituals of perfection?

"I see you've noticed Matthew's hobby." June took a seat next to her husband.

"I paint to relax and think through my sermons," Brother Rawlings said.

"That one there," June indicated an oil painting above the sofa, "is how he sees heaven."

"Lots of clear blue sky, peaceful, green. The vision came to me while reading First Chronicles, chapter 16, verse 31, '*Let the heavens be glad, and let the earth rejoice.*' "

To Mike it didn't look that much different from Jodean's garden in the early morning hours when everything was still hazy with silver mist.

"And that's our daughter." June pointed to a photograph on the small table next to Mike's chair.

Brother Rawlings leaned forward. "She's in Phoenix, Arizona…"

"…working for a radio station." June finished the sentence, and added, "She sees and hears about all kinds of exciting things out there. Her last letter said she's going to try to get transferred to California and, if she does, she wants us to come for a long visit."

"A long visit." Brother Rawlings repeated June's words.

A while later, Brother Rawlings said a brief prayer of thanks over a platter of pot roast and potatoes June had set on the table.

"How long have you lived in Cooperville?" Mike helped himself to the potatoes.

"Let's see now. We..." Brother Rawlings thought for a moment.

"...replaced Brother Jake Blue in '28." June passed a basket of bread.

"In 1928, yes. Brother Jake died without warning. Heart attack. I didn't know him well. But from the way his death affected this town, I've assumed he was a saint."

Mike had to bite the inside of his mouth to keep from smiling. Brother Rawlings slurred his *s*'s and nearly spit when he said *saint*. Mike pictured children ducking behind church pews to mock the man.

"It must have been hard replacing someone so well thought of," Mike said.

"In some ways it was, but the bank closed down about that same time and..."

"...people were glad to have Matthew to turn to..."

"...And I reminded them that God is merciful and to have faith."

"How about you, Mrs. Rawlings," Mike asked. "Was it hard for you to move here?"

"Oh my goodness, no. The people..."

"...are so friendly here. But then June is the outgoing sort. That's one of the things that attracted me to her forty years ago."

They looked at each other from the far ends of the dining table and Mike watched a lifetime pass between them. The skin around June's eyes resembled over-washed lace. Her body appeared as soft as fluffed pillows. Brother Rawlings wore tiny wire glasses hooked over big ears. His face was big and square-jawed.

By the time Mike drove away from the curb, he'd decided that June and Matthew Rawlings were one body with two talking heads. They took turns finishing each other's sentences the rest of the evening, so he had no idea whether or not he could use the information he'd gleaned, how he'd separate their thoughts.

But it had been a relief not to have to put up with a lot of shaming mumbo-jumbo church talk. When Brother Rawlings walked Mike out to the truck, he casually invited him to church services, as if inviting him to go fishing, and that was the end of it.

Mike made it back to the tank house by nine-thirty that evening. Walking across the dewy yard, he noticed a light on in the open upstairs window. He heard Cora Mae growling and carrying on. He froze and held his breath to listen, but try as he might he wasn't able to make out what she was saying. There were no other voices, no sounds other than the low drone of night insects. A shadow moved close to the window curtain and leaned down. It was Cora Mae and this time Mike heard every word.

"You let him put his hands on you, didn't you? Answer me girl."

The hair on the back of Mike's neck stood on end. He strained to hear a reply. Nothing. Cora Mae straightened and moved away from the window snarling words he couldn't make out. After that the light went out and a door slammed so hard the thin curtain over the window puffed from the force of air.

Mike clamped his jaw teeth. Something wasn't right. He couldn't take his eyes off the window. Why hadn't he heard Jodean? Where had she been for the last few days? Who was the *he* Cora asked about? Was it *him*? Was Cora Mae mad because he walked Jodean home from the street dance? John Rice? Could Cora Mae have been asking about John Rice?

Mike stared at the window straining to see movement or light – *anything* – until his eyes hurt. He went into the tank house, hung his hat on a hook behind the door, took off his shirt and trousers. He did it all moving around in the dark with one eye on the upstairs window. The longer time stretched, the more worried Mike became that Jodean was in trouble.

This is crazy, he chided himself. He was developing a wild imagination, getting nosy like the old biddies in the beauty shop who didn't have anything better to do.

He climbed to the loft but couldn't sleep, so he went back down again and slipped into his trousers. He tried to read but the words ran together on the page. His head hurt from trying to concentrate on his notes instead of Jodean's window. Around one in the morning, Mike jumped as if shot. He'd dozed and thought he'd heard someone call out to him. He stood at the screen door and waited to hear it again. A damp wind blew through the trees, churned the shrubs along the back of the house. Rain began to fall, slowly at first, big drops that made loud plunking sounds on the roof. A low one-note wail sounded on a gust of wind, not from the house but from somewhere behind the car shed down near the swimming hole. He ran his fingers through his hair, rubbed the back of his neck. *Losing his mind, he thought.*

Then he heard it again and swung around toward the house, trying to determine for sure where the sound came from. Rain fell in earnest, torrents of it. For reasons he couldn't name, Mike ran for the car shed. A flash of lightning crackled overhead. The whole countryside, all the way down to Cooperville Spring Creek, lit up in blue light. Mike knew he wouldn't find anything out there. He leaned against the shed and pressed the sharp pain in his side, heaved for air. He looked at his hands, squeezed them into fists. Regardless of whether or not he was nosy or crazy or hallucinating – Jodean needed help. Of that much, he was sure.

MIKE WATCHED THE storm move off to the south allowing the first slanted rays of sunlight to glint on Jodean's window. Around eight-thirty he heard Cora Mae moving around inside the house. Blind from lack of sleep, he left the tank house, crossed the yard and banged on the porch screen door. When Cora Mae didn't answer, Mike banged again and called out, "Mrs. Travis!"

He heard the radio scratching between stations so he pulled the screen door open, crossed the porch to the kitchen door window and rapped on the glass. "Mrs. Travis!" Through the filmy curtain he saw her coming and took a step back.

She peeped through the curtain then opened the door a couple of inches. "Jodean's not going to be fixing you any more meals."

"I need to talk to her, Mrs. Travis, about my rent coming due."

"If you can't pay then move out." She started to shut the door.

"Is something wrong with Jodean? Why haven't I seen her in the garden—"

"Listen, it's none of your business what our comings and goings are. Now leave me alone or move out!"

She slammed the door and turned the lock. Through the glass pane Cora Mae yelled, "I'm going to call Emmet or Neal if you don't leave me alone."

Mike sat on the steps, studied the ground for a second or two, then stood and yelled Jodean's name toward the upstairs window as loud as he could. Nothing. He hurried to the shed, fired up the truck and took Cooperville Spring Creek road out of town. It was after nine when he swung off the road at Red's place where he found Ada on the porch braiding Jean's hair.

"Hi ya, Mike. You just missed Red. He's gone out on horseback to check fences after that rain last night."

"It's you I need to talk to, Ada."

She gave him a double look and shooed Jean off the porch to join the other kids playing tag. "You don't look so good," she said.

"I didn't get much sleep last night."

"Have you eaten?"

Mike shook his head. "I'm worried about Jodean."

Ada pinched her eyebrows together and invited him inside for scrambled eggs and skillet toast.

He explained the situation while she banged around her stove. Listening to his own words, his voice, hoarse with fatigue – it came clear to him how much Jodean had occupied his mind in the last weeks. How much he wanted another chance to put his arms around her, not just to dance, but to hold close so they could be quiet together, breathe together. It frightened him to think she was like air and could blow away, slip around him, through him, never to be seen or held again. He gulped Ada's coffee to clear his throat. He felt god-awful inside, like clabbered milk.

Ada sat across the table looking at him, listening like she thought he was addled. When he finished telling her why he worried about Jodean, not seeing her for days, Cora Mae's caterwauling and all the door slamming, Ada let out a big sigh and leaned forward on her elbows.

"There's no telling what's going on where Cora Mae is concerned, Mike. The woman is shameless. I wish Red was here." She stood and moved his dishes to the sink. "Maybe the best thing is for you to go on back. I'll round up the kids, stop by the beauty shop and act like I want a quick shampoo or something."

"Has anything like this ever happened before?"

"No. But nothing would surprise me. Cora Mae Travis looks at the world from a whole different place than the rest of us. A place she's invented so she'll never see anything wrong with it. She makes the rules as she goes along, changes them to fit her wishes. Trouble is, she thinks her world is ours, too. She has no idea how warped her thinking is. Probably never will."

Mike stopped in the doorway on his way out. "Don't be too long."

"I won't."

A little of the worry lifted from him as he drove back to town. Ada's breakfast helped but most of all he was relieved to find help. When he turned into the drive along the rock wall, nothing had changed since early morning except the angle of sunlight. He parked beside the tank house and stood under Jodean's window to watch and listen. He said her name out loud a few times but got hot and blinded by the sun. In the tank house he found it hard to be still. By the time Ada rolled up in front of the house, a good three hours had passed since he'd talked with Cora Mae that morning.

He heard Ada and Cora at the front door. They moved inside the house. Mike waited. He caught a snatch of what Cora Mae said, like "*what could I do*," and another time, "*she won't tell me what to do*." Their voices moved upstairs. Mike walked out of the tank house, watched the upstairs window. What was taking Ada so long? Why were they suddenly quiet?

The window curtain moved aside. Ada stuck her head out of the window, "Hurry, Mike. *Hurry*!"

He was at the back door in four strides. It was locked.

"Ada! I'm locked out!"

Ada didn't hear him for her loud arguing with Cora Mae. Mike yelled at the top of his lungs. When Ada banged back down the stairs and flung the door open, the look on her face was grave. "I have no idea what's wrong with her. It's bad, I..."

Ada's face twisted with worry. Mike moved her aside, found the stairs and climbed the steps two at a time. At the door to the only room upstairs he stopped dead in his tracks. The stench of vomit hit him like a club. Sunlight peeped through a crack in the soaked window curtain and sparkled in a puddle of clear rainwater on the floor.

On the bed, flattened like paper between wads of dirty sheets, Jodean appeared bloodless, white-lipped. Her matted hair clung to her head. Her curled hands hooked over each of her collarbones as if clawing herself. Bruise-colored rings circled her eyes that stared at nothing.

Mike steeled himself against the awful quaking in his gut. When he stepped to the side of the bed, Jodean's eyes fluttered and rolled. He touched her forehead. She gave no response.

"Shut up! Just shut the hell up and get out of the way!" Ada exploded as she ran back up the stairs.

Cora was on her heels. "How am I supposed to know what she needs if she don't say nothing! Tell me that! What do you think I am, some kind of mind reader or something?" Cora wiped her face with her headache rag.

Ada spread a clean sheet across the end of the bed, then moved across from him. "Let's get her to my car."

Mike moved back the sheet covering Jodean. Her nightgown was splattered with dried vomit, one knee was drawn to her chest. Ada moved the vomit soaked pillow from under Jodean's head, coughed and covered her mouth and nose.

He gently worked one hand under Jodean's shoulders, felt nothing but bone and fever. He glanced at Ada. She seemed paralyzed all of a sudden. Neither of them could have acted on the situation alone. Each found strength in the other's need to help Jodean. Had he been alone, finding Jodean like this, he might have gone into a mad rage and killed Cora Mae Travis with his bare hands.

Mike lifted Jodean to the clean sheet. Her body convulsed and shuddered when he tried to straighten her leg. Ada quickly wrapped the ends of the sheet around her, swaddling her like a baby. Mike scooped her into his arms, rushed down the stairs and out the door into the fresh air. Ada was right behind him. Cora Mae whined non-stop from the top of the stairs.

CLYDE CHEEVERS LEANED on the gate's cross brace to scrap mud off his shoes. Then, with his hoe slung over his shoulder, he headed for the house. The rain had been almost too much, too fast. About ten percent of the cotton plants were beaten down but, all and all, after a morning in the fields he decided it helped more than hurt.

His wife was in the shade of the cottonwood tree serving up beans and slabs of ham to the Mexican family that came to help chop cotton. Clyde sat on a weathered bench next to the water pump to think. He had never considered sending out a chopping crew without going along, but maybe it was time to do just that. Somewhere along the way he went and got old. He'd have to put somebody in charge, of course. Clyde glanced at Arturo. Arturo, his wife, and two of their grown boys drifted by at planting time and, thankfully, stayed on to help with the hoeing.

His gaze traveled beyond the group sitting in the shade, out to the blue hills in the north and west, to each outcropping of rock and earth that cushioned him from the rest of the world. It was like casting glad eyes on a beautiful woman, those hills. A man never gets enough of it.

He waited while his wife handed everyone a cold baked sweet potato to put in their pockets to munch on if they got weak-kneed working the second half of the day. Clyde angled his head with a little jerk. Didn't seem right to keep them in the fields till dark, but if he didn't, he wouldn't get as good a yield. If he didn't get a good yield, he'd not have enough to pay them. One by one the workers stood up from the ground and started back out to the fields.

"Señor Arturo? Puedo hablar con usted?" *Can I have a word with you?*

Clyde offered Arturo a percentage of the cotton sale if he would agree to supervise the workers and see to it that they didn't slack off.

"Sí, señor Cheevers. Sería un honor. Le agradezco su gesto de confianza." *I'd be honored. I appreciate your gesture of confidence.*

When Clyde turned toward the house, his wife, having overheard the conversation with Arturo, looked at him with big eyes. He ignored the expression on her face and told her he would eat on the porch. After that he moved his rocking chair outside so he could sit and sip his coffee and regard his fields, cotton shin high, green as could be, and those hills. Those beautiful hills.

Aging isn't so bad, he decided. Fighting it was.

Just as he got good and comfortable, Hannah Odell from up the road drove into the shade beside the house. Her feeble looking old aunt hunched in the seat next to Hannah with a sour look on her face. Hannah stepped out of her car and called a *hidy* to him and said the aunt had finally remembered where she'd seen the woman in the newspaper picture and did he know who she should tell.

"I sure's hell do. Uh, where? Where does she know Miss Beck from?"

"Claims she saw her at the railroad station in Fort Worth a couple of lifetimes ago. Clyde, it took some effort for her to get through the details, if you can call it that. She gets impatient when I ask her a lot of questions. I have no idea if what she says will do any good, but you can count on it being gospel. I've tried to slip things by her, you know, like you would to get a little kid to go bed, but she calls me to task every time."

"Right. Well, I'll contact Tubby Whittaker in Cooperville and explain the situation, let him arrange some kind of interview. That okay with you?"

Hannah nodded. "It'd be better if he or whoever could drive out here. She doesn't like riding in cars too much and, well…"

"I'll take care of it, Hannah. Tubby's going to be real thankful."

Hannah shrugged. "I hope it helps."

She glanced at his rocking chair then looked away. He was glad she left it at that.

Clyde dialed Tubby's office. Tubby answered on the sixth ring.

"I's about to give up on you," Clyde said.

"You caught me going out the door. What's on your mind?"

"Got a woman here, Hannah Odell, remember her?"

"Yeah, yeah."

"Says her aunt remembers seeing Miss Beck at the train station in Fort Worth way back when. Hannah seems to think you might be able to get some decent information out of her. But y'all going to have to come out this way to talk to her. She don't like automobiles."

"I'll check with Neal and Emmet, decide on a day and give Hannah a call." There was a moment of dead silence on the phone then, "I'll be damn."

"What is it, Tubby?"

"Looking out the window here. Ada Kasper just that minute turned down the alley next to Doc Skaggs' office. By-god, I bet she was doing fifty when she turned the corner. Woman's gonna kill somebody one of these days. She's got a car full of kids, too."

"Hope it's not one of her kids sick."

"Well, I'll get back to you about the other. Okay, bye."

Clyde looked at the telephone receiver buzzing in his hand. Tubby Whitaker ended all his telephone conversations the same way. *Okay bye,* then *blam* – he'd slam the receiver down before a fellar could say *boo.*

MIKE HELD JODEAN as close and still as possible. He could tell by the shudders rippling through her fevered body each time the car lurched that it caused her pain. After a few heart-stopping, two-wheel turns, Ada slammed on the brakes in an alley behind the doctor's office, told him to wait, then ran inside. The door boomed shut behind her.

"Where'd Momma go?" Jean asked from the back seat.

"To get Doc Skaggs," Pete answered.

When Pete had seen Mike coming out of the Travis house with Jodean limp in his arms, the boy jumped out of the car and held the door open. The other children went big-eyed and quiet as mice, shifting their attention from Jodean's white shut-off face to their mother running down the walk with Cora Mae huffing and yelling at her heels like a terrier.

"Is she dead?" Ted asked peering at Jodean from the back seat. Pete shoved Ted and told him to be quiet. Tootie Sue started sniffling.

The alley door Ada had gone into opened and a crisp, starched man in his middle fifties followed her out into the sun. He opened the car door, leaned in to look at Jodean. He lifted one of her eyelids, then pressed his hand to her forehead.

"Jodean," he said, "open your eyes and tell me where it is you're hurting." When Mike shifted so the doctor could see her better, Jodean let out a groan.

"Every time she moves that leg it hurts her," Mike said.

The doctor pressed her stomach just below her waist. She sucked air and tangled her face.

Doc Skaggs grunted. "Let's get her inside."

"Pete," Ada said, "you take the others to the waiting room and I don't want to hear a sound out of any of you." Her words were stern but she hadn't managed to hide her apprehension and it showed on the faces of her children.

Mike carried Jodean to a small curtained area just inside the door. A nurse, as starched and white as the doctor, pointed to a hospital bed, indicating that Mike should put her down. He paused, drew his arms up to hold Jodean closer.

"Lay her down." The nurse looked him in the eye.

Mike leaned forward and eased his arms out from under Jodean. Her eyes rolled open. She bit her lip to stave off the pain and focused on him for an instant. Mike's chest ripped wide open.

The nurse touched his arm with a sympathetic nod. When he turned to leave, he bumped into Ada. He hadn't realized she'd been right there at his elbow.

"You two run along to the waiting room," the doctor said drying his hands. He shifted his eyes from Ada to Mike. "I'll find you there after I've had a time to examine her."

"This is Mike LeMay," Ada said. "He's been renting Cora Mae's tank house."

The doctor shook Mike's hand, patted him on the back and said it wouldn't be too long.

To Mike, the wait was an eternity. When the kids weren't watching, he and Ada exchanged glances across the small cramped waiting room. She hugged her ribs and chewed the inside of her mouth. Pete sat next to Mike but Tootie Sue gave him a wide berth. The child still didn't understand why he grabbed her the way he did the day she stepped on the hornet's nest. He guessed she thought he'd tried to drown her.

A stream of liquid dripped from her nose. Ada fished in her purse, withdrew a handkerchief and tossed it to Pete, who was nearest Tootie Sue.

"Come here," Pete said, but Tootie Sue shook her head *no* without taking her eyes off Mike. Pete sighed and went to her and wiped her nose and told her to blow. "Mike isn't going to hurt you," he said. "He saved Jodean's life."

Ada popped out of her chair when she saw the doctor coming down the hall. His eyes were downcast. Mike didn't know the man, wasn't sure how to read his face, but he appeared in deep thought, as if mapping a complicated route to some place important.

"Appendicitis," he said when he looked up at Ada. "Ideally she should be taken to San Antonio for the operation, but frankly...I'm not sure she'd make it." Ada covered her mouth.

"I have the nurses preparing her for surgery now. They've moved her upstairs. Give them about fifteen minutes more, then you can take the elevator up if you want to see her before we start."

"Doc, I— Is she—"

"I'd feel a lot better about doing the operation myself if she wasn't so drawn down and weak but I think she'll pull through, Ada. She's got to have a certain amount of fight in her to have withstood..."

When the doctor's voice trailed off, Ada nodded agreement. Doc Skaggs touched her shoulder and moved off down a narrow side hallway.

Ada bit her bottom lip again trying to hold back tears. It didn't work. Mike turned to the children. "Why don't we walk around the block to City Café for ice cream?"

Jean and Ted squealed, each grabbed one of Mike's hands. Pete looked at Ada for approval. She nodded carefully, tears about to spill over the rims of her eyes.

"Pete," Mike said, "you get Tootie Sue's hand and lead the way."

On the way out the door he glanced over his shoulder. Ada had covered her whole face with her hands.

Outside in fresh air and sunshine, Mike thought it interesting how kids could dilute a situation. But nothing right now could ease his fear for Jodean.

Jean's pointed little fingers dug into his hand each time she jumped over a crack in the sidewalk. Ted asked Mike where his kids were. When he explained he didn't have any, Ted said, "Oh" and shot him a look of pity.

Mike watched Pete's back as he led the way with Tootie Sue dragging along beside him. His dark hair was cropped short showing off a well-shaped head. The boy was really something, like a miniature granddaddy taking over where his parents had to leave off. He was big for his age too, with his overalls riding high above his ankles. And tiny Tootie Sue tripping along beside him, like a shaggy puppy, with all that strawberry hair hanging in her face and not a care in the world. Except, of course, to avoid the strange man who tried to drown her. She stopped and oohed at a doll in the drugstore window but Pete soon gave her arm a tug and they were on their way again.

Jean tripped on her shoelaces and fell to the sidewalk. When Mike helped her stand, the feel of her warm little body, so like Jodean's, made a lump as big as a grapefruit rise up in his throat.

CORA MAE SAT at the kitchen table dumbfounded by the turn of events. Someone knocked on the front door, tried the handle.

"Cora Mae! Jodean! Y'all got the door locked. Cora Mae! What y'all doing in there?"

Cora Mae opened the door slowly. Her face was red and swollen. "They took Jodean away."

"What? Oh, Cora, honey, you look awful."

"Jodean got sick and Ada took her away."

Frances stepped inside and took Cora Mae by the elbow. "Good Lord! Tubby said he saw Ada driving like a mad woman. What happened?"

"I don't know what's wrong with her—" Cora Mae stopped short and shot Frances a sober look. "I did everything I could think of but she just kept vomiting. Ada showed up this morning and she went and got Mike and they hauled her off. I don't even know where." Cora Mae's face wadded into a frown.

"There, there." Frances hugged Cora Mae and patted her back. "Tubby said Ada stopped at Doc Skaggs. If you want, I'll take you there."

Cora blew her nose and wiped her face. "You can't imagine the mess Jodean made upstairs. It's just awful and me too upset to do anything about it."

"Oh, for heaven sakes, honey. You can't be worrying about such things at a time like this. After we see about Jodean, we can stop by the boardinghouse. Maybe one of the housekeeping girls there can come clean for you."

Cora reminded herself to keep her tongue in check. She didn't want anyone to suspect, as she did, that Jodean could be pregnant. The Black Draught she'd given the girl hadn't worked. There'd been no blood in the bed after they carried Jodean out. Castor oil would've been better had she been able to find any in the house. She sighed and shook her head. The shame would tear her in two if it was true. If Jodean didn't have a monthly and ended up big as a sow. Pregnant. Cora Mae knew her nerves just couldn't take it.

"Come on now," Frances said. "Let's get your face washed and find your shoes. Everything will be all right. You'll see."

MIKE CARRIED JEAN piggy-back on the return trip to the doctor's office, which he now realized was the first floor of a small hospital. Tootie Sue whined and yanked on Jean's foot but each time he offered Tootie Sue a ride, she shrank away from him.

Pete and Ted were singing *This Old Man* when they all filed through the doctor's office side door. Mike was the last one in with Jean still riding on his back when he recognized Cora Mae's braying somewhere inside the building. They rounded a corner. Frances and Cora Mae were sitting opposite Ada. The only empty chair was next to Cora Mae. Mike slipped Jean off his back and leaned on the doorjamb until he caught Ada's eye.

"She's still in the operating room," Ada said. Tootie Sue climbed on her lap and said something in gibberish. Ada smiled and looked at him. "Thanks, Mike."

Cora Mae made a loud blowing noise into a handkerchief. "Lord knows I've tried to make that girl happy."

Mike turned and walked out.

THE SUN LOOKED like nothing more than an orange lump low in the west when Mike got word about Jodean. He'd hated to abandon Ada the way he did but he couldn't stomach Cora Mae another minute.

Ada swung by the tank house on her way home to tell him Jodean came through the operation okay but would be a long time recovering. The doctor said she would be in the hospital about two weeks and would have to take it easy for quite a while after that. Cora Mae had gone home with Frances for supper. Ada invited him to ride out to their place to eat but he declined. He didn't say as much, but he thought it would be a while before he could stand the idea of eating. After Ada left, he climbed in bed and slept like a dead man.

The next day, to fill long hours of worry, he decided to write his brother, James, and try to get some news about his mother. He mentioned Jodean and her troubles but wadded that page, tossed it and started over. Later, when he moved to the sink to get a drink, the wadded page on the floor caught his eye. He picked it up and straightened it out. Why did it bother him to mention Jodean? Why did it scare him, make him uncomfortable? He wadded the page into a tight ball a second time and threw it against the window screen.

By the fourth day after rushing Jodean to the hospital, he had exhausted his pile of interview notes, typed them into readable text and caught up on his letter writing. Including a letter to Tom Coker in San Antonio asking him to find information on Joseph Dunlap, address or occupation, anything. In all that time the Travis house seemed shut off and dark, as if Jodean had been its breath and blood.

He walked to the creek evenings and sat on the rocks at the deep pool. The old carp was always there rolling big eyes at him. Mike studied the thicket across the way, listened to the tick of heat in the air, the high buzz of insects. Nothing could make Jodean stay at the back of his mind. The minute he relaxed, things she'd said or done repeated in his head. He wanted to see her – needed to see her – but he wasn't sure Jodean was well enough for company. Or, if she would want to see him. He hoped to run across Ada in town but didn't. And the Kasper's didn't have a phone so he couldn't call.

At two o'clock each afternoon, Frances parked in front of the house and honked three times. Cora Mae would climb into the car and they'd be gone an hour, he assumed to see Jodean. The only other sign of life from the house was Cora's radio – Fibber McGee and Molly, laughter, preachers yelling damnation and brimstone, a

Martha White Flour commercial – sounds and voices from a world away coming to a place he had made real on the pages of his manuscript.

Though he ached for news of Jodean he wouldn't bother to consult Cora Mae. As far as he was concerned, it would be like talking to her radio. A lot of noise came out of Cora Mae's mouth but nothing ever made it past her ears and into her brain.

Finally, one afternoon after Cora Mae left for the hospital with Frances, Ada turned into the drive. She said she had been to see Jodean and that she was coming around some, could sit against a pillow and talk a little bit.

"She asked about you Mike."

"I didn't know if I should go see her. If it'd be okay."

"I think so. Maybe tomorrow morning."

His heart swelled in his chest, pounded against his ribs. The next morning he used his pocketknife to cut a rose from one of Jodean's bushes on the north side of the house and headed for the hospital on foot. Halfway there he began to feel foolish carrying the rose. Jodean might get the wrong idea. But then, what was the right idea? He tossed the rose against a planter outside the doctor's office.

There were four rooms upstairs from the doctor's office, two on each side of a wide hall. The same nurse, who shooed him out of the room when he carried Jodean in the back door, looked up from a clipboard. She gave him a quick smile and pointed at the last door on the left.

Jodean's face was turned to the open window. The room smelled like overripe apples, sweet and airy.

"Jodean?"

She was white as chalk, even her cracked lips, but the terrible knot of pain was gone from her eyes. She blinked as if trying to clear her eyes.

"Jodean."

She focused on him. "Ada told me what you did…that you went to get her. I-I don't remember."

Her hand moved, turned palm up, then she closed her eyes and said his name.

"I gave her a sedative about an hour ago," the nurse said coming into the room with her clipboard. "That's why she's so drowsy." She took Jodean's pulse and then left.

Mike touched Jodean's fingertips and when she opened her eyes and found his face, she looked directly at the thing making his chest swell and rip and knot, and he let her look. He resigned himself to being found out and was relieved. He leaned over her, touched her cheek.

"Mike." She said his name a second time, like it was a blessing and he knew she'd received his heart. Weakened as Jodean was, she had taken his heart into her own. And he willingly let her have it.

NEXT MORNING JODEAN watched Mike come through the door with a fistful of sweetheart roses. He looked so embarrassed she wanted to laugh but it hurt too much. So she bit her lip against the pain and thanked him. He said he'd weeded her garden and picked a few tomatoes. She wanted to ask if Cora Mae was cooking for him but facts and dreams got mixed up in her mind. Her lips felt thick, her throat dry.

Two days later he brought a ladies' magazine and told her all about how his grandfather had migrated to North Carolina from Nova Scotia. He worried about not hearing from his brother or mother, mentioned that the sun had gone down behind a bank of clouds and did she think it would rain for three days like she'd told him that first day? She watched his mouth move as he talked, listened to the slow, thick sound of his voice and sometimes got so mesmerized by it she forgot to pay attention to what he said and would fall asleep.

One day he came to visit later than usual. He said he'd stopped by the newspaper office to collect the photograph of Effie Beck he'd loaned them and was held up talking with Rudy. A nurse came in about that same time and told her she needed to walk. Mike held her arm while the nurse tied her robe. Her legs felt like water. Sharp burning pains shot from her abdomen up to her shoulders, down her arms and out her fingertips. Mike and the nurse each took an arm and led her to the hallway.

"Well," Cora Mae said, coming out of the elevator with a basket on her arm. "I see you're getting back to your old self." She ignored Mike and the nurse.

"Doc Skaggs said I could go home soon if I walk a little every day."

Mike and the nurse turned her and she managed to make it back to the end of the hall two more times before declaring she was exhausted and ready to return to the bed. Cora Mae glowered without saying a word.

Jodean sensed a difference between Mike and Cora Mae. Just now, Cora Mae crept to a corner of the room while Mike helped her back to bed. Come to think of it, yesterday Ada's hair all but stood on end when Cora walked through the door. Jodean remembered being very sick and frightened that Cora Mae wouldn't hear her calls for help with the radio blaring. Then later, she had no idea how much later, she just quit caring, sort of fell into a pained state where there was no time or light.

From the look on Cora Mae's face, someone would have to pay for the way things had changed. Jodean eased back onto the pillow, exhausted, knowing it would probably be her.

Cora Mae put away the clean nightgown she'd brought in the basket and collected a soiled one from the bottom drawer of the side table. When she straightened, she fingered one of the sweetheart roses Mike brought.

"Everybody at the shop says to say hi."

"Have you been able to keep up?"

"I'm managing." Cora Mae licked her lips. Jodean thought of lizards.

"Can I give you a ride home, Mrs. Travis?" Mike asked.

"Frances offered to give me a ride soon as she finishes getting groceries."

He left then with one last glance from the doorway.

Cora Mae walked to the window and folded her arms across her chest.

"What is it, Momma?" The last clear thought Jodean had, before the feverish abyss drew her under, had been Cora's relentless suspicion that she was pregnant. "In the porch swing, Momma?" she had asked appalled. "You think John Rice got me pregnant in a porch swing with you watching our every move from the crack in the curtains?"

Each day Jodean felt stronger and with returning health came the realization that Cora Mae, in an effort to cause her to miscarry an imagined pregnancy, had nearly killed her by forcing Black Draught laxative down her throat.

Jodean relaxed her back flat against the hospital bed, willed her muscles not to draw up. Cora Mae continued to stare out the window. The set of her mouth was grim, her face hard and stern. It dawned on Jodean that even Cora Mae, the woman who raised her from infancy, assumed she was unhealthy, damaged in some way. Cora Mae believed the old adage that fruit doesn't fall far from a tree. The person who knew her best of all suspected the worst, was as leery of her worthiness as anyone in Cooperville.

Jodean finally understood what Ada had always tried to tell her.

"Momma?"

"That man gives me the creeps coming into your room like that."

"From what I've heard, I'd be dead if it weren't for Mike."

"Listen." Cora Mae wheeled away from the window and bared her teeth. "If it hadn't been for *me* you'd be in the gutter this very minute, you hear? And another thing…" Her voice was little more than a husky, evil whisper. She leaned down into Jodean's face. "No matter how sick you are, I'm sicker. You know that. You know how delicate my health has always been."

Jodean could only stare and wonder why Cora Mae had said such a thing. Why did it matter so much to be the sickest? Were they having a contest to see who would have to take care of the other? Why had she not seen the truth before now?

Cora Mae was terrified. Cora Mae was pitiful.

Doc Skaggs came through the door with a big smile on his face. "Well, well, I hear you've been walking."

Jodean nodded. "But it sure hurts."

"I expect so." He pulled back the sheet to press on her side.

"Doc Skaggs," Cora Mae said. "Uh, while you're here, I was wondering if there's anything you can give me for my nerves. You see, with Jodean laid up I've been working all the appointments myself and, well…"

He side-glanced her. "Take a few aspirins when you go to bed Cora Mae."

"But I thought you might know of something stronger."

"I'm letting Jodean go home tomorrow. I want her to have complete rest for another couple of weeks until I see her again. She's not to work. Someone will have to prepare her meals."

Cora yanked on the waist of her dress. "Can I talk to you a minute?" She shot Jodean a pointed look before adding, "In private?"

Jodean wondered what Cora Mae was up to. Maybe she was sicker. But who would know for sure the way she carried on all the time.

She turned to the window and curled into a tight ball, exhausted. The room lacked air because Mike had left. She tried to hold onto the presence of him, the way the room filled with color and shadow when he was there. At first he confused her, the way he'd jabber about anything, everything and then get real quiet and stare at her with those telling eyes of his. When it was time for him to go he'd hold her hand and open his mouth to fill his lungs, and then close it and exhale through his nose.

Once when she struggled to sit up he rushed to fluff her pillow and she wanted to press her face to his shoulder and ask what had happened to make everything so different. How had things shifted when she wasn't looking? But each time she tried to make herself ask, her insides turned to mush. Maybe all these feelings were caused by the high fever Doc Skaggs said she had.

Before dropping off to sleep she pictured Mike in the kitchen the day before the festival. He'd filled the whole house with his man-presence. He smelled like Brylcream and had fine blonde hairs on the backs of his hands. She'd noticed little things like the swirled pattern of hair on the crown of his head as he sat at the table rolling cookie dough. He left little trails of flour on the floor, even on the drawer knobs. She'd have thought he was building Hoover Dam the way he concentrated on rolling the dough and placing each ball just so on the cookie sheet.

Part of her wanted a clear definition of what was taking place between them. She had a feeling Mike already knew. He'd seen it coming when she was too sick to notice. Should she try to stop what was happening before it went too far? Before her heart got chopped in two as had happened with John Rice. And even before John Rice. Whenever a young man new in town came calling on her, just as they were warming to each other, learning what there was to know about their personal histories, he'd take a polite leave without explanation.

Jodean closed her eyes. She could hear Cora Mae's garbled talk echoing out in the hall. It was hard to think clearly after all the sickness and drugs, hard to sort through what she was supposed to be worried about.

MIKE LEANED AGAINST a signpost in front of C.J.s Grocery reading the day's newspaper. He glanced up in time to see Emmet turn off High Street and head his way. Earlier in the week Tubby had stopped Mike coming out of City Café and asked if he'd go along with Emmet to interview Hannah Odell's aunt. He hoped Mike's interviewing experience might help draw important information about Effie Beck out of the woman.

Emmet eased his car to the corner and stopped. Mike climbed in and they were on their way.

"Appreciate you coming along," Emmet said.

"No problem, but I wondered why Tubby didn't ask Neal since he's an official."

"Neal had some business to take care of." Emmet gave Mike a quick side-glance and pushed his glasses up his nose with his thumb. "He didn't elaborate. I checked with Clyde Cheevers, too, since

Hannah Odell is his neighbor, but he hired some new field hands and can't get away either."

"Got any idea where we should start questioning?"

"None. Thought I'd let you do most of the talking."

Mike hadn't been back to the main highway since he hitched a ride with Clyde Cheevers on the road that cut south to Cooperville. It was interesting to see the countryside from a different angle now that he wasn't so much a stranger, had shared a little history with the town. Not only that, two months ago his vision had been clouded with anger and hunger.

Emmet pointed at an abandoned cotton gin north of the highway without comment. None was needed.

The thing that made Texas different from other states Mike traveled through was the amount of space between hills. It gave a man the feeling that there was plenty of room to grow. The thought reminded him of certain breeds of fish that grow as large as their surroundings will allow. If they're kept in a bucket, they stay small as minnows. Put the same fish in a pond and it'll grow as big as Jodean's carp. No telling what could happen to the same fish in an ocean as big as Texas.

Mike felt close to the land – not squeezed – but pressed close to it, seduced by the persuasiveness of a solid foundation.

Emmet geared down as they approached Pole Cat Creek. The town wasn't all that different from Cooperville, a little smaller maybe. They navigated a dog-leg turn through town that eventually took them east again. About five miles out, Emmet turned onto a dirt drive that, like so many others, disappeared into a grove of trees in the distance. When they rounded a bend, a farm house came into view and behind it some of the richest rolling hills Mike had ever seen. Not indigo and distant like the hills to the west, but late summer green, flecked with golds and browns. Emmet parked in front of the house and turned off the ignition.

A woman about the same age as Mike's mother stood at the screen door drying her hands on her apron.

"Morning, Emmet. Sorry y'all had to drive all this way."

"Oh, now don't you go worrying about that, Hannah. Part of the job, you know. This is Mike LeMay. Tubby's got relatives in town so he asked Mike to take his place."

Hannah led them through a maze of rooms. The house was huge and elaborate with beautiful ornate fireplaces in each room. They walked through the kitchen and out a narrow hall to a solarium and it was there that Hannah introduced Mike and Emmet to Aunt Nola who had been watering a bougainvillea. Aunt Nola's smile displayed mostly pink gums. Like Breezy Parker, she looked permanently bent in the middle, but her eyes were clear and direct.

Hannah helped her move to a chair padded with old quilts and pillows. Aunt Nola's shoes had been cut away to allow extra room for her twisted toes. A condition probably due to a combination of ill-fitting shoes and a lifetime of hard labor as a rancher's wife.

Aunt Nola held up a crooked finger and wagged it at Mike. "I'll warn you straight out. I'm old, not stupid."

Hannah turned her face to hide a smile. Mike cleared his throat and looked at Emmet for support. Emmet nodded a go-ahead.

"Aunt Nola, your niece tells us you know something about Miss Effie Beck, whose photograph appeared in the newspaper the week of the Pickle Festival."

"That's right. I saw her in Fort Worth at the railroad station."

"When was that?"

"Why, three weeks to the day after Mr. Fowler died."

Mike looked at Hannah who explained, "Mr. Fowler was Aunt Nola's father-in-law. What year was that Aunt Nola?"

"Nineteen aught six. Hannah, why don't you offer these gents some coffee?"

"That'd be nice," Emmet said.

"Tell me," Mike continued, "what was Fort Worth like in 1906?"

"Smelled like cow shit everywhere you went. The stockyards, you know. And there's balls nearly every month of the year. Big damn deals, girls planned for year round."

Mike squirmed in his chair. Aunt Nola was toying with him. More than likely, the old woman hadn't had this much attention since her wedding day. "Did you participate?"

"Hell no. I didn't have time for that silly stuff."

"She never lived there, Mike," Hannah explained setting a tray of cups on a side table. "She was in Fort Worth to meet the train that day. What do you take in your coffee?"

"Nothing, thank you."

Aunt Nola shook her finger at him again. "See, I knew I liked you, young man. I like a feller drinks his coffee straight. Puts hair on him, I always say."

Hannah rolled her eyes.

Mike tried again. "Why don't you tell me about seeing Effie Beck."

"Well, she was skinny as hell. Blubbering her head off and about squeezed that little girl to death before the nuns could get her on the train."

Mike took a swallow of his coffee to keep from asking *what* little girl. If he gave Aunt Nola full rein maybe she'd get the story out in one piece and they could go home. He waited but she didn't take the bait.

"Nuns?" he asked.

"Yeah, nuns. See, me and my husband were there to get our boys. Every year the children were all taken by the time the train got this far south, so we decided to drive to Fort Worth, see if we couldn't—"

"She's talking about the orphans," Hannah clarified. "It was an Orphan Train."

"That's what I'm saying," Aunt Nola barked. "Listen. Me and my husband figured we was about the luckiest people alive. They was the best boys in the world." Aunt Nola hunched back into the chair like a small child.

Hannah reached to pat her arm. "They were killed in France a week before the armistice."

Seeing Aunt Nola's sudden sadness made Mike want to give up and accept that he'd never know any more about Effie Beck than what he'd already learned. But then Hannah offered everyone more coffee and the old woman rallied.

"We were all done signing the adoption papers. They were brothers, you know. So scared. I held their hands while my husband found out from the nuns everything he could about the boys' past before the train pulled out... In case they ever wanted to know. We never made a secret of where they came from, thought if we did it'd seem like we were ashamed and we weren't. Besides, they were old enough to remember how they came to us. We loved them like our own."

Aunt Nola sobered. Her half-answer game lost its fun. She continued with a big sigh. "Anyway, I heard this awful carrying on and turned around and it was that woman in the picture, that Miss Beck. She was holding a little girl. Both of them were crying. A nun kept telling the woman everything would be all right, not to worry, not to worry. Then this other nun comes up and takes the little girl."

"It sounds, from the way you're describing it, that Miss Beck was leaving the child with the nuns. Yet weren't the nuns there to *offer* adoptions?" Mike asked.

Aunt Nola curled her bony shoulders. "I'm just telling what I saw. I couldn't wait to get away from there. All that crying was making our boys nervous and I figured they'd been through too much as it was."

Mike took Effie's photo out of his shirt pocket. "Take a look at the photograph again. It's a little clearer than the newspaper. How sure are you that it's the same woman? After all that was such a long time ago."

"Remember now, I never saw the woman after she got old like me. My memory of how she looked is of the age she was back then." Aunt Nola looked at the picture. "That's her. I got one that looks just the same."

"One what?"

"Picture. My husband, he was a photographer. Had a tidy little business going all around taking family portraits while I took care of the ranch. Sometimes he sold a few pictures of this or that to the Fort Worth newspapers." She paused to dab at the corners of her mouth with her handkerchief. "Uh, where was I? Oh. He took a picture of me and the boys and the nuns that day before all the commotion and crying started. That woman was a little to the side of us waiting on the nuns."

Mike looked at Hannah for confirmation.

"I don't remember ever seeing a picture like that," Hannah said to Aunt Nola.

"That don't mean I don't have it in that flat box of mine, the one you put under the sofa. Go get it and see for yourself."

Hannah shook her head, rolled her eyes again and left the room. Mike followed her leaving Emmet to entertain Aunt Nola.

In the parlor, Mike helped Hannah drag the box out from under the sofa. Among the assorted papers and tied letters they found a large photograph album. While Hannah flipped through it, Mike noticed a big brown envelope with a return address for the Catholic Foundling Society in New York City.

"Do you mind if I open this?" he asked Hannah.

She glanced at it and waved him on. It turned out to be the boys' adoption papers. Mike took a note pad out of his shirt pocket and wrote down the return address and the date of the adoption.

"Well, I'll be dipped. Aunt Nola never ceases to amaze me," Hannah said. She slipped a photograph out of the glued down corner tabs and handed it to Mike. It was just as the aunt said. A young version of Aunt Nola flanked by two little boys and two nuns stared at the camera, while a little to the left and behind them, a dark haired woman looked on. A little girl in the woman's arms was wearing a light colored bonnet and crying so it was hard to make out her features. But the woman indeed look very much like the one in the photograph found in Effie's trunk.

"How old would you say the little girl is?" Mike asked.

Hannah studied the picture. "About a year old, fifteen months, maybe."

"Can I take this with me?"

"I suppose, as long as you promise to bring it back."

When Mike and Hannah returned to the solarium, Aunt Nola dozed with her chin on her chest. Emmet looked bored as a toad staring out the window. He jumped self-consciously when he heard them coming. Mike whispered good-byes and gratitude to Hannah on their way out the door.

Heading back to Cooperville, Mike relayed to Emmet the information about the adoption agency address and the photo. Emmet showed no interest whatsoever. Maybe that's what made him an attractive choice for police chief. Not much excited Emmet.

Excited was an understatement for how Mike felt. What was Effie Beck doing in Fort Worth with a child? Why had she been so upset, near hysteria as Aunt Nola explained it?

"Wait a minute, Emmet. Breezy said Effie Beck left town for a time because of some sickness. I assumed tuberculosis. But if the baby in the photograph was around a year old." Mike slapped his leg. "Effie Beck was pregnant! And I'm betting Joe Dunlap was the baby's father."

"Uh huh."

Mike might just as well have been talking to himself. It was inconceivable that Effie Beck had held so much of the town's attention – be it in an odd hurtful way – yet she could disappear for a year, longer maybe, and no one had been aware of it. Except Breezy, of course. On the other hand, there were distances to consider. Travel between town and ranch, on horseback or in a wagon, didn't happen very often back then. Some farm and ranch people made it to town no more than once a year. Taking that into consideration, it made sense that Effie wouldn't have been missed.

Mike held Aunt Nola's picture next to the one he and Tubby had found. He had to admit it looked like the same person. The expressions were very different, but the hair, the tilt of the head, the eyes were the same.

Emmet cut east off the highway onto a paved road that took them through fields of cotton and past the Bat House. Mike knew they were nearing town when he got a whiff of the pickle factory. In the road ahead a scene of chaos and confusion was taking place. A red light blinked on and off atop the sheriff's car. Several men, including Neal, were down a sharp drop on the opposite side where rain run-off had washed the road bed. Emmet slowed to a crawl. Two men carried Otis Bartel up the slope. He was in bad shape with a big gash on the side of his head and two black, swollen eyes. Neal waved Emmet over while the others dealt with Otis.

"Somebody beat the pulp out of him last night," Sheriff Neal said.

"Did he say who?" Emmet asked.

"Says he doesn't remember a thing. Probably a gambling debt due or some such among the WPA workers. I figure it's nothing to worry about."

Easy for Neal to say, Mike thought, as he watched the men stuff Otis in a car and drive away.

When Neal and Emmet finished their exchange, Mike asked Emmet to drop him off at the post office, adding that he'd walk the rest of the way from there. He found no letter from his brother or mother. It worried him.

Back outside the post office, late afternoon sun heated the air until it crackled with static and he suddenly realized how tired he was. At the tank house he emptied his pockets and looked once more at Miss Beck's young likeness in the photographs.

Jodean's curtains were closed. When she opened them, as she did late every afternoon since she'd come home from the hospital, he'd call up to her and ask if she'd like to take a drive.

Mike rubbed his face. Between Effie Beck and Jodean Travis, he felt bewitched, as if the mystery of one and the allure of the other had him under a spell. He smiled to himself at the thought, but down deep he had an itchy, edgy feeling that something regrettable was near at hand. He dreaded his own curiosity. At the same time, he knew he'd try anything to find out all he could about the little girl in the picture. She'd be, he guessed, around twenty-five, twenty eight years old now – living anywhere the nuns and railroad tracks might have taken her.

Anything was possible. Anything.

PETE JUMPED ONTO the back of the hoopie with Bullet then tapped the top of the cab with his knuckles. Red fired up the engine and yelled at Pete to hold on.

Red had been putting Pete off since the day before, when the boy first complained that Pot Roast, his bottle fed bull calf, broke out of his pen and disappeared. The boy was worried sick, wouldn't stop begging Red to drive him around to look for the calf.

Red seldom used the old hoopie anymore. It was a lot of trouble to switch the battery from the car to the hoopie. He drove toward the tank, thinking the calf would have met with the herd there. When they didn't find the calf at the tank, Red followed a cow trail to the north where, sometimes in the heat of day, the cows would hole-up in a thicket near the creek. No sign of the calf.

Two hours later, Red rolled onto a ridge overlooking the entire Medina River valley. He got out of the hoopie and slipped his hat off his head. The sun had a deep-day slant to it. Heat shimmered in the oven dry air. Bullet barked as if to ask, what now?

"What now?" Red asked Pete. As soon as the question left his tongue, something jabbed his consciousness, a poke-in-the-ribs kind of feeling. It was to be the first time he'd rely on his son's instincts, which Red had always known would someday be sharper than his own.

"Can we look on the other side of the road?"

"Son, I don't think Pot Roast could get to the Beck place. There's two fences to cross."

"I've seen him work through barbed wire with my own eyes, Daddy."

Bullet barked from the bed of the hoopie, wagged his tail, and in his excitement, nearly fell off. Red climbed back in the cab and yelled once again at Pete to hold on. When Red pulled onto the road he saw a pickup coming from town. It was Mike and Jodean. They stopped in the middle of the road.

"Taking the lady out for a little drive, are you?" Red called out.

"Doctor's orders," Mike smiled.

"Y'all haven't seen a bull calf running loose have you?"

Mike shook his head. "Want us to help you look?"

Red looked over at Jodean. She had about as big a grin on her face as he'd ever seen. And Mike had that eye-twinkling twitch only a woman can cause in a man. He was pretty sure neither one of them knew it yet, but they'd been bit good by the love bug.

"Nawh. Me and Pete here, we'll find him."

"Don't mind helping out now."

"Nawh," Red winked at Mike and put the hoppie into gear.

When he stopped at Effie Beck's west gate, Pete hopped off the hoopie to swing it open. Red drove through then waited. This time Pete got in the cab with him. They bumped up and down ravines and over rocky wash-outs. It was dusk by the time Red convinced Pete that the calf hadn't crossed fences. As they navigated through a thicket, Bullet started a barking spell. Red geared down to get through a low spot, but the tires spun on gravel and the hoopie slid sideways a few feet.

Red moaned, jerked the gearshift to low and gunned the motor. A rear wheel dropped into a deep rut with a rattling jolt.

"Damn! You okay, Son?"

"Yeah, but I bet we'll have to get the tractor to pull the hoopie free."

Bullet jumped off the back of the hoopie. His relentless yelping was high pitched and piercing.

"Shut the hell up dog!" Red yelled.

Bullet ran about thirty yards back the way they'd come and continued to bark.

Pete said, "I think he scented something."

Red found a downed tree limb to use to jack the hoopie a little. "Pete, might be if you get in and gun the motor while I do this we can get out of here and be home in time for supper."

"Momma's gonna be mad."

"Well now, I don't reckon she has to know anything about this."

Bullet came back, ran around the hoopie barking his head off.

"What if she asks?"

Red yanked his hat off and threw it at Bullet.

"Come on, Bullet," Pete said. "Maybe if I go see what he's barking about he'll hush."

While Pete followed Bullet out of the thicket, Red found a good-sized rock to roll over to the side of the hoopie to use for leverage. With any luck he could—

"Da-a-ddy!"

It was the most blood-curdling scream Red had ever heard from one of his kids. A terrorized plea that made his toes curl inside his boots.

"Da-a-ddy!"

Bullet's hysterical barking nearly drowned out Pete's cry.

Red took off in a scramble the direction Pete had gone. Just as he reached an open field, Pete lunged out of nowhere and grabbed Red around his ribs.

"What is it, Son?" Pete was white as a handkerchief. "Pete?"

Red patted Pete's back, looked all around, saw nothing unusual. The meadow they had just driven across was still and unchanged except for Bullet's yelping. Summer grass, about knee high, and trees along the edge of the ravine outlined the field like a natural fence line.

"Pete?" Red held the boy at arm's length to study his face.

"I-I think it's Miss Effie."

PART III

RED PARKED IN a shady spot between the church yard and road. Ada sat next to him sad and drawn down, as if drained of emotion. The kids stared, quiet as dust, at their parents from the back seat without a clue how to behave on such an occasion. All of them watched Paddy Blue gimp up the church steps. No one else was around.

A breeze whispered through the trees. Ada reached out and touched Red's face. "We're early. Why don't the kids and I wait here for a little while? You go on and see if Paddy needs help."

The church smelled of mold and perfumed Sunday ladies. Bright bars of light gleamed through the stained glass window behind the pulpit. Red gave his eyes time to adjust to the dark dampness, then felt along the wall to his right and tripped the two ceiling fan switches. When they groaned into motion, dust cartwheeled like orbiting stars through the bars of rainbow light.

Paddy shuffled from window to window, straining against the swelled dampness to get them open. He hummed a hymn as he went about his work and ended up standing shoulder to shoulder with Red. He'd unknowingly left a trail of thick black dirt footprints from Effie Beck's fresh-dug grave along his path.

Together Red and Paddy propped the church's double doors open and walked back down the steps. Tubby, Emmet, Rudy Cochran, C.J. from C.J.'s Grocery, the high school coach and a couple of the football team's players gathered around Miss Effie's black-draped coffin cart ready to act as pallbearers. Red and Paddy were the only ones to notice a small, white spotted dog relieving himself on a wheel of the cart.

Red hated that he hadn't been much help to Emmet and the others, but his grief was all-consuming, and turned his mind to cement.

Three days ago, in that grassy meadow turned orange in waning sunlight, he realized the minute Pete said he'd found Miss Effie that the woman had tried to get to him for help. Her confusion must have been as weighty as the grief he felt now in mourning her. That she had crossed two fence lines in a raging thunderstorm was proof enough of how frightened and worried she'd been. He just couldn't shake his guilt. Sometimes it was worse than his grief. His heart sank even more.

He walked back to the car, opened the door and took Pete and Tootie Sue by the hand. Ada held onto Jean and Ted. Jodean, still pale and thin, walked by and kissed Red on the cheek and gave Ada a hug. Cora Mae followed Jodean into the church without saying a word.

Neal and Faye walked by. Faye looked worse than Jodean, if that was possible. Her puffy eyes scanned each one of the kids but avoided the adults. She cupped Tootie Sue's chin in her hand and Red glimpsed three perfectly matched bruises just above her wrist, each about the size of a nickel. Frances and a dozen or so people filed in after Faye and Neal. Red looked down to watch Pete's face when the pallbearers carried Miss Effie's coffin up the steps.

He and Pete would never be the same after what they'd seen. Rotting flesh, bones scattered by coyotes, shreds of Miss Effie's ancient black coat. Her bucket flung to the side of what was left of her. The smell.

Red thought he could see into the years ahead – himself stooped and gray, Pete referring to this season as Effie Beck's Summer. It would become a notch on the timeline of their lives. *So-and-so was born two years after Miss Effie Beck disappeared ... The new Medina River bridge was built the year we found Miss Effie ... The best cotton crop came in so many years after Effie Beck's Summer.*

The experience would bind him and Pete together as men as well as father and son. Red put his wide, callused hand on Pete's shoulder and felt the fabric of the man he would become.

Brother Rawlings moved to Red's side and indicated they should go inside. Paddy removed the black cloth from the coffin that the pallbearers had placed on a stand at the front of the church. Someone, Faye Lackland most likely, had draped cedar and yaupon garland over the coffin. A vase of Jodean Travis's tiny pink roses sat on a fern stand between the coffin and pulpit.

Leave it to the ladies, Red thought, to make everything nice and proper. He sucked in his bottom lip and bit down. Pete's big eyes, filled with gloom, centered on Red's face.

Glory scooted across the piano bench to whisper in Brother Rawlings' ear. He whispered something back. Footsteps scraped on wooden floors, Tootie Sue sneezed and, across the aisle, Cora Mae blew her nose. It wasn't much of a surprise to Red that the church was less than half full. Miss Effie interested people a lot more alive and missing than dead and found. He didn't know what that told him about his town, but glancing at the faces around him, Red thought he was seeing a pretty good reflection of the woman's life.

While Glory plunked away at a slow hymn, Brother Rawlings stepped up into the pulpit that stood high above those gathered in the pews. When he opened his Bible, Red looked up and let his dread evaporate into the twin caverns of the preacher's big nostrils.

FROM WHERE MIKE sat near the back of the church, it appeared Red was dealing with everything pretty good, but that was probably show for Ada and the kids. When he and Jodean came upon Red walking the road toward home the day he and Pete found Effie

Beck, he looked like a man cut in two. He kept repeating, "We found Miss Effie, Miss Effie," between hiccups of air. Bug-eyed little Pete looked dumbstruck.

Mike managed to calm Red enough to get him to explain where they'd found the woman. Though everyone more than half expected she was dead, Mike could see the news paralyzed the whole town. Not so much from grief as downheartedness, a loss of spirit.

Mike hadn't bothered to mention his talk with Aunt Nola to Tubby or Red. He decided to wait until after the funeral, give everyone time to recover from Miss Effie's gruesome discovery. More than likely, Emmet had filled Tubby in on the basics of the conversation with Aunt Nola anyway, and Mike couldn't see that there was a need to hurry. Still, he'd taken it upon himself to write the Catholic orphanage in New York and talked with the railroad clerk about getting a record of passengers for the days leading up to the adoption of Aunt Nola's boys.

Jodean sat two rows ahead of him. He stared at her delicate neck where it sloped to her shoulders. He intended to show her the photographs of Effie Beck the day they'd been out driving, to see if she had any opinions or insight to offer about what he'd learned. But at the last minute, before leaving the house, he'd forgotten to slip them back into his pocket.

Jodean touched her neck, then glanced over her shoulder at him. Color flooded his face.

At one point the day they'd taken that drive, before bumping into Red and Pete, Jodean asked him to stop so she could pick wildflowers, and he brought up the subject of Miss Beck then. He explained why he thought she had a child, a little girl, and that Aunt Nola indicated it had been agony for her to hand the little girl over to nuns running the orphan train operation. If that was so, Mike had asked Jodean, who could the child's father be and where was the little girl now?

But Jodean took a sudden sinking spell and dropped her flowers. Mike leaned down to pick them up and when he straightened, she had a panicky, faint-hearted look on her face. It puzzled him.

"Jodean? Are you sick again?"

Then he too dropped the flowers and put his arms around her and held her close until her trembling settled. He kissed her hair, her temple and her cheek. He wanted to keep on kissing until he reached her mouth, but he knew things weren't right for that.

She pressed her face to his chest. He asked if she was all right and she nodded against him but said she needed to go home.

After that, they'd run into Red and Pete a second time and Mike found himself at a loss. Jodean, white and trembling, Pete wild eyed, Red repeating Miss Effie, Miss Effie and shaking his head. Thank God Ada had been home and knew what to do. She instructed Mike to drop Jodean off then report the discovery to Emmet and leave the rest to him.

Brother Rawlings read a scripture from the Book of Matthew, the one about God's house having many rooms then asked everyone to stand for a hymn. Mike tore his eyes away from Jodean to peer out a window. There, in the back of a mule-drawn wagon Breezy Parker sat, regal and respectful, in his old porch chair. Jericho, wearing a suit coat over his overalls, sat on the wagon seat with the reins resting on his knee. Breezy's head bobbed to the hymn's rhythm and, though Mike couldn't hear, he assumed the old man was humming.

He had a hunch Effie Beck would have approved.

When the hymn ended and everyone settled back in the pews, Brother Rawlings ceremoniously closed his hymnal and Bible. "I've talked to a good many of you in the last few weeks about Effie Beck and have come to the conclusion she made her way in our world the best she could. She was a brave woman, steadfast, and overcame adversities most of us cannot fathom. She was expert at animal husbandry, at reading weather signs, industrious. Unlike most women, she had little opportunity to be nurturing, childless and living alone the way she did. And ...," Brother Rawlings' eyes traveled over the occupied pews. "I suspect she hid behind a show of anger."

He looked down at his hands with a smile playing at his mouth. "I wonder what she thought of us. She probably had an idea of the right way to live but was limited by life's predicaments. Some of you feel Miss Beck harbored a mean spirit. Others, that she was tenderhearted.

"Perhaps Effie Beck is best described as the unloved who gave up on having anyone love her back? If so, that says as much about us as it does her. Were we forgiving of her harshness? Did we choose to focus on her extraordinary skills of perseverance? Were we unmerciful in our judgment of her?

"According to town officials, Miss Beck leaves no great family tree, but all the same, she leaves a root system the rest of us can tap into. Make no mistake about it, the woman set examples for all of us. God blessed Cooperville with Effie Beck's presence. Now, may God bless Effie Beck and welcome her into His paradise."

For a full minute the church was so still Mike felt he was sitting in a photograph. Brother Rawlings whispered *Amen* and indicated everyone should stand for another hymn.

Those who were able walked behind Paddy's coffin cart the quarter mile or so to the cemetery. Others, including Jodean, doubled up in cars for the short distance. Mike walked behind Red and Ada and Brother Rawlings, but waited on the outskirts of the small crowd until Jodean climbed out of one of the cars. He offered her his arm, which she grasped with both hands. Everyone recited the Twenty-third Psalm as the pallbearers lowered the coffin. Brother Rawlings stepped forward and tossed a handful of dirt into the dark hole. One by one each of the mourners stepped forward to do the same before moving towards the cemetery gate where June Rawlings waited to invite everyone to stop by the manse for coffee and cake.

"You all can ride with us," Frances said as she approached Mike and Jodean.

Cora Mae hurried over, "Thanks, Frances. Don't think I could make it otherwise."

"You go ahead," Mike told Jodean. "I'll wait for Red and Ada."

Jodean's eyes were shiny and wet looking, but she let go of his arm. Something had a hold of her. She had that far-away-in-a-fog look, like the day he carried her into the hospital.

When he turned back to the cemetery, Red and Paddy were shoveling dirt over the coffin. Jericho rolled up with Breezy still sitting in the back of the wagon. He grabbed a shovel out from under his wagon seat, jumped down and began shoveling, too.

After a while, Mike tapped Red on the shoulder and offered to take his shovel. Red let him have it, then moved to the shade of a massive live oak tree where Ada and the kids waited.

When they were done, Red palmed Paddy and Jericho on the back and looked over at Breezy, watching from his wagon throne.

Breezy said, "She be jus' fine from here on out, I reckon."

Red placed his big Montana slope hat back on his head. The muscles in his face worked as he looked at the ground and took a deep breath. "Me and Ada are heading home. I don't much feel like cake and coffee and chit-chat. Besides," he glanced at Ada. "I still need to look for Pete's calf."

"DROP ME OFF at the boardinghouse," Faye said to Neal as they drove home from the funeral. "You don't have to wait for me. I can walk home."

Neal passed Front Street without turning. "Now why the hell you want me to take you there?" he asked.

She tucked a tea towel around the plate of leftover cookies on her lap. She wanted to take them to Eula and her children to cheer them up after what had happened to Otis. He'd missed close to a week's work after he was found beaten by the side of the road.

Neal looked across the seat at her, curled his mouth. "I asked you a question, Faye."

"I want to take these cookies to Otis and Eula's kids."

"I don't believe you." Neal propped his right elbow on the back of the seat and reached to stroke her neck. His left hand remained on the steering wheel in a relaxed pose. "You know better than to lie to me. No telling what the consequences might be."

This was the last straw for Faye. She turned her face to him and spat her words. "You—I know it was you who beat Otis. You lay a hand on me and you'll hang, Neal Lackland. I'll tell."

Neal dug his thumb into the soft muscle under her jawbone. "Careful Mrs. Lackland. Careful."

"No, you be careful. I know now that by keeping quiet all these years I've helped you ruin people's lives. That makes me as guilty as you..." She gritted her teeth when Neal tightened his grip. His eyes never left the street but the muscles in his face balled up, his eyes darkened.

He stopped at the corner of East and High Streets and squeezed her throat hard one more time before letting go to wave out the window at the Alvins. He turned the corner, skirted the playground and pulled into the circle drive in front of their house. He got out and walked around the car to open Faye's door. She didn't move. Neal hitched his pants, looked up and down the street. "Faye..."

When she continued to sit, he reached in and grabbed her by the arm and dragged her into the house. The plate of cookies scattered across the car seat and onto the floorboard.

Faye had long since learned not to fight back. It didn't hurt as much. But this time everything had shifted. Maybe because of the old woman they'd just buried whose life seemed such a waste. But Effie Beck had persevered, Brother Rawlings said. Faye tried to love Neal but, like Effie Beck and everybody else, she needed something warm to hold onto and care about even if it was just a *thought, a thread of hope.*

As soon as they were inside, Neal clamped his hands on her shoulders and shook her until she thought her head would roll to the floor. He shoved her against his big leather chair. The terrible jerking motion, the snapping of her neck blocked her thoughts. She bounced to the floor. Faye steeled herself and stood, to face Neal.

She'd been food for his parasitic needs for so many years now there wasn't enough of her left to satisfy him anymore. She supposed she'd always known that sooner or later he'd consume her, leave only enough behind to be carried around in a feed sack, bones and hair and hide like Effie Beck when life was done with her.

In the beginning, she told him it didn't matter that he couldn't finish his lovemaking, but then more and more their private times became a carnival-like sham and Neal could appease his carnal need only by hurting. It had begun slow enough, with him getting out of hand only occasionally. For a time, Faye convinced herself the pressures of being sheriff caused him to explode uncontrollably. She made excuses for his behavior so she wouldn't have to face the horror of his dark side.

When the kids were still little and Neal and his cohorts planned their big buck hunts, it would take him half a day to clean and pack his guns. The smell of barrel bluing and gunpowder would always remind Faye of the nights before those hunts. Those were the worst nights and it crossed her mind often that she was Neal's first kill each season. He wanted to do everything – anything – he could to bring blood.

Neal pressed her against the chair again, groped her breasts while staring out the window at a black fantasy playing in his mind.

The worst of it, the demon thing that turned Faye inside out, was the hunger she had for love, for a man's weight nearby, reassuring. Not over her, threatening, menacing. She'd come to hate her longings because they'd been created by Neal's unwillingness to see himself as an ordinary man with imperfections like everyone else.

He moved his hands around her hips and squeezed so hard pain shot down the backs of her legs. A groan escaped her throat. He liked it.

Faye prayed that her mind would survive what Neal was doing to her body, prayed she'd have enough sensibility when he finished to know, to *understand*, the time to leave was at hand.

TWO DAYS LATER Faye waited for Neal to leave for the courthouse before driving to Ada's to return the cookie tray. But that was just an excuse. She really wanted to tell Ada what she planned to do. For as long as Faye could remember, the relationship she had with Ada and Jodean, though distanced by adulthood, had been her touchstone. She realized most people thought she existed above the town's concern because of where she lived and who she was married to. But Ada and Jodean looked at her situation from a different, more sympathetic angle.

Bonds formed in youth, no matter what the ensuing years brought forth, were lasting. Those bonds sought truth first and never took anything at face value. Few summers passed without Faye recalling sweltering midnights on a porch swing with Ada and Jodean when they were school girls, and wondering what grown-man penises looked like and wishing for titties. Yes, Faye reminded herself, Ada and Jodean would understand what she was about to do.

Faye turned west out of the circle drive in order to bypass town. The last thing she wanted was for Neal to see her. At the end of Oak Street she turned left, passed the Travis house, and waved at Mike push-mowing Jodean's lawn. Jodean was coming out of the front door with a glass of tea in her hand. Faye would have to catch Jodean another time or maybe have Ada fill her in when the time came.

On Cooperville Spring Creek Road, Faye mashed the accelerator and ran her fingers through her hair. Maybe wind and speed would blow dread from her bruised mind.

She thought of the packed suitcases hidden in her daughter's closet, the one, five, and ten dollar bills she'd rolled and stuffed in the flour canister — enough to get her to her sister's home in Dallas. As soon as she cleared up a few last minute tasks, like returning this tray to Ada, she'd leave Cooperville. Forever.

She punched the accelerator all the way to the floorboard, felt the car fishtail a little.

Maybe it had made things worse not having the kids around all summer. Neal had fewer restraints on his behavior with them gone, but the children were getting old enough to sense the tainted air between their parents. She was trapped between the fear of staying with Neal and the fear of leaving him. She had no doubt he'd come after her wherever she went and no telling what he'd do when he found her. As far as she could determine, one kind of death wasn't that much different from another.

A pair of Mexican doves flushed out of the weeds by the side of the road as Faye sped by. She swerved hard to the right to miss hitting them. A plume of dust spiraled from behind her car, tears stung her eyes, everything blurred. *One kind of death couldn't be that different from another. Dead was dead.*

Out of nowhere a golden, white-maned horse reared up in front of the car. Faye hit the brakes hard and swerved left. The car went into a spin and she lost track of right, left, up or down. She glimpsed a big cowboy hat flying through the dust cloud. A man yelled *goddamnit to hell* just before the car smashed into a tree. Her head whipped forward, smacked her mouth on the steering wheel. She screamed. Air rushed in and out of her mouth. She screamed again and again.

RED ROLLED TO the side of the dusty roadbed where Sampson, his prized Palomino horse from his rodeo days, had thrown him. He cleared his eyes of dust, coughed and hauled himself from the ground.

"Faye. Faye. You all right?"

Faye Lackland screamed and choked on sobs. He rushed to the side of the car and saw blood dripping from her mouth onto her hands. The muscles in her face were twisted up. She huffed between sobs and screams. He pulled his handkerchief from his hip pocket and yanked the door open.

"Settle down now, settle down," he said. But she couldn't hear him for her screaming. He reached down and turned her face toward his. Finally, she came to see it was him and stopped screaming but her breath came and went in quick little huffs.

"Sh-h-h, now." It was all Red could think to say. He dabbed at her bleeding mouth. "You busted your lip is all."

She started shaking.

"Come on, let's see if there's anything broke." He took her elbow and gave a little nudge. She stood but used both hands to steady herself against him.

"Are you hurt, Red?" Faye asked between sobs. "Oh God, I just wanted to die. I didn't mean to hurt anybody."

"Hush that talk now." Red put his arm around her shoulder. "I was throwed from horses enough in my rodeoing days to know how to fall, remember? Course, old Sampson may be clear to China by now."

When he tried to wipe at the blood on Faye's mouth a second time, she threw her arms around his neck. Her hair, soft and honey-colored, brushed his cheek. He patted her back, waited for her to stop crying, then tried to move away. She smelled real good, like that expensive perfume in Leroy's drugstore, the one that lets the ladies have a free squirt. She wadded his shirt in her balled fists, clinging.

"Faye, you gotta let me get a good look at you." Red tried to move back. "Faye?"

She rubbed her face against his neck.

"You can't be doing that now." He stepped back, stumbled on a tree root and crashed to the ground with her landing on top of him. Her crying turned soft and weepy, little tears that were the saddest things he had ever seen. He rolled to his side and eased her down on a grassy patch and smoothed hair off her face.

"Why were you driving like that?"

She kept weeping and trembling. Red tried to figure how he could stop it and make her feel better. "Sh-h-h," he wiped her tears, kissed her cheek and checked himself when a wicked stirring tightened his groin.

He sat up. Faye had gone all quiet beside him. In their tumble to the ground, her skirt had twisted up so he could see her legs.

Red shook his head *no* but kissing began anyway. While it was happening, Red felt as if he watched from a tree limb overhead. It couldn't be real, him kissing Faye Lackland by the side of the road like this. Scared-rabbit Faye holding onto him now like he was her last hope.

She unbuttoned his shirt. He kissed her wet eyes then touched the smooth white skin of her thigh.

ADA MARVELED AT the endless gibberish of her children. In one morning alone they'd gone from playing cowboys and Indians, to Tarzan and the apes, to movie-making and the circus, and were now back to cowboys and Indians. Pete pretended to be Hopalong Cassidy, Jean, his girlfriend. They shot stick guns at Ted, the bank robber outlaw from behind the water trough.

She set the laundry basket on the ground and shook out the first of dozens of shirts she'd washed that morning. Tootie Sue, who'd been assigned the role of Gabby Hayes, rode a stick horse in circles, oblivious to what the others were doing.

That morning before sunup, Red pecked Ada on the cheek and saddled Sampson, his favorite horse from the old days. He wanted to try one last time to track down Pot Roast and thought he could cover more ground if he was on horseback. To Ada it seemed that's all Red had done the whole summer – look for lost or needy souls.

Pete stood behind the water trough and looked out toward the gate.

She'd been worried enough about her quiet oldest child losing his pet calf, Pot Roast. But add to that the experience of finding Effie Beck's corpse like he had... She wanted to go to Pete and gather him into her arms and hold him there, make a cloak of herself so all her children could wear her protection forever.

At Effie's funeral Ada overheard Frances and Cora Mae talking about how bad things happen in threes and wondered if Pete or Red could take a third blow after losing Pot Roast and finding Effie Beck.

Ada followed Pete's gaze across the pasture and out to the road. Sampson was running full out, riderless through the gate. Pete shot her a startled look.

"Get the kids in the car!" she yelled. Oh God in heaven, she never should have thought about bad things in threes. *Red, Red.* She ran for the house and had the car keys in her hand before the screen door could slam shut behind her. She ran back out the door and jumped off the porch. *Red.* She could withstand just about anything, except...

She slammed the car door, mashed the clutch to the floorboard, then jerked the gearshift. Pete's eyes were glued to her face.

"Where would your daddy have gone to look for Pot Roast?"

"He was going out Butter and Egg road, near the Brady place."

Ada bit her lip and popped the clutch. The car lurched and ran over the laundry basket. One of the kids screamed from outside the car.

"Ted! Momma, we forgot Ted!" Jean yelled.

Ada slammed on the brakes and Pete flung his door open. Ted scrambled inside, Pete shut the door and Ada took off a second time.

Red. Please God not my Red.

"I want every one of you to look out for your daddy. Ted, you look out the back, Jean out the side window behind me. Pete you look out that way!"

"He's okay, Momma. Daddy knows everything," Pete said.

Two miles out, Ada spied a car beside the road. Maybe someone had stopped to help Red *if* he was hurt. When she got a little closer, she could see it was Faye's car and that it had hit a tree. Ada swallowed hard and slowed down. She could feel her heart beat in her ears. She stopped and got out. There wasn't a soul in sight, but she heard a rustling sound.

"Red? Faye?" Ada picked her way into the weeds and tall grass beside the road. The driver's side door of Faye's car was open. "Faye," she called out a second time.

"Ada!"

She spun around to see Red scramble up from the tall grass. His face was flushed, eyes big as wagon wheels. Faye was behind him struggling with her tangled clothes.

"You see, darling—she—Faye was—Sampson threw me and…"

Faye started crying. Ada looked back at Red.

"It was just her lip a-bleeding, but she was real scared… and I…"

Faye moved beside him. "It isn't what you think, Ada. This is my fault—"

Ada held up her hand to stop Faye, then shifted her eyes back to Red. His belt dangled unbuckled, his shirttail stuck out to one side.

"Ada? Darlin'?"

Ada balled her fist, reared back and let go enough fury to tear a mountain apart. Red's head popped back then whipped forward before he dropped to his knees and grabbed his nose. Tootie Sue let out an ear-piercing scream from the car. When Ada wheeled around she bumped into Pete. His eyes were full of tears.

MIKE THUMPED HIS fedora and dipped his chin to Leroy who was sweeping the sidewalk in front of his drugstore.

He'd finished mowing Jodean's lawn, showered and now hurried to get to the post office and back before she finished her morning chores. She had managed to keep her chores simple like Doc Skaggs ordered. But that didn't mean, of course, that Cora Mae eased up any on her complaining. The important thing was that Jodean let most of it fall on deaf ears. It hadn't been easy, but Mike finally talked her into a driving lesson.

He knew it was too early to expect a letter from Tom Coker about Joseph Dunlap or from the railroad clerk in Fort Worth about passenger lists, but he did hope to hear from home. As it turned out, the only piece of mail in his box was a check from the government. His monthly pay for the FWP work, which was almost finished. Mike thought about what he'd do, where he'd go when he finished his interviews in Cooperville. Rudy Cochran hadn't mentioned anything more about a job at the *Cooperville Gazette* and yet, if he did, Mike wondered what he'd tell Rudy? Did he want to stay in Cooperville? Shouldn't he go back home, see to his family?

He left the post office and headed for the bank on High Street where he cashed his check and asked for a dollar's worth of dimes. From there he struck out for the train depot.

Cooperville had slumped into a lethargic quandary. When he passed the courthouse, the older gentlemen, the ones Doris said qualified to sit on the dead pecker bench, whittled without their usual chatter. And no one lingered to talk in front of City Café or the newspaper office. No spitting or chewing anywhere that Mike could see.

With the Pickle Festival over and Effie Beck found, there seemed little need for stirring around, nothing to fuss and stew about. Sad that people needed something to celebrate or complain about in order to connect.

At the depot, Mike dropped a dime in the pay phone, closed the booth doors and gave his mother's telephone number to the operator. Evelyn, his sister-in-law, answered after the third ring. Mike recognized her slow, hollow-sounding voice in spite of the scratchy connection.

"Long distance from Mike Lemay." The operator sounded like she had a cold.

"Yes. Hello, Mike?"

"That'll be sixty cents, sir," the operator said.

"Hold on, Evelyn." Mike fed coins in the slot. "Evelyn, how's Mother? I've been looking for a letter for weeks."

"We know you have, Mike. It's just that things could change any minute and we haven't been sure what to tell you."

"What does the doctor say?"

"That she had a stroke and isn't getting enough air to her brain, that she don't want to go on living."

Mike leaned his forehead on the grimy phone booth wall. "Is she there? Can I talk to her?"

"Sure thing Mike, but I warn you, she don't make sense most of the time. I read your letters to her and tell her about the money you send but—" The phone crackled, made snapping sounds. He missed some of what Evelyn said but let her keep going. "Hold on a minute and I'll go get her."

Mike heard mumbling in the background then the receiver moved across something rough. "Hello?"

"Hi, Ma. It's Mike."

"Mike who?"

"Your youngest boy, Ma." Mike heard Evelyn coaching in the background. The operator interrupted and said he needed to put in more money.

"Hold on, Ma."

"To what?"

"The phone. Wait 'til I put more money in the pay phone."

"I don't have no money 'cept what my boys give me. The baby, he's in Texas, don-cha know?"

Thick sludge filled Mike's throat. He closed his eyes. "I love you, Ma."

"Such a sweet boy."

"Mike? Mike, you still there?" Evelyn asked.

"Evelyn, should I come home?"

"Only if it's what you want. Jobs is still hard to come by."

"I have another month, at least, before I'm finished here."

"Then I'd say you better keep at it long as you got pay coming."

"Evelyn, I—"

"Please deposit thirty-five cents for the next three minutes, sir," the operator interrupted again.

"Evelyn, listen, I'm—"

"Don't worry none now, Mike. We'll let you know if anything changes. I'll tell James you called. He'll be real sorry he missed you."

"Tell—" The telephone line made a noise like wind blowing through it, then went dead. Mike looked at the receiver and thought how magical the thing was to put his family right up to his ear like that and then suck it back again, quick, in a crackling wind.

Jodean was on the front porch when he turned the corner on his way back from town. As he got closer, her eyes moved over his face and he could tell she'd read his state of mind. That's how she was, what drew him in whether he wanted it or not. He wondered if she read everyone like that – so aware of another's mind.

He waved then parked the Ford in the shed so he could check a tire he thought might be low. Jodean walked around from the front of the house and joined him there. "Did you get to talk to your momma?" she asked.

"Some. She didn't know who I was."

Mike used a foot pump to add air to the tire. Jodean waited until he stood and turned to face her. The muscles in her forehead squeezed into a tiny V between her dark eyebrows. "Are you going to leave soon?" she asked.

"I need to finish my job here before I decide what to do." He returned the foot pump to a shelf. She was reading him again. Mike stepped closer, cupped her sweet open face in his hands and kissed her lightly. She kissed back and the rest of the world fell away while the two of them spiraled up from the ground on a warm current of air. When they moved apart, Jodean pressed her palms to his chest and hitched a breath.

Instead of taking Spring Creek Road, Mike drove east through town then north to the highway, where he parked the shoulder. Few cars passed by on the straight stretch so he thought it would do for teaching Jodean how to shift gears. He motioned her to move close to his side. She grinned like a schoolgirl and moved across the seat until her arm pressed against his.

After a little instruction on how to maneuver the gears and clutch, he got out and walked around to the passenger side. She scooted under the steering wheel.

"Okay," he said. "Clutch and shift. That's it. Now ease out on the clutch." She let up on the clutch too fast. The car bucked forward and died.

They laughed unselfconsciously leaning into each other's shoulders.

"I can do it if I take my shoes off." Jodean shot him a saucy grin. Mike pealed with laughter. She elbowed his ribs.

"I've been meaning to ask you about that..."

"Oh?"

"Why don't you like shoes?"

"I'm not sure. Daddy said I always kicked them off from...day one." There was a blink of time between Jodean's last words, as if a thought struck her mid-sentence, but then she continued. "I hate having my feet pinched all day. I like to feel the cool gritty floor in the kitchen or the cushion of grass in the yard, smooth rocks at the creek. Always have."

Once she got the hang of shifting and driving on the straight stretch, they drove to Horse Pen Canyon where they stopped and got out of the car. She told him tales of Indians driving wild ponies up the river valley to the narrow pass between walls of limestone. "They blocked off the pass by wedging tree limbs between the tumbled boulders there, see?"

Mike squeezed his eyes against the sun's glare to look where she pointed. Unspoiled land sloped to the west with the wide green path of the Medina River tacking across it all the way to the horizon. Violet rocky hills, above which vultures wheeled on thermals, shimmered in the heat. Mike felt distilled to a moment. The sight, the sound of Jodean's voice, hot air fanning them, all of it attached to the back of his skull and he knew that no matter what happened from that moment on, he'd be able to recall anew this place and instant and relive it with the same razor-sharp clarity that he felt right then.

"...Then there was the time Daddy said—"

"—I love you Jodean."

Her face went flat all of a sudden. "You can't Mike. You don't know enough about me."

"I know all I need to."

"You're wrong."

Her response jolted him. Had he misjudged the way she'd returned his kiss back at the shed? Had he fooled himself into thinking she'd let him into her heart that day at the hospital?

"I'll explain another time. Let's not spoil today," Jodean said.

She touched his arm and said she was too tired to drive anymore. Out of confusion, more than anything else, Mike let her comment drop. He held the truck door open for her and said, "You need to understand, I'm sure of how I feel."

The subject dropped. He doubled back down the canyon trail to Butter and Egg Road. Jodean explained the road got its unusual name because Breezy had used it for as long as any of them could remember to deliver his butter and eggs to ranchers along the way. But Mike wasn't in the mood for history lessons. He continued to puzzle over Jodean's strange reaction to his declaration of love.

A few miles from town they spotted Faye Lackland's car curled around a formidable oak tree. Red was trying, without much luck, to pry the bumper with a heavy limb while Faye gunned the motor in reverse. When Mike pulled to the side of the road and got out to help, it was obvious that more had been damaged than Faye's car. Her eyes were red and tear-soaked, her bottom lip blue and swollen, blood dried on the front of her blouse. Red didn't, wouldn't or couldn't meet Mike's eyes. Dried blood caked his red nose. He kept sniffling. Mike glanced back at Jodean as she rushed to ask Faye what had happened.

"Jodean, please, can you take me to talk to Ada? I have to talk with her."

"I'm—I'm not sure I can drive all that good yet." Jodean looked at Mike and then they both turned to Red for an explanation. He drew back a little and observed the ground.

Faye bounded out of the car and lunged toward Mike. "Will you drive me?"

"Faye, there's no call for you to talk to Ada," Red said. "It's between her and me."

"I'm leaving Cooperville first chance I get. I may never see Ada again. I have to talk to her, Red. I have to."

Red blew air out of his mouth and nodded. "Go on Mike. Jodean, Ada's going to be needing you, I 'spect. I'll stay here, keep working on this bumper. I don't think there's any harm done to the engine. Maybe by the time you all get back here, I'll have it loosened enough you can pull the car back to the road."

Mike said, "I have a crow bar in the truck if you think that'll help."

"Damn right."

Mike fetched the crowbar for Red while Faye and Jodean climbed in the cab of the truck. He couldn't stand to look at either Red or Faye. The pain of whatever had happened to them was so great it wasn't going to go away for a long, long while.

By the time Mike, Jodean and Faye rolled to a stop beside the water trough outside the Kasper house, the sky had faded to late day blue. Pete sat on the porch steps with his elbows propped on his knees and his chin in his hands. Behind him, Ada moved through the door and crossed the porch.

Faye turned to Mike and Jodean. "I'll send the kids out here. Maybe y'all could keep them out of earshot for a while."

Ada folded her arms across her chest while Faye approached. Ada said something to Pete and the boy jumped up and started yelling under the steps. The other three kids climbed out from under the porch and ran for the truck where they packed in on top of Jodean and each other.

"We're going for a ride," Mike said.

"Where to?" Jean asked.

"Where would you like to go?"

"California."

Mike shot Jodean a look. "You asked," she said.

"I need to feed Miss Effie's chickens," Pete said.

Mike, grateful for Pete's suggestion, circled the yard and a few minutes later swung into the Beck drive. He glanced over at Pete. The boy's eyes were heavy with worry as he got out of the cab and headed for the chicken shed. Ted and Jean followed Pete squabbling non-stop about who would be in charge of the bucket of feed.

Tootie Sue whined until Jodean took her hand and walked her around the yard and onto the front porch. Mike pulled a blade of grass to chew then trailed behind Jodean.

"Do you think it's okay to go inside?" Jodean asked.

"Don't know why not."

She turned the doorknob and pushed. Emmet had said it would be silly to lock the house because it contained nothing of value and any hobo bum or drifter could easily bust a window to get in out of the weather. Except for an odd pewter light filtering through the grimy windows, everything looked exactly as it had the day he and Tubby found the photograph.

In the front room Jodean turned in a little circle and then moved into the kitchen where her eyes darted from object to object, corner to corner. She touched the back of a chair, looked at the plate and chipped cup, along with the fork and knife, that had been set in place on the table with obvious care.

Then she moved to the sink and leaned forward to peer out the window. When she drew back, she sniffed and looked all around, her eyes coming to rest on a little shelf above the stove lined with small bottles of spice. Jodean picked one up, blew dust off the label, then unscrewed the lid and sniffed. "Ginger," she said.

"In there is the trunk where we found the photograph," Mike said. He could tell the house intrigued Jodean as much as it had him the day of the search. And ever since, he tried to determine just who Effie Beck was, not only in relation to the town, but to himself as well, which was absurd when he stopped to think about it.

Jodean moved to the doorway of the bedroom where Tootie Sue had already discovered the trunk. She mashed an old hat down on her head and tugged on the corner of a stained tablecloth buried deep in the trunk.

"Now just look at you all dressed up," Jodean said. Tootie Sue wrapped the cloth around her shoulders and looked at Mike with a shy grin. Tootie Sue leaned back into the trunk to get something else that caught her eye. When she straightened, she held the baby shoe out at arm's length saying, "Me, me," then squatted and tried to put the shoe on.

"Silly girl, that shoe is too small for you." Jodean took the shoe from Tootie Sue and was straightening the laces when she suddenly froze and handed the shoe back to Tootie Sue. She looked at Mike, "I hear Pete calling. We better go see about the others."

She started for the door but Mike blocked her way. "The day you were picking wild flowers, remember? A look hit your face then, just like it did now. Why? What is it?"

Tootie Sue tugged on his pant leg and held up the shoe. Clear liquid ran down her nose to her mouth. "Me?" she said.

Jodean sidestepped. "You're making a lot out of nothing, Mike."

"Explain to me what *nothing* is."

She grabbed the shoe from Tootie Sue and pitched it in the trunk and slammed the lid. Tootie Sue let out a squeal. Jodean scooped the child into her arms and headed outside. Mike's blood heated. He'd been walking around with his lovesick head in the clouds long enough. One way or another he'd get to the bottom of Jodean's flip-flop moods.

They said nothing to each other on the way back to the Kasper place. Faye and Ada were still on the porch steps. Ada sitting much like Pete had been with her knees drawn to her chest and Faye standing on the bottom step. Both women glanced up at the truck.

"You kids wait a minute." Jodean said before Pete could open the door.

Faye turned back to Ada, held out her arms, hands palm up and bounced them with each word she spoke. Ada said something back without looking up. Faye slumped to the steps, sat next to Ada and leaned down to peer into her dropped face. For a minute or two, both women appeared paralyzed. Finally, Ada stood and gave Mike a nod. Jodean opened the door to let the kids out. When Faye made her way to the truck, she told Jodean she should stay with Ada while Mike drove her back to her car. "Ada'll explain," Faye added.

Jodean glanced at Mike. "Go ahead," he said. "I'll pick you up when I drop Red off back here."

But he wished she'd gone along to take Faye back to her car. He didn't know what to say, still couldn't look her in the face for fear it would cause her more pain and embarrassment than she already felt. He couldn't imagine what had happened.

Red was leaning on the fender of Faye's car when they returned. He'd managed to free the tangled bumper and, in a matter of minutes, using a stretch of chain, they pulled the car back to the road. Both men insisted on following Faye into town in spite of her protests.

"If we run into Neal, let me explain what happened," Faye said. They agreed, but in the end they saw no one. Faye turned into the circle drive at her house and waved to them as she got out and went inside.

Mike headed back out of town to take Red home.

"Guess you're wanting to know what happened," Red said.

"Only if you need to run it by me before you face Ada."

"Between me wallowing in my grief and Faye running from her fears… We lost sight of ourselves for a while. She'd been driving crazy-like hoping to kill herself when I crossed the road on horseback looking for Pot Roast. Sonofabitch!" Red hit the dash with his fist. "How could I let a thing like that happen?"

Mike didn't bother to ask *what* thing. When he turned off the road at the Kasper house for what felt like the hundredth time that day, Jodean came out of the house. At the same time Red popped the pickup door open and got out. The two paused halfway between the house and the truck but said nothing to each other when their eyes met.

On the way back to town Mike told Jodean what Red had said.

Jodean let a big sigh and kept her eyes straight ahead. "Ada thought Red'd been hurt when Sampson showed up without him. Faye told her she was desperate wanting, hoping for somebody to rescue her from her awful life when Red just happened to cross her path."

Mike turned on the headlights and wondered at what point it had gotten dark. They drove the rest of the way in silence. He parked the Ford in the shed and turned off the ignition. It was pitch dark. Jodean yanked on the door handle and bounded out of the truck. He did the same and met her at the shed door.

"Don't say anything, Mike." She hugged her arms to herself. Her voice wavered.

Mike wanted answers but couldn't make himself force her. "I'll let you pick the time to explain why it's so impossible for me to love you. In the meantime, I plan to do everything I can to find out what you're holding back, what you find so painful to tell me. Consider yourself warned."

He could see her head move up and down in the inky blackness. "And…nothing I find out will change how I feel."

He drew her into his arms and rested his chin on her head. Finally, she unlocked her arms and wrapped them around him and squeezed before pulling away to run for the house.

CORA MAE TOSSED burned breakfast toast in the sink just as Jodean came through the kitchen door. She hated that the girl caught her struggling so.

Jodean poured herself a cup of coffee. "How many appointments do you have today?"

"Mrs. Harden, the one who doesn't wash her hair between appointments, smells like a henhouse, is coming at nine-thirty. Then Frances and that Eula woman."

"I feel better, like I can help a little. If you shampoo, I'll set."

Humph, Cora thought to herself. Been long enough since she had that operation but she's still milking the attention. Ungrateful little snit. But Cora Mae knew she had to hold herself back. Jodean's pale, thin look drew a lot of sympathy. And that damn Mike didn't help any, pawing over her the way he did. Give him time. He'd learn the truth of things and be off in a flash. Then who would Jodean have left to turn to? Her momma, that's who. Cora Mae thought about what a taxing time it had been, carrying on with the beauty shop by herself the way she had, headaches and all. She put four more slices of bread on the broiler tray.

"Isn't this June Rawlings' regular day?" Jodean asked.

"Said she wants to skip this time." Cora would be damned before telling Jodean the uppity preacher's wife said she wouldn't be back until Jodean was well. At least June was too goody-goody to complain to Jodean about a bad haircut. Cora Mae poured herself more coffee and scooped eggs from the skillet.

"The toast, Momma, it's ready."

Cora Mae jerked the broiler drawer out, retrieved the tray of toast and then kicked the drawer shut with a little more force than she'd intended. She put a slice of toast, along with some bacon and eggs, on a plate and set it in front of Jodean. Jodean popped out of her chair, poured a second cup of coffee, grabbed the plate and dashed out the back door.

Well, damn if she wasn't taking it to Mike. Cora kicked at the broiler drawer again and the whole kitchen rattled.

If that wasn't bad enough, later, when Mrs. Harden came in she wanted to know if she could pay for her hair appointment with a dozen eggs. Jodean had the nerve to say "that'd be just fine," without so much as asking if it was okay.

While Jodean set Mrs. Harden's hair, Eula walked in. All Cora Mae could think, looking at Eula's face, was how plain.

"Ada looking after your kids?" Jodean asked Eula.

"Yeah. She took 'em to the park, said she'd bring 'em by here in about an hour. This is sure nice of y'all. I mean to give me a free appointment and watch after my kiddos and all."

Cora Mae turned to the shampoo bowl, adjusted the water then tapped Eula on the shoulder so she'd lean back. Eula reclined and added, "Otis says people here are real nice."

Frances huffed through the door and let out a dramatic sigh. "Have y'all seen Faye's car?"

"No. Why?" Cora Mae splashed Eula in the face when she glanced around at Frances.

"The front of it is all mashed in. Tubby said she hit a tree. Looks like Neal hitched the bumper out of the way of the tires with a piece of rope. It's just kinda hanging there."

"Now why do you suppose she'd do a thing like that?" Cora Mae asked as if Faye would intentionally run into a tree.

Eula blew water out of her nose.

"Tubby said she was dodging doves on the road." Frances dropped her big handbag in the empty set chair. "You know anything about it, Jodean?"

Jodean turned the hair dryer on and motioned Mrs. Harden over.

"Humph," Frances huffed, but the effect of it drowned in dryer noise.

An hour later, with Mrs. Harden sent on her way, Jodean gave Eula her comb out. Cora Mae was finishing Frances' set when Ada came bounding up the front steps with her four and Eula's two kids in tow.

"Why, I didn't see your car, Ada," Cora Mae said.

"We decided to walk from the park. I'm trying to tire the kids out so they'll take a nice long nap this afternoon."

"Say," Frances piped in. "Maybe you know what hap—"

"—I'll be finished with Eula in a minute or two," Jodean interrupted. "Pete, why don't you take the little ones to the kitchen. You all look like you could use a cool drink of water after walking all the way from the park."

Ada glanced at the kids' blank faces turned her way and nodded at Pete to go ahead.

"Looky there," Frances shouted pointing at the window. She leaned down to get a better look under the half drawn shade. "It's Faye in her wrecked car. By golly, I'll ask her myself what happened. Tubby never gets anything right."

Cora Mae raised the shade the rest of the way up and noticed Ada stiffen. Something, by damn, was going on and she'd bet Jodean knew all about it. Faye came through the door carrying that stupid basket of children's books. Now *that's* what she wanted an answer for. Why all those kids books?

Faye's eyes stayed on Ada a beat longer than was natural. "I—I didn't see your car out front."

"I walked from the park with the kids."

Faye turned away quickly to face Eula with a shaky smile. *Finally*, Cora Mae thought, the titty-pull she and Frances had been waiting for. And right here in the beauty parlor!

Faye moved to the set chair and held the basket out to Eula. "Otis said I'd find you here. I'm leaving town and don't expect to be back anytime soon. I thought you and Otis might like to have these little storybooks. My children have long since outgrown them—" Faye's voice caught in her throat. She swallowed hard. "Maybe your children…?"

Eula took the basket. "Why, that's mighty sweet of you."

Faye whirled around but stopped dead when her eyes met Ada's. Ada looked away and Faye gave them all a quick good-bye and was gone in a flash.

"Well, I nev—"

"Hush!" Jodean barked at Cora Mae.

"I should think," Eula said, unaware of the sparks in the air, "that you all are sure going to miss that fine lady. I don't know what my Otis would've done all these months without her help."

All eyes locked on Eula. Frances' mouth gaped.

"Y'all don't know?" Eula scanned their blank faces.

Cora Mae leaned forward. "Know what?"

"Well, I 'spect Faye didn't say anything on account of she didn't want to embarrass Otis. You see, he never had a chance to go to school. Never learned to read or write properly. Faye Lackland has been teaching my Otis to read so he could get promoted to foreman." Eula peered out the window at Faye moving down the walk.

Ada bolted for the door. Jodean scrambled right behind her. Frances and Cora Mae joined Eula at the window. The three women on the sidewalk outside the beauty shop hugged each other and sobbed like little babies. Cora Mae felt cheated. Damned cheated.

"Yessirree," Eula said, thumbing through a little red book with a rocking horse on the cover. "I 'spect y'all gonna miss Faye Lackland round here."

IT HAD BEEN a week since Jodean slept the night through. She stretched out flat on her back in the narrow bed and kicked the top sheet off her legs. She was hot and sticky, no air moving anywhere, inside or out.

She still couldn't believe Faye left town. Not that anyone blamed her. It was a shock because no one ever left Cooperville by choice like that. Neal walked the streets dark-faced and grim now and Faye was never mentioned in his presence. People behaved as if nothing had changed. Somehow that didn't seem fair to Faye because everyone cared a lot more for her than Neal.

That day in front of the beauty shop Faye told her and Ada she expected Neal would sooner or later come looking for her, and that she was scared. But since she didn't have any kind of life anyway she figured she wasn't risking much. Jodean couldn't imagine most of what Faye was talking about, but Ada explained a lot of it later.

Ada had the heart of a giant to forgive Faye the way she did. Even though Ada hadn't said the actual word, Jodean could tell Faye felt it. They all felt it the minute they threw their arms around each other. Forgiveness, giving it and receiving it, was an essential element for love and understanding. Sort of like what Brother Rawlings said at Miss Effie's funeral.

Jodean rolled to her side and stared at a wide band of moonlight beaming through the tied-back curtains. The hall clock at the bottom of the stairs tick, tick, ticked. Somewhere down the street a dog barked three or four sharp warnings then fell silent.

She thought of Mike. The first day she'd seen him through the screen door of the tank house, crumpled with sleep, thin and sad. He'd changed so much since then. And he, in turn, had changed her, though she wasn't sure just how.

If only he'd stop worrying about Effie Beck's past the way he did. But then, why did that bother her so? After all, the baby shoe was just a ridiculous coincidence.

She hoped Mike would stay in Cooperville, maybe get a job here and keep everything the same. Rides through the hills on Sunday afternoons, walks to Spring Creek late after a hot day, talks on the porch swing Saturdays after he mowed the lawn, feeling the heat of him sitting close by.

She recalled Mike's kiss, the way it made her legs go limp. She imagined him kissing her again and again, until his kisses reached her collarbone and then the valley between her breasts.

She drew her knees to her chest, willed her body to stop longing for Mike. But it didn't do much good. He was there on the back of her eyelids and she couldn't sleep for the sight of him. The quiet but sure way he moved around town, a wayfarer in a foreign place. The way he worried about his family back in North Carolina. The way he could make her skin go slack by just looking at her.

She sat upright for a minute then got out of bed and moved to the window. The tank house loomed like a tall, milky-blue tower in moon glow. Jodean wondered again how Faye found the courage to change her life.

MIKE TORE OPEN the envelope before leaving the post office. It was a letter from Tom Coker, the one he'd been waiting an eternity for. He scanned the usual jargon about turning in reports on time and making sure he stuck to the interview format outlined in the FWP instruction manual. About halfway down the first page his eyes locked on the name Joseph Dunlap.

"Hey there, young fellow." Clyde Cheevers slapped Mike on the shoulder.

Mike gave him a weak smile.

"Me and Tubby was just a while ago wondering where you been. He says you're about to give up air trying to find out about that Beck woman."

"Tubby exaggerates," Mike said, backing toward the door.

Clyde threw his head back and laughed. Mike wouldn't have thought the comment was that funny. He waved the letter and apologized for rushing off, adding he had to see about some business right away. Clyde looked a little dismayed, but nodded and tipped his hat.

Back at the tank house, Mike shut the door and sat down, eager to glean any information the letter offered. As it turned out, old Joe Dunlap was dead, which of course he half expected. He'd died in a tuberculosis sanitarium in Otoe, Oklahoma, on May 30, 1915. He'd never married, and no next of kin had been listed on any of his records.

When Mike finished the letter, he let it flop in his lap and rested his head on the chair back. He'd hoped for a clue of some kind to the man's background, anything that could lead back to Effie Beck or the little girl in the photograph. Mike leaned forward again, elbows on knees. An irritating niggling told him he had all the information needed to figure out Effie Beck's frame of mind when she left Cooperville all those years ago.

Why was she in Fort Worth the day Aunt Nola adopted her boys, why did she come back and why did she hang around town at night? He just couldn't make the puzzle pieces fit.

He moved to the shelf above the window and grabbed the folder he'd titled "Effie Beck Lost," a phrase from Brother Rawlings' funeral sermon that had echoed over and over in his head. Mike turned it upside down and dumped everything on the floor. Joe's letters, the two photographs, newspaper clippings asking for public help in finding Miss Beck, the notes he'd made after talking with Aunt Nola – then tossed the letter from Tom on the pile.

The next thing he knew, he was on Spring Creek Road headed for Breezy Parker's place. Why? He couldn't have said for sure. When he arrived, Trudy was picking purple hull peas in the garden at the side of the house. She had moved Breezy's porch chair to the shade of a cottonwood tree next to the garden. He was shelling peas and telling the smallest of his grandchildren stories about a black king in Africa who had been their great-great uncle.

Trudy waved at Mike but the children at Breezy's feet took off when they saw him approach.

"Here now. That ain't no way to do," Breezy scolded the scattering children. "Sit yourself down, Mr. Lemay." Breezy indicated a straight-back kitchen chair with a big bowl on the seat. Mike sat and started shelling peas from a burlap bag on the ground between them.

"You don't have to do that," Trudy said. She walked out of the sunny garden with a bucket of peas. She pushed her poke bonnet off her head and emptied the peas into the burlap bag.

"It'll give me something to do with my hands," Mike said.

"Got the fidgets, have you?" Breezy asked.

"Worse, Breezy. I can't get Effie Beck off my mind."

A few of the children started squabbling behind the henhouse and Trudy took off to scold them. The next thing Mike knew, she had them in the garden picking peas. To Mike, Trudy was the closest thing to a fairy godmother he would ever likely see. Even in her scolding he heard infinite and everlasting mindfulness, a deep inborn caring power. His own mother had been like that once.

"Why you got Miss Effie on your mind?" Breezy asked. He reached for another handful of peas.

"A woman from Pole Cat Creek says she saw Miss Effie years ago with a baby girl, not quite two years old, at the railroad station in Fort Worth. The woman and her husband were there to adopt two boys off the orphan train. She even had a picture with Miss Beck in the background. Now, Breezy, I got to wondering if Miss Effie couldn't have been ... well, with child when she left here with the sickness her daddy said she had."

Breezy continued to shell his peas without looking up.

"I think Joe Dunlap, the medicine show man, could have fathered the child. I checked some sources and found out he died in Oklahoma of TB."

"That right, now?"

"Is there anything more you can tell me about Effie Beck? Anything to help me find out if she had a child, or where that child might be?"

"No, sir." Breezy stopped shelling peas. "Might be you digging up a whole lotta mess," he said, turning steady eyes on Mike. "What else you got on your mind?"

Mike studied Breezy's face. The old gentleman was a mind-reading soothsayer. Of course, Mike wanted to blurt out *Jodean*, but didn't dare. He wasn't ready to admit that she'd bewitched him, wheedled him down just by moving in and out of his days, that the sight of her siphoned his common sense. Her scent stayed in his nostrils long after she was gone, and late at night he'd wake thinking he could taste her mouth. He felt feverish most of the time. Infatuation? Surely. Nothing genuine could feel so intense. It would kill a man after a while.

On the other hand, Mike had never been more sure of himself, more purposeful. Somehow giving his heart to Jodean had unburdened him, freed him to accept things he couldn't do anything about and gave him enough backbone to change the things he could. But it scared the hell out of him, like he'd lost some of his powers along with his heart.

"Breezy, it looks to me as if Cooperville keeps Jodean Travis at arm's length. She's always asked to judge the Pickle Queen contest, a position reserved for out-of-towners, visitors, anyone not associated with the town. Why?"

"Some folks call it like they sees it from their eyes, not necessarily from truth's eyes."

"What is the truth?"

"Miss Jodean, she a fine little lady."

"Exactly. So why hasn't some man scooped her up?" He didn't know why he bothered asking except that he liked the old man.

"May be none of 'em smart enough."

Mike tilted back and balanced on the back legs of his chair.

"Where you folks at, Mr. Lemay?"

Mike explained that his father lost the family farm in the Crash and died a shriveled-down man not long afterward, and that his mother's mind went south with the migrating birds the following spring.

"Hard times ain't the punishment, don-cha know. They's the lesson. You got to decide which counts the most, what you lost or what you learned from it."

A car horn blasted. Breezy jumped and nearly dropped his bowl of shelled peas. Trudy yelled, "You chil-ren done it now! I'm gonna blister me some black hide!"

The two older children had put the youngest up to blowing the truck's horn. Breezy got tickled watching them scramble, but his laughter turned into a coughing spasm. Trudy patted his bony shoulders a few times on her way to the truck with a cottonwood switch.

"Trudy, wait," Mike called out. "No harm done. As a matter of fact, let me take them for a ride."

She stopped dead in her tracks, shot him a puzzled look.

"You and Breezy come along too," Mike added.

She shifted her eyes to Breezy, who was still trying to clear his throat. He wiped his watery eyes with his handkerchief and sucked a clear breath. "Las one in da automobile is a rotten egg."

A free-for-all broke out as they all piled on the back of the truck and squirmed for a place to sit. Trudy hopped on, too, but left her feet dangling over the rear edge.

"Whew-wee, ain't this sompin' now," Breezy said. He sat in the cab with Mike and stared ahead with an expressionless face, but Mike could tell he was having the time of his life.

"Lord, lord," Trudy shouted as she waved to Jericho out in the cotton fields when they drove by. Jericho's laughter trailed the truck like the sound of drums in a deep forest. For a fleeting instant Mike felt connected to all things that mattered.

An hour later he delivered Breezy and his heirs back to the house. He helped Trudy settle the old man on the front porch where he preferred to be when evening approached.

"We ain't got much, Mr. Lemay," Trudy said. "Little bit of ham bone, some cornbread, and 'course purple hull peas. Will you stay to eat?"

He turned down Trudy's offer. It was odd though, that on the way back to town he felt as if he'd feasted. Breezy's parting remark stayed with him, made him want to think hard on all the things that had happened since he and his family left their farm under a cloud of utter despair. With a watery-eyed wink, Breezy had repeated the phrase, "*this ain't the punishment, it's the lesson.*"

When Mike turned into the drive at the Travis house, Jodean was crossing the yard on her way to the tank house. She stopped when she saw him coming and waited until he parked in the shed.

"Momma's canasta ladies need me to fill in for the coach's wife so I left your supper in the oven."

She was wearing a pale yellow sun-dress with wide straps that tied on each shoulder. Her fragile-looking collarbones ended on either side of the valley at her throat.

"Will you be back in time to walk down to the creek?"

"It'll be after dark."

He knew what she was doing. Avoiding him, his questions. At the same time, she seemed to accept that sooner or later he'd find out what he wanted to know.

"Maybe tomorrow," she said.

He reached to touch a small mole high on her cheek, but she took a step back. A little later he watched her walk down the sidewalk with Cora Mae.

After eating the dinner Jodean left in the oven, he plopped in his tank house chair and stared at the pile of Effie Beck notes scattered on the floor. When it got too dark to see, he yanked the pull string for the light and emptied his mind so all the chaos of the last weeks could sift down to an ordered list of facts. But, just as he thought he could see a chain of possible events in Effie's life, Jodean popped into his head and his mind would be off and running in her direction.

The next thing Mike knew, a hot poker-like pain shot up the back of his neck and he jerked awake to find Jodean standing under the dangling light bulb. She'd taken off her shoes and one shoulder of her sun dress had slipped down to her elbow.

"It's late," she said. She tapped the papers on the floor with her bare toes. When she looked at him again, her face was slack, her mouth open and moist. She reached up and tugged on the light string, throwing them into shadowy darkness. She moved to his side, let her fingers drift over his arm. Every rational thought Mike had up to that moment rolled away. Like a man craving oxygen, he drew her into the curve of his body. Air groaned through his vocal chords and blew moist and warm on her face.

RED THOUGHT THINGS couldn't go on like this another day longer. It was time for Ada to forgive him or tell him to take a long goddamn hike. Even the kids suffered under the black cloud that had blown overhead the day Faye hit that tree. The look on Ada's face when she realized what had been going on flashed across his mind every time he blinked, and bile surged from his belly and burned his throat. He, by-god, couldn't take much more. And just as painful was seeing the droop of Pete's young shoulders. The boy still hadn't looked him in the eye, and Pot Roast was still lost. Red couldn't remember when something or someone wasn't missing, felt he'd been on the lookout all summer, if not for Effie Beck then Pot Roast.

He heard a screen door pop shut. Red raised up onto his elbow in the hayloft where he'd been sleeping since the Faye fiasco. It was Pete coming out of the house, headed for the barn with the milk bucket. As bad as Red wanted to talk to the boy, tell him how sorry he was for worrying all of them, he knew he shouldn't until he tried to talk to Ada one more time. Amazing how that woman could toot her bugle without drawing a breath or uttering a word. He climbed down from the loft, reaching the last ladder rung as Pete moved by.

"Pete?" The boy gave no indication that he'd heard. "Your mother and I need to do some talking. Soon as she finishes her breakfast chores, I want you to watch after the others while we take a ride."

Pete positioned himself on a three-legged stool next to the milk cow and started cleaning her udders.

"Did you hear what I said?"

Pete nodded.

"Then you and me will have a talk, too."

At the water trough between the house and barn, Red took off his shirt and pumped water over his head and face. He could see Ada moving around in the house, hear Tootie Sue whining. Using a bar of soap, he worked a lather and washed his neck and ears. Maybe if Ada saw him washing first thing in the morning like this she'd be impressed. She'd had her panties in a wad so long he couldn't be sure what she thought anymore, but anything was worth a try.

He dried off, buttoned his shirt, then slipped into the kitchen where Ada worked strips of bacon around a big skillet. He moved to the stove to pour himself a cup of coffee. She sidestepped just enough to let him know none of her feelings had changed. Her mouth had a gray ring around it. She looked ashen, sick. Red turned to Tootie Sue sitting at the table with an empty plate in front of her. She stuck out her bottom lip and covered her face with a rag. A sonofabitchin' shame when even Tootie Sue couldn't stand to look at him.

Jean came into the kitchen and joined Tootie Sue at the table. Ted hung back at the door.

"You kiddos are going to stay with Pete while your momma and me go for a ride."

Ada spun around from the stove.

"We're going to talk, Ada Ann. I've had enough of this." Her eyes looked bleary and tired. Red finished his coffee in three long gulps. "I'll go saddle Gyp."

When he walked Gyp out of the barn, all four kids were lined up on the porch steps. He looked from one little face to another and ended eyeball to eyeball with Pete. Ada stepped out of the house wearing a pair of his pants, something she rarely did, even when helping brand or doctor cattle. She was a beautiful woman in spite of the hardships of ranching life, and through some of the worst years in memory at that. He held the stirrup for her and gave her a hand up, then swung himself up behind her. Old Gyp let out a windy sigh when Red tapped her belly with the heel of his boot.

Ada felt warm and soft against his chest. She'd brushed her hair off her neck and pinned it in a knot on the back of her head.

Once they were clear of the first clump of trees, Red said, "I'd walk through fire for you, darlin'."

"Why'd you do it, Red?"

"You make it sound like I planned it. It just happened, like a freak accident."

"Have there been other times?"

"God no, Ada. You know that."

Somehow, not facing each other made it easier to talk. Having their hips move in tandem with the horse's sway reminded Red of how good they moved together in other ways. He reined Gyp off the trail and up a low hill. When he did, his arms moved against hers and he could have sworn she relaxed into his chest a little. He pulled Gyp to a halt in a grove of trees near the west tank. Mist hovered above the greenish water, and heavy dew made the ground look crystalized. Red dismounted first then looked back up at Ada still astride Gyp. "Tell me you believe me."

"Why, Red? *Why?*"

"I felt so bad about Miss Effie, almost like somebody coldcocked me." He helped her dismount. "Then there was Faye. We all know she's had it hard. Hard in a different way from Miss Effie, but just as bad. She was crying and shaking and begging me to help her. The truth of things just got all scattered for a while, Ada. It didn't mean anything. I swear."

"Why do you think it's your job to fix everybody's problems?"

"I wish to hell I knew how to answer that." Red's throat nearly closed off, tears welled in his eyes.

"Me and the kids are what you're supposed to worry about first."

"And I do, Ada. I do. You know it's the truth. It's just that all the wrong things came together at the wrong time."

Red let his voice trail when Ada turned her back to him and walked a few steps away. She slumped to her knees on a dry patch of ground where the sun had dried the dew. She looked awful.

"Ada? Don't do this to yourself, to us. I love you. I'm not making up some horseshit excuse here because nothing will excuse what I let happen. The question is can we put this thing behind us?"

"I don't know. I honestly don't know." Her eyes filled with tears.

"You're a good woman, Ada. You've never left me wanting for a thing." He knelt on one knee beside her and smoothed her hair, touched her cheek with the back of his hand. "Ada?"

"I think we have to try." She swallowed hard. "We owe it to the kids."

"And ourselves."

Any little bit of color she had in her cheeks faded with a sigh. She leaned her forehead against his shoulder. Red's heart flooded with relief. He wrapped his arms around her. No woman would ever stir him the way she did. He laid back onto his side and guided her down beside him. The feel of her pressing against him was different. He drew back a little to study her face.

"Red? Honey?"

"What is it?"

She sat up suddenly.

"Ada, for the sake of everything we've had going for us, we got to try."

She pressed her fingers to her mouth. Her breathing quickened.

"Stop doing this to yourself—" Before he could finish, she started waving her hands as if to fan her face.

"What is it?"

"I feel sick."

"Huh?"

She turned away from him and vomited.

Well, sonofabitching dogshit, he'd gone and done it now. "Ada..." he held her shoulders. She heaved again and again, dry choking heaves. When she was done, she leaned back into the curve of his body and sobbed. Red gave up. All he could do was weep right along with her. God only knew how much he loved his broken-hearted queen.

Ada sniffed, then wailed, "I'm pre-g-g-nant!"

MIKE REMINDED HIMSELF of a wallowing hog. Since the night Jodean came to the tank house he'd not been able to reel his mind back in. He daydreamed impossible plots that put him back in the loft with her again. At times he realized he'd been staring at the same word on a typewritten page for long minutes or had watched ants trail the window frame for most of the afternoon.

Jodean had been eager, desperate almost, and yet shy. It surprised and worried him, but impossible to back off and ask questions once she was in his arms. No matter how much he thought himself an honorable man, the thunder of their coming together still rumbled in his ears and flashback images of her willing body fired him all over again.

He set his notes aside with a quick glance at the last line. He hadn't written a single, rational thought in hours, had let his lovestruck fantasies go on long enough. Maybe Red would be at City Café, or Tubby had had time to talk to a lawyer about what to do with the Beck ranch. And come to think of it, he needed to check his mailbox, something he'd let go for days.

He walked by the front of the house, heard Cora Mae's radio and noticed big black clouds forming north of town. The smell of hair solution, or whatever it was called, wafted in the heavy hot air outside the beauty shop window like always, even when the ladies weren't in there. It made him think of Jodean and her fingers all tangled in his hair. But, that kind of thinking would get him nowhere. He hurried to town and found Red and Tubby leaning over cups of coffee at the City Café counter. The skin around Red's eyes still had a hint of bluish-green from Ada's blow. Tubby, content with Red's explanation that his bruises were from Sampson having thrown him, sipped coffee and yawned.

"Hear tell," Tubby said rubbing his eyes, "… there's been a hell of a storm north a ways. Old man Farley says his son, the one that ranches out near Sweetwater, called to say they had a tornado blow through. Leveled the place. The boy had to drive to Abilene to find a working telephone. Twelve inches of rain."

"Well, goddamn, you'd think we could get a little rain around here. Wash the dust down some," Red said.

"I 'spect we'll get some of it. Even if we don't, you can bet the river is gonna rise from the runoff upstream." Tubby yawned again and announced he was going home to take a nap.

Mike turned to Red, "How's Ada, the kids?"

"A whole lot better. I never did get a chance to thank you for your help."

"Any idea what's going to happen to the Beck place?" Mike asked.

Red shook his head. "Tubby was just saying it'd probably go to the state, then auctioned off. Sure would like a chance at it." He looked over his shoulder then back down at his coffee. "Fat chance I'd have coming up with the sonofabitchin' money."

Red didn't look much in a mood to accept news or an opinion out of the ordinary, so Mike made no mention of the little girl in Aunt Nola's photograph or of his suspicions that Effie Beck might have had a child.

Red slid off his stool, said he had to put his mind to rounding up his cattle soon, that he was off to check on-the-hoof prices at the feed store. He threw a few coins on the counter and tipped his hat to Doris. Mike noticed a new gimp in Red's gait, but then it could be that he still suffered in a downtrodden way for what he'd done to Ada.

To Mike's surprise, when he stopped by the post office, he found a letter from the railroad clerk in Fort Worth and the Catholic orphanage in New York. If nothing else, his collection of clues and information would finally be complete. He might learn where to start looking for the little girl in the photograph. Then he'd give up his Beck madness once and for all. By all rights, the job belonged to Tubby and Emmet anyway.

He walked east on Main Street to City Park. In spite of midday heat, gangs of knobby-kneed boys gathered at the baseball diamond. Mike skirted the ball field and crossed to the gazebo benches to read his mail.

In the letter from Fort Worth the clerk explained that his office didn't have a name list for orphaned children accompanied by the nuns. But, he did have a list showing how many children had been passengers along the way.

On July 7, 1909, when the train crossed the Texas state line at Texarkana, twenty-three orphans were listed under the name of the orphanage in New York. Seventeen orphans were on board the next day when the train arrived in Dallas. The day after that, July 9, two orphans and two nuns left Dallas for Forth Worth.

Mike heard the crack of a bat and looked up from the letter. A tall, lanky kid was hell bent for first base while a second boy, half the age of the first, slid into home.

He remembered July 9 was the same day Aunt Nola adopted her boys.

The Catholic Foundling Society letter revealed even less than the railroad clerk's. They informed him that a privacy policy to protect the orphans and their families was strictly upheld. That was that.

Except for a cursory note written in longhand at the bottom of the page. It stated that children placed in Texas between 1899 and 1920 had been visited at least twice during the first three years after adoption.

"Those in charge of the visits," the note continued, "during the time you mentioned, were convinced that all the children enjoyed a healthful family life. Of the six adopted in Texarkana, four are still living, but records of the seventeen adopted in Dallas are incomplete, not surprising since most appreciate our privacy policy and wish to be disassociated from the orphanage."

By *protect* Mike assumed they meant to guard against discrimination toward the orphans.

The last sentence read, "The only item on record about the three adopted in Fort Worth is a note stating that two, who had been brothers, were killed in France during the war."

They would be Aunt Nola's boys. Sister Lena signed her name at the end of the handwritten portion of the letter. He returned the letters to the envelopes. He'd hoped for concrete details like names, histories, faces, but all he got was numbers.

A cheer rang out at the baseball diamond. The long-legged kid who'd made it to first base tried to steal second and got tagged. A bunch of kids on the bench stood and grasped each other by the shoulders.

Mike cut through a vacant lot on his way back to the Travis' backyard where Jodean furiously swept porch steps in that way she had of attacking a task. Everything routine - work, sweep, hoe, smile, cry - took on a peculiar hue all of a sudden. His measure as a man up to the day he first stepped foot in the Medina River valley had been one of unbearable failure. He'd dealt with it by growing thick scabs of guilt, cynicism and anger. Like ice on a hot sidewalk, his dark side had slowly melted away. And, he now knew, the melt began the day he'd eaten a slice of Effie Beck's ginger cake and gazed across the vastness of Texas.

He paused in a patch of shade. Jodean moved down the porch steps to the walkway with her head lowered, bobbing with the effort of making her broom fly. A black curl flopped across her forehead and hid her eyes. She was humming.

Loving Jodean Travis made it easier to see the world from a different angle.

On the cusp of this awareness, dread flooded Mike. Whatever was happening between them would eventually exhume trouble that made Jodean afraid.

Mike thought he was about to wake from a jumbled, hard-to-remember dream in which important things happened but he'd glanced away for a moment and missed what they were. The answers he so desperately wanted were so close.

CORA MAE SAT up and peered over the back of the sofa to see why Jodean laughed. Lum and Abner had just gone off the air and she hoped to get a nap before Glory Hughes arrived for her regular appointment.

Mike was outside making Jodean laugh. Damn his sorry-assed hide. Funny that Jodean could sweep the sidewalk and play slap and tickle with him out there in broad daylight but couldn't do Glory's hair.

Stupid Sheriff Neal had gone loony since Faye left. He told Cora to stay away from him and his office. She'd smelled whiskey on his breath that day at the courthouse when he snarled at her like a mad dog. All she'd wanted was a little help with her situation.

So she was forced to form a plan all by herself and who could blame her, alone like she was. She'd have to wait for the right time. Maybe tomorrow when Jodean was gone to C.J.'s for the week's groceries.

Brother Howard's Healing Hour came on the radio but somehow it didn't matter. The little girl she'd loved and given a home to, fed and taken care of to the point of sacrifice was outside flirting with a worthless drifter. Lord Almighty.

Cora watched Mike take the broom away from Jodean, prop it against the tank house, and pick her up to swing her around in a circle. Jodean screeched like a fool. He put her down with a quick kiss, then pulled on her arm and waved toward the creek. Jodean shook her head and looked at her bare feet. Mike turned around, bent his knees a little and, to Cora Mae's horror, Jodean jumped on him piggyback and they took off through the apple orchard. Beyond them, the sky was dark as night. A storm coming. Cora Mae damn sure hoped the electric didn't go off and cause her to miss her radio programs.

She moved through the house cursing the day Mike Lemay walked into her life. She could still hear Jodean laughing in the distance when she fetched her headache rag out of the refrigerator. She wiped her eyes and blew her nose.

That's all right, she told herself, let them have their fun. Ol' Cora Mae is about to take things into her own hands, with or without Neal Lackland's help.

JODEAN COULDN'T BELIEVE it. Mike kicked off his shoes and jumped in the carp's pool feet first with her still clinging to his back. When he kicked off the bottom to come up for air, she laughed so hard she sucked water down her throat and started a coughing spell. Then, between fits of giggles, he took her breath away with a long kiss.

Mike.

Oh, God help her. She lost all control, all inhibition when he touched her the way he did just now. The two of them were like drops of rain on a windowpane, coming together on their zigzagging way through life. She could no longer separate herself from him, tell which heat was his and which was hers. They slipped from their clothes unhurried, without modesty, as if they'd done it a hundred times, then tossed them layer by layer onto the grassy bank.

Sooner or later he would leave town. She was sure of it. Because of his job or family. Or, because he'd find out about her past. But at least she'd have this memory. She'd remember the feel of him inside her, moving, the deep groan of his soothed passion and the soft puff of his breath on her face.

"I love you, Mike," she whispered as her body convulsed and quivered out of control. But the crackling heat of him drowned her words.

THAT NIGHT BETWEEN fifteen-minute intervals of sleep, Mike's head seethed with images of railroad officials, nuns, and trains roaring across the countryside with the faces of sobbing children pressed to passenger car windows. An hour before dawn, he woke with a start when he dreamed nuns were pinning numbered squares to orphans' clothes. The last child in line was the little girl in Effie Beck's arms... number twenty-four.

He untangled himself from the sheets and almost fell scrambling down the loft ladder. Then he cracked his little toe on the leg of the chair when he reached for the pull string. He squinted against the glare, grabbed the Effie Beck Lost folder and flopped in the armchair.

He seized the letters from the railroad clerk and re-read with a keener eye for details revealed in his dream-crazed half-sleep. He added the number of children who did *not* get back on the train after each stop. The number came to twenty-one. It clearly said *two* orphans and two nuns left Dallas for Fort Worth. Aunt Nola's boys brought the count to twenty-three.

Yet, Sister Lena's note just as clearly stated, "The only thing on record about the *three* adopted in Fort Worth..." Her note clearly said *three*.

Mike was dumbfounded. Here was proof enough, for him anyway, that Effie Beck had indeed given up a baby girl for adoption in Fort Worth. And, someone adopted the baby right after Aunt Nola and her boys left the station. That meant the child likely had *not* been hauled all the way back east somewhere to get lost in America's sea of citified humanity. The little girl might still be in Texas somewhere.

While the chain of evidence was still clear in his mind, he sat out to write it all down in a report, as much for his own understanding, as for the authorities who would make decisions about Effie's after-death affairs. He wanted to see the events spelled out, wanted to know that the clues fit as well as his dream-crazed mind told him they did.

He started with the photograph he and Tubby found in the trunk. He placed it on the floor to his left. Then he placed the letters from Joseph Dunlap in chronological order to the right of the photograph, and ended with the letters he'd received from Tom the day before.

He stopped dead still, eyes locked on the last letter from Joseph Dunlap. He whispered, "Damn." The shock of a new revelation dumbfounded him.

The last letter from Joseph was mailed from Oklahoma City *to* an address in Fort Worth. Not to Effie in Cooperville. Mike figured Effie had gone to see him to tell him she was pregnant - the travels Breezy mentioned. Then, when Joe's job took him to Oklahoma for a matter of weeks she probably stayed behind to give birth and take care of the newborn. There was no way to know that detail for sure.

When Joseph sent the last letter from Oklahoma City, he essentially told her he didn't plan to marry or take responsibility for the child. His exact words were, "This is a nomad's life, not suitable for a family man..." Effie knew she couldn't take care of the child alone with no job, no home. She certainly couldn't go back to Cooperville to face her father as an unwed mother.

Mike leaned back in his chair. He could swear he heard the shrieking blast of Effie Beck's anguish as if she'd been sitting right here beside him.

First thing in the morning he'd head for Tubby's office, show him the report and tell him about his assumptions. If he was right, all they had to do was post letters in all the small-town newspapers, or big cities for that matter, requesting that any woman adopted in July 1909 contact Tubby or Emmet.

Mike rubbed the stubble on his chin and ran his fingers through his hair. He should feel better than he did. Maybe there's a benefit in not knowing a thing. Breezy, who understood so well the art of held-back information, had said once that all things happen according to it's own time. Was it time to learn the truth about Effie Beck, time to reveal her secrets?

He slumped deeper into the chair. A thought crawled across the back of his brain, raised the hair on his arms.

No. No, not Jodean. He'd have known. *Somehow.*

He reached back into the folder and withdrew the photograph of Effie Beck and the child in her arms. Jodean would have told him.

If she knew.

Mike stood suddenly with thoughts rushing his mind. Jodean was adopted, he'd bet on it. Yes, everything fit. The way she was ostracized, was so unlike Cora Mae physically. The day she told him he couldn't love her. Her dread of shoes...the little girl in the photograph with a missing shoe. And the way Jodean responded to the shoe in Effie Beck's trunk. My God, could it be? Did Jodean know? Suspect?

He put the photograph and letters back in the folder and tied the string. Violet light glowed low on the horizon in the east. Mike wished he could stop the day from coming.

Pipes knocked and whistled when he turned on the faucet for his cold, musty-water shower. While shaving he heard Jodean's voice and moved to the screen door to see if she was calling out to him. He glimpsed her moving down the sidewalk toward town calling out to Cora Mae, who apparently stood on the front porch where Mike couldn't see her. He'd hoped to talk to Jodean before she got busy with whatever her day held. In his heart he knew he'd dragged out the morning to keep from confronting her or Tubby or Emmet. Anyone for that matter.

He rinsed his face and patted it dry. A low rumble of thunder rolled across Cooperville. The overcast sky made the day gloomy. Air hung heavy in the tank house, thick with humid heat.

"Yoo-hoo!" Cora Mae came down the walkway toward the tank house.

"Good morning," she said when he stepped to the tank house door.

Why the hell was Cora Mae so cheery? She'd not been to the tank house since the day he'd rented it.

She smoothed her hair. "I was wondering if you could help me get some things down out of the attic. Patterns. That's what I need. Crochet patterns. See, all the ladies are going to make... Oh, well, I know you don't care about any of that."

"I'll get my shoes and be right there."

Inside the house she led him to the attic door in the hall ceiling outside Jodean's bedroom. He tugged the dangling chain and unfolded the ladder.

"Now, it's a couple of boxes I'm needing, like dress boxes, about so big." Cora held her hands about eighteen inches apart.

In the attic, light filtered in from a vent at the end of the roofline. Mike brushed a cobweb off his head. A stack of boxes behind a rocking chair with a torn cane bottom looked promising. He showed one of the boxes to Cora Mae standing at the bottom of the ladder.

"Not that one."

He climbed over several wooden crates full of canning jars.

"As I remember," Cora called out to him, "one of the boxes was tied with ribbon."

He found three boxes in a neat stack and carried them to the attic opening.

"Yeah, that looks like it could be them."

He climbed down careful to balance the boxes and held them while Cora removed the lid off the box on top. It was stuffed full of bits of tissue cut in various shapes. She nodded, replaced the lid then set the box aside and flashed a smile. She untied the ribbon around the second box but somehow managed to knock it from his hands, spilling the contents across the hall floor. Mike was stunned by what he saw.

"Why, would you just look at this," Cora Mae said as she held up a baby dress. "I forgot all about these things. You see this here's the little dress Jodean wore the day her daddy brought her home."

Mike squatted for a closer look at a baby shoe. A right-foot baby shoe that landed on top of some papers.

"And Lord, don-cha know that girl has kicked her shoes off from day one..."

Mike sat on the floor, leaned against the wall. One of the papers was an adoption certificate from the Catholic Foundling Society in New York dated July 9, 1909.

"You didn't know, did you?" Cora said. "I just thought with you doing all that interviewing and such that somebody would've explained things to you. See my husband, Buddy, wanted kids real bad, but I was just too delicate – my headaches and all. And, anyway, for the longest time he'd go to the train station to see about getting one of the orphans from the Baby Train, but they's always all gone by the time the train got this far south. So this one time he decided at the last minute to drive to Fort Worth. You all right, Mike?"

He couldn't move, couldn't comprehend, couldn't imagine what all this would lead to. He held proof of Effie Beck's secret and Jodean's past in his hands.

"So he drives to Fort Worth. I felt poorly that day and decided not to go along, you see. Anyway, there wasn't but one little girl left when he got there. Jodean, of course, and the train was just a fixing to leave the station. That there's the little bonnet Jodean wore the day Buddy adop—"

"Do you know who her real parents are?" Mike held the baby shoe in one hand and the adoption certificate in the other.

"Why, me and Buddy, that's who!"

"I mean her birth mother."

"Course not. That stuff is kept secret, even if me or Jodean ever wanted to know. Why you asking? What difference does it make, unless you plan to marry her, which might not work because you can't find out about what *kind* she came from, you see. Her *people*, good blood or bad, if you catch what I'm saying. That's why I always tried to protect Jodean. Why, don-cha know there's not a man in the county that'd marry a woman who might have come from... Well, you understand."

"Does Jodean know about this box?"

"Of course she does. I've never hidden the truth from her."

Mike grabbed the dress out of Cora's hand and put it, along with the papers and shoe back in the box and shoved himself off the floor.

"Where you think you're going with that box?"

"Where did Jodean go this morning?"

"Why, uh… C.J.'s. Now you come back here with that box!"

Mike ran out the back door, grabbed the truck key, the Effie Beck Lost folder from the tank house and headed for the shed. He tossed everything into the space behind the cab seat. He hadn't realized it was raining until he backed out of the shed.

Cora Mae watched him from the back steps. The old horse's ass had planned the whole charade like she'd planned Jodean's whole life. Nothing terrified him more at that moment than to tell Jodean what he now knew to be fact, that Effie Beck was her birth mother, but tell her he must. She had every right to know even if, like him, she dreaded the truth. The truth might be the very thing to help Jodean buck up to Cora Mae's manipulating once and for all. Give her a chance to make the best of the rest of her life.

On the other hand, she might hate him for telling what he knew. She understood he'd find out sooner or later that she was adopted from the orphan train, had even prepared herself to see him leave like John Rice and God only knew how many others before him.

Everything fell into place. Why Jodean got upset that day he mentioned that Effie Beck had been in Fort Worth the same time as one of the orphan trains, the baby shoe that Tootie Sue tried to put on her foot. Jodean recognized it, surely.

Rain fell in earnest as Mike drove slowly along Main Street looking for Jodean. He spied her on the sidewalk to his left. She was rushing to get home out of the rain. He slammed on the brakes and made a U-turn in the middle of the street. She jumped and looked at him puzzled, then leaned down to look in the cab window. "My gosh, Mike, is something wrong?"

"Get in out of the rain." He leaned across the seat and opened the door. She scrambled in and waited for an explanation. He opened his mouth but he stopped short.

"Mike?"

"No matter what, I love you. Do you understand?"

She gave him a blank look then her eyes moved beyond him to watch as Neal Lackland roared by with his siren blaring. Mike reached into the tight space behind the seat where he'd shoved the box of baby things. Jodean went white and looked away. She traced the path of raindrops working down the window glass with her finger.

"I know you're from the orphan train but I don't care. I love you."

She shook her head. "I don't expect you to, Mike. My birth mother could have been a whore, my birth father a bum, or…"

"I think I know who they—"

Paddy Blue clanged the fire bell in front of the Pickle Factory. Two men ran out of Hank's filling station on the corner and hopped in a truck and took off. Rain fell in torrents.

Jodean dropped her head. "Take me home."

Mike reached in the box and showed her the baby shoe. "You recognized the mate to this shoe the day Tootie Sue tried to get you to put it on her foot."

"Stop it! There're shoes like that in almost any house that's had a baby in it." She grabbed for the door handle but Mike clutched her arm before she could bolt.

"Please, please just take me home, Mike." The bag of groceries in her lap toppled to the floorboard when she tried to pull away. The last thing he wanted was to have her feel trapped, and yet that's exactly what happened.

"Don't do this, Mike."

Before he could reply, Paddy Blue clopped by in his cart. Brother Rawlings, riding in back with three or four other men, waved at Mike to roll his window down.

"New bridge collapsed!" he yelled. "Men are trapped and they're calling for all the help they can get."

Mike turned back to Jodean. "Think you can drive home?" She nodded with big frightened eyes. *Damn*, how could he leave her at a time like this? He touched her face then got out of the truck and climbed on Paddy's cart. The rain was icy cold and in seconds he was soaked to the skin. Jodean watched him roll away.

Ten minutes later Paddy pulled up to what was left of the new WPA river bridge. Rain fell so hard Mike could barely see the opposite bank. He had never seen anything like it. The air literally was water. No thunder, no wind, no lightning. Just rain and lots of it. The Medina River boiled with great muddy whirlpools and was a good twenty feet out of its banks. Massive oak trees on the opposite bank leaned with half their roots exposed and would soon wash away.

"Must'ta rained like a sonofabitch upstream," Red called out, joining them. "Seems we got a drought and grasshopper plague or a goddamed frog-choking flood. Beats all I ever saw."

Tubby, red-faced and puffing, yelled at Red above the roar of rain and rushing water. "Git on down there to the bridge pilings. They need a man who can swing a rope wide and true."

"By god, I'm that man."

Two sections of the new bridge, the ones connecting it to either bank, had washed completely away along with eight or ten feet of the bank itself. A WPA worker held on to the bridge center-section railing, the only part still above water. Straining to see better, Mike realized the guy was holding onto a second man who looked injured and in grave danger of being sucked away by the current.

Neal, who stood where the bridge had once connected to dry land, peered downstream at some men in a treetop in the middle of the furious rush of water. One of them was Otis Bartel.

Emmet met up with Red, handed him some rope and yelled something, but voices were lost in water noise. Red moved dangerously close to river's edge to swing his loop. Just as Mike thought he'd throw, he drew it in and looped it back into his left hand. Warming up, Mike guessed, but it made him nervous as hell to watch the two men who were about to be washed away. A barrel riding the current slammed into the bridge midsection.

The whole scene was incredible. Men he'd passed on the sidewalk daily were unrecognizable in their drenched state, some covered with mud, others, like Leroy the druggist, packed shovels and rope over their shoulders, paced, ready to help as soon as someone figured out how.

Red swung again, wider and wider until finally he gave the rope flight. It fell short. Rain poured off his big hat as he drew the rope back in. He circled the loop overhead a third time. Mike couldn't comprehend how he managed in the heavy rainfall.

Red yelled as he circled the rope overhead, "I roped the meanest, shitty-assed bull in Oklahoma once. This old river's a pussy cat compared to that." He released the loop. It landed about three feet upstream from the men on the bridge. They grabbed it as it floated into the railing. The crowd roared and clapped and Red tossed the free end of the rope to a string of men lined up ready to haul the stranded men to safety.

Red struggled through shin-deep mud to gain solid ground. He pointed with his chin at the other men trapped in the tree. "Too far to throw a rope."

"I's afraid of that," Tubby yelled. Emmet and Paddy Blue had joined them. They all stood with their shoulders hunched against the rain. Paddy's lips were purple from cold. Emmet looked blind with his thick glasses fogged and muddy. A crashing rumble came from the bank on the other side of the river. A huge live oak leaned into the water and, like a willing lover, succumbed to the river's rage.

"I suppose…" They all turned at the sound of Neal's voice. "We could launch a boat, keep it tied to shore mind you, and try to work our way over to them."

"And you'd be the first one in the boat. Right, *Sheriff?*" Bart Steves sneered as he joined the circle of men. He held up a huge crossbow for everyone to see. "Made it in shop class last year."

The thing looked to Mike like it could drop an elephant fifty yards away.

"Damn, boy, you all right!" Red slapped Bart's back. While Bart tied a lightweight, thin rope to an arrow, Red discussed aiming tactics.

"We can tie heavier rope on the end of this lightweight stuff, then Otis can haul it out and tie it to the tree for a high line," Red suggested.

The deafening drum of rain was unlike anything Mike had ever witnessed. His hands were so numb from the cold he could hardly tie off the two ends of rope Red handed him. The men in the tree screamed and gestured wildly.

"Oh, merciful God," Brother Rawlings boomed. A roiling automobile bobbed in the current like a toy headed straight for the tree-trapped men.

"Aim high for the bank on the other side of the men," Red instructed Bart. "That way it'll fall right above them."

Neal assumed his arms-across-chest pose near the water's edge. He was wearing a heavy poncho and rubber boots. In the blink of an eye, three feet of the riverbank where he stood gave way. He clawed at the muddy bank, screamed and rolled his eyes in wild fear at the rush of water. Paddy lunged for him but slipped. Mike grabbed Paddy's collar and they flopped like fish back onto the muddy bank. The movement gave Mike a chance to grip Paddy around his chest.

Neal screamed again when the suck of deep water took him farther out. Beyond him the automobile rolled upside down as it narrowly missed the men trapped in the treetop. Neal's head bobbed out of the water about thirty feet upstream of the tree. He gasped and disappeared again. Otis let out a roar then with one leg hooked on a sturdy limb, leaned as far out over the water as he dared.

"Well I'll be a flea-bitten goddamned sonofabitch." Red swiped his wet face with his sleeve to get a better look.

Otis caught Neal's poncho hood and hauled him from the angry river. "Kick your boots off. Kick your damned boots off!"

The other two men struggled to help Otis pull Neal to a safer position in the tangle of tree limbs. One of them managed to knock Neal's heavy boots off.

Red turned back to Bart. "Go on now, let her fly."

Bart licked his lips, aimed high and squeezed the trigger. The arrow sailed straight and true and the line landed exactly as Red had hoped, arm high above the stranded WPA workers. They hauled over the heavier rope and tied it to the largest limb within reach to create a high line.

Otis used his pocket knife to cut the lighter weight rope into sections to tie around the high line giving the men some measure of safety for the swim to the river bank. The first two men positioned themselves on the upriver side of the high line and looped their arms and head through the loops Otis had made. One at a time, they moved themselves, hand over hand, along the rope to the bank where Red cut each man free of the lightweight safety loop.

When Otis nudged Neal, he shook his head "*no*" like a kid and jerked away. Otis grabbed Neal's poncho, gave him a good shake and then looped a length of lightweight rope around Neal's belt and the high line. Then he thrust Neal back into the river and yelled at him to hurry. Neal had no choice but to save himself.

As soon as Neal's feet touched the slippery bank, he started sobbing. Mike and Brother Rawlings locked arms to pull him to safe ground. Neal was still laying face down in the mud, a shivering, sobbing hysteric, when Red fished Otis out of the river twenty minutes later.

Doris and Glory drove up and yelled out the window that the ladies had hot coffee and dry blankets waiting for them at the school cafeteria.

"Have you seen Jodean?" Mike asked.

Doris shook her head.

"I reckon I'll beat it on home," Red said when Doris drove away. "This rain keeps up, I might not be able to navigate the roads. Spring Creek Bridge is sure to wash out, too."

"Do you mind dropping me off?" Mike asked. Red motioned him into the car. When they slowed in front of the Travis house Mike let out a groan.

"What is it?" Red asked.

"The truck is gone. Red, you're not going to believe the mess I've stirred up."

"Don't count on it. Remember trouble, especially with women, is my middle name."

Mike gave Red the whole ball of wax about Jodean, Cora Mae and Effie Beck. For the most part, Red listened with a shocked look on his face, asking only an occasional question.

"I'll be a hornswoggled goddamned idiot," Red said when Mike finished. "I guess it takes a stranger in town to see through all the surface stuff. I mean, I grew up knowing about Jodean, and then I didn't pay any attention to her situation once we were all grown. And sweet Miss Effie. Think of the suffering she must have gone through. Her only child, too."

"Where do you think Jodean could be?" Mike asked.

"My guess would be the Beck place."

Without waiting for Mike's go-ahead, Red put the car in gear and sloshed out of town. When they got to Effie Beck's house, Red pointed to the truck parked next to the henhouse.

"Want me to wait?" Red asked. Mike shook his head no and stepped out of the car into rivers of icy water that continued to pour from the sky.

MIKE HOPPED ONTO Miss Effie's porch and drew his arm across his tired face. Rain dripped from his nose and chin, sloshed in his shoes.

The house was dark as twilight, smelled musty and sour. There was a small wet shoe print in the doorway to the kitchen. Other than that, no sign of life, no sound above the rain drumming on the tin roof. He moved into the kitchen. His report papers were strewn across the table. Jodean must have found his Effie Beck Lost folder stuffed behind the seat where he'd thrown it along with the box of baby things. Her wet shoes had been placed at the back door next to Effie's father's antiquated boots, the ones held together with ducking cloth.

He heard movement to his left and turned to look into the dim bedroom. Jodean curled child-like on the bed with a baby shoe in each hand, a faraway look on her face. On the floor next to the bed, scattered in a damp heap, was the rest of the stuff from his Effie Beck folder.

Mike said her name. Her eyes stared at air and were so striking that their color didn't register with him so much as the look of anguish.

"Why?" She whispered without moving.

He eased down onto the edge of the bed.

"Answer me that, Mike. Why? Why didn't Effie Beck tell me?"

"Maybe she thought you'd be happier not knowing."

"She cared about me, though. I know that now. Evenings, I used to see her down around the spring watching our house. I remember seeing her at the oddest times, the oddest places. But when I mentioned it to Daddy, he'd say she was a lonesome, odd old woman and that I should be respectful."

A tear dripped over the bridge of her nose. She turned to look at him. "Did Daddy know, do you think, or Momma?"

Mike shook his head. "Not likely. But I think Miss Effie might have planned to wait and watch from a distance until the Baby Train left with you on it. I think she saw your daddy drive up late, just in time to talk to the nuns. It's a good guess she watched him carry you away and was relieved to know you'd be close by."

Mike paused and touched her hair. "Just think of the irony, Jodean...so hard to believe."

Jodean pointed at Aunt Nola's photograph on the floor. Mike leaned down to pick it up and she pointed at the baby girl's feet. Her left shoe was gone, the shoe he found in Effie's trunk. Mike nodded. He had missed so many details.

"The only time my daddy talked to me about the baby train, he said the nuns told him my name was Jo but Momma hated it so she added the *dean* part."

She curled back into a ball and wept. Mike brushed her cheek with the back of his hand. He couldn't imagine her despair or how to put words to her grief. Abandoned? Discarded? Betrayed?

"Do you think Effie Beck named me that after Joseph Dunlap? He signed his name Joe in some of the letters."

"I hadn't thought about it but, yes, that makes sense. She must have felt pretty desperate." Jodean glanced at Mike as if she hadn't understood his point.

He explained what he thought could have happened, what he put in his report for Tubby and Sheriff Neal. "I'd guess Joe was intimidated by Effie's father. Red said the situation was pretty bad. And I got a feeling from his letters that he liked his freedom. Effie would have been pretty naive about men like that."

For a minute Mike thought the rain had eased a bit. "We better head back to town," he said. "Spring Creek Bridge is liable to wash out."

Jodean shook her head with a sniffle. "I want to stay here." Hysterical, choking sobs shook her whole body.

"Wh-y-y?" she cried hard into the musty pillow. Nothing Mike did came close to softening her heartache.

He gathered her into his arms and rocked back and forth until the worst of her crying eased. "Come on. We better get out of here while we can."

She shook her head. "Stay here with me."

Emotions he couldn't name swamped his mind. If he could siphon her pain, give her peace, he'd do it freely. Anything. Yet, what could he realistically offer Jodean? He was little more than a drifter come to town, mad at the world and its Creator, whose family back in North Carolina looked to him for hope and help.

He pulled back a little and tilted his face away from her. Rain plipped from the eaves outside the window to a puddle between some rosebushes. The brooding indigo sky continued to weep as if mourning all that had happened. Jodean couldn't go back and undo what she'd lived. Nor could he.

Mike recalled the day he'd first walked along Cooperville Spring Creek and heard sighing in the thicket across the way. It was as if Effie's deepest secrets were being whispered to him then in the hope that someone, at last, would listen.

Effie Beck? Mike sure didn't believe in ghosts but, looking back, it seemed as if he'd been getting Effie messages all along. Signs, like his need to run down to the carp's pool the night Jodean got sick and he didn't know what to do. He overlooked so much because of his own private misery.

Jodean shuddered, air rasped in her throat, then she rolled aside and pulled back the dusty, tattered quilt. He slipped from his cold wet clothes, used his wet shirt to wipe mud from his arms and neck. Even though it was early evening, they both slipped into deep, exhausted sleep.

Mike stirred around two in the morning and realized the rain had slowed to a soft drizzle. Jodean whimpered in her sleep and then got still as stone. It mesmerized him to listen to her slow breathing, the sound of life going in and coming out. *Effie Beck's daughter* right here in Effie Beck's house.

He thought about the tolerant, forgiving relationship between Breezy and Effie after she clubbed Jericho the night he and his brothers tried to steal chickens. And Effie's acceptance of the town's conditional compassion, in spite of how much she must have hated it in her later years. She had no choice but to be a woman of great privacy and independence.

The next thing Mike knew it was morning and he smelled coffee. He could see Jodean at the kitchen table sipping from a cup with the report papers stacked in a neat pile to her right. She must have heard him move because, without looking up, she poured a cup of coffee and brought it to the bedroom. Her face looked very different, unmoved, and at peace.

"Is this place mine now?" she asked.

Mike shrugged. "As soon as the courts acknowledge the evidence and a judge makes some sort of declaration. At least that's my guess. I'm no lawyer."

"How long will it take before it's official?"

"Don't know. Maybe Tubby and Emmet can talk the judge into speeding the process or give you permission to... I don't know, rent or occupy based on the information from Aunt Nola and the Orphan Society. I've heard these things can be worked out."

Her gaze traveled around the dank room and ended on the portrait above the bed.

"My grandparents?"

Mike nodded.

"This is not the best of my dreams, Mike." She sighed, looked at him with clear shining eyes. "But, it's not the worst either."

Mike clamped his jaw teeth. Life had badly splintered Jodean Travis, but like her birth mother she'd managed to hold herself together.

RED REINED SAMPSON hard to the right and let his rope fly. Pot Roast bucked and jerked against the rope. His hungry bellowing had eventually led Red to find him.

Pete ran out the back door when he heard Pot Roast, huffing and complaining as Red alternately herded and dragged him to the holding pen. The boy's face split with a grin. The calf shouldered Pete then gave him a good push with his head.

Pete filled a trough with feed for Pot Roast while Red dragged a bale of dry hay out of a shed. It had been weeks since the Medina River flooded out of its banks, backed up to the creek and soaked much of Reds hay fields. Still, he dared not complain. Rain was a good thing any way he looked at it.

"Pete?" Red motioned him to sit on the hay bale next to him.

"Son, I know you don't understand what happened between your mother and me and Mrs. Lackland. Not all of it anyway. I'm not sure I do. But remember when I told you Pot Roast would think you were his momma once you fed him? That's kind of what happened between me and Mrs. Lackland. She was real heart hungry the day she ran her car into that tree. And scared out of her wits, too, I guess. I don't know how else to explain it to you. I tried to help her and she – Mrs. Lackland – grabbed onto me, thinking I could go on helping her, like Pot Roast here, thinking it's you that'll go on feeding him. I know it wasn't my place to help her once she was out of danger…but I… Pete, I faltered in not telling her right from the git-go that I wasn't the one to put things right for her. As bad off as that lady was, I was wrong not to turn around and go get your momma to help her."

Pete stared at the ground.

"Don't get me wrong, now. Mrs. Lackland is a fine lady like your momma. She was scared and mixed up. Life has a way of buffaloing us grown-ups sometimes."

Red took his hat off. Pot Roast was in a heavy-breathing doze with a full belly. Flies lit on his ears but he didn't twitch.

"I guess," Pete said, "if Momma doesn't hold a grudge, I shouldn't either."

"Your momma's a saint, Pete Kasper." Red reached over and hugged his son to his heart-thumping chest. "Come on. I bet the Saint is ready to skin the both of us for being late to the supper table."

After supper Red shooed Ada outside to sit in the cool breeze on the porch while he and Pete cleared the table. The heat bothered her more than she let on.

Later, when Red joined her on the porch, she said, "Still can't believe the way everything has turned out for Jodean. Who would have ever thought?"

Red draped his arm over Ada's shoulder. "Tubby said she'll be our official neighbor by the end of the month when the last of the legal mess is taken care of. Did you see how she's got the place cleaned up?"

Ada nodded. "Yesterday while you were out working the cattle, I took her those blue curtains that belonged to Granny Kasper. I don't have a use for them anymore. Mike was there working on the front porch – almost had it leveled when I left."

"Amazing. Jodean Travis, Effie Beck's daughter." Red shook his head in wonderment.

"She told Cora she'd work two days a week and that she wanted to keep a percentage of the hair-doing money for herself. Cora Mae caterwauled of course, asked who was going to clean house and take care of her."

"What'd Jodean say?"

Ada smiled, "That she guessed Cora Mae would have to pick up after herself, that she was sorry it would seem unfair after all this time of not lifting a finger."

Red and Ada turned when they heard someone turn onto the drive. Mike stopped beside the trough and got out of the truck, a grim look on his face. Red moved to the steps and shook his hand.

"I got a telegram from my brother. My mother is pretty sick. I need to go home."

"Sorry to hear it, Mike."

Mike looked past him to Ada. "I'm on my way to tell Breezy good-bye, then I'll stop at the Beck place to tell Jodean. I'll have her drive me out to the highway so I can hitch a ride. I'm worried she'll think—"

"—You're leaving her." Ada finished for him.

"Will you look in on her later? I can't honestly say when I'll be back. My mother may linger and I don't want to promise Jodean something I can't follow through on."

"Trying to do the right thing sure makes life harder, don't it?" Red said.

"Do what you have to," Ada said. Mike kissed her cheek and shook Red's hand. When he turned to leave he nearly tripped over Tootie Sue, who was playing with a rag doll on the steps. He touched her head. She looked up at him with a big smile.

MIKE PARKED UNDER the cottonwood tree and gave Jericho and Trudy a wave. They were in the side yard between the house and garden scrubbing kids in a big wash tub. Breezy was sound asleep in his porch chair with his chin resting on his chest. He drew himself up and opened his eyes as Mike approached.

"Guess you think I's sleeping."

"Hadn't formed an opinion one way or the other."

Breezy laughed and stomped his foot. After a stretch of quiet he said, "Leaving us, are you?"

Mike shot him a look.

"I know these things."

"Did you know about Jodean Travis and Effie Beck?"

"Mr. Lemay, the truth floats out there round our heads all the time. Alls we got to do is look at it to know what it is. I didn't want to see it till that little girl had a chance to look for herself. Be like snooping if I had."

Mike remembered discovering his own truth the night of the street dance, that of his self-serving self-pity. He leaned on a porch post, listened to a mockingbird sing its heart out and watched road dust float in sun-gold air. Trees in the distance shimmered. The hills looked weary.

Mike still couldn't make himself believe in a just God. Not yet. But he was open to the idea.

By some small miracle Jodean had a home of her own and a measure of peace about who she was and where she'd come from.

Mike learned about forgiveness from Cooperville. Jericho forgave Effie Beck. Ada forgave Faye and Red. Otis didn't exactly forgive Neal for the beating but he must have figured two wrongs didn't make a right. The sheriff will suffer shame enough after the blubbering idiot he'd made of himself the day the bridge washed out.

As for himself? Mike thought he'd carried around guilt and hung onto hopelessness so long that it, not the hard times, had boxed him in.

For the time being, it would have to do to thank the sun when he saw it rise in the mornings and the stars that sprinkled twilight across the land at night. He felt no greater for his best deed, which wasn't much, nor more evil for his blackest thought. He was only a small part of the great hum of life and it wouldn't miss him once his own noise died out.

"Breezy, do you think it was luck that brought me here?"

"Hard to say."

"Yeah, well. It's all over. The wondering what happened to Effie Beck, what was to become of her ranch, finding her child."

"Time to decide which way you want to go with your own life now, I reckon."

Mike held out his hand. "Be seeing you, Breezy."

Breezy took Mike's hand and used it to pull himself up from the chair. "I be here or in the graveyard yonder when you come back."

Mike draped his arm across Breezy's shoulders but didn't dare squeeze the fragile brown bones as hard as he was inclined to. He rushed then, with burning eyes, down the steps and gave the Parker family a last wave from the Model A truck.

Jodean was planting purple sage bushes around the mailbox pole when Mike parked on the road in front of the Beck place. He got out of the truck. She looked at his suitcases in the back.

"It's my mother, Jodean. I have to go."

She tilted her open face to him. He reached in his shirt pocket and withdrew the folded telegram. She ignored it.

"Jodean, I'll be bac—"

"—You don't owe me promises."

He pulled her to him and locked his arms around her, buried his face in her dark silky hair. "I'll do everything I can to come back soon. I swear it."

"I've always known you would leave."

"When my mother—"

"Just look at us. How one summer changed us."

"Rudy said he—"

"I'll drive you out to the highway."

"Stop this." He held her shoulders. "I know what you are thinking but you're wrong. Jodean, I love you and I'll come back. I just can't tell you when. I'll write you every day. That I *can* promise."

She didn't say a word. Instead, she climbed in the Ford, fired it up and nodded at him to get in. At the crossroads, they got out to wait for a car to pass. Mike set his cases in the weeds.

"You write down in that notebook of yours what was done to me and Effie Beck, Mike. Some day somebody might make sense of it all." Jodean's eyes filled with tears and she turned her head away for moment. "I'm glad to know my history, Mike. People who don't know their history drift. I don't have to drift anymore. I can plan."

An ancient hoopie appeared on the horizon. Jodean watched it. "Red is going to show me how M-Miss Effie rounded up the cattle." Her voice sounded wet. "Next week Bill and Bart are coming to help with the corral."

"I left my forwarding address with Rudy at the newspaper office." Mike stuck out his thumb. Jodean pressed three fingers to her mouth. When the hoopie squeaked to a stop, Mike tossed his cases on back next to a boy holding a pig.

Jodean flew into his arms. Mike choked on the knot in his throat and could say no more. He moved back to look into her wet eyes one last time before climbing onto the hoopie. He sat on a wood crate and tapped the rear window.

As the hoopie rolled away, Jodean looked as if she was being pulled backward into the disappearing valley. She raised her arm in a sweeping wave.

"I was just wondering," Mike said to the boy holding the pig. "How many men get to start life over. Fresh. A second chance."

He supposed that's what had happened to him. He had shed a life of hopelessness and assumed another that now waved an open palm at him.

He stood and waved back.

Living was nothing more than a long string of days clumped together here and there to make up seasons. The trick was to not get sucked under by the bad spells, to keep in mind that seasons change.

He needed to set a course and endure like Effie Beck. Like Effie Beck's daughter.

"Got far to go, Mister?" the boy with the pig asked.

"Yes, a long way."

Mike waved again at the small figure at the end of the dusty road. "A long, long way."

READING LIST

First Person America
Ann Banks

From Can See to Can't: Texas Cotton Farmers on the Southern Prairies
Thad Sitton and Dan K. Utley

Hard Times: An Oral History of the Great Depression
Studs Terkel

The Orphan Trains: Placing Out in America
Marilyn Irvin Holt

Orphan Train Riders: Their Own Stories, Vol 1
Orphan Train Heritage Society of America, Inc.
Stories written by Riders and their descendants, compiled by Mary Ellen Johnson

Acknowledgements

I wish to thank the community of writers across this country who freely gave advice, shared expertise and were quick to cyber-pat me on the back when I despaired that this book would ever come to pass. You know who you are and how much I counted on your midnight emails for survival in this wobbling, maddening business of writing novels. Thank you for perspectives I had not considered. Thank you for saving me hours of research when I had only minutes to spare. Camaraderie is everything, isn't it?

In addition, I thank my sisters, Cathy Casey Berger and Renee Casey Rabke, for running away with me on occasion and for laughs and shared secrets.

I thank Susan Clayton Luton and Linda Jo Clayton - my touchstones who add equilibrium to my everyday life, just because I know "they are there."

And finally, for all those before you and me who endured throughout one of this country's most devastating eras - that of The Great Depression and Drought - may we never forget.

www.karencaseyfitzjerrell.com
kcfitzjerrell@gmail.com
http://www.facebook.com/kcfitzjerrell